REMEMBER US

BY EMMA NICHOLS

Britain's Next
BESTSELLER

First published in 2017 by:

Britain's Next Bestseller
An imprint of Live It Publishing
27 Old Gloucester Road
London, United Kingdom.
WC1N 3AX

www.bnbsbooks.co.uk

ISBN: 9781521841808 (PBK)

To keep in touch with the latest news from Emma Nichols and her writing please visit:

www.emmanicholsauthor.com
www.facebook.com/EmmaNicholsAuthor
www.twitter.com/ENichols_Author

Remember Us is the sequel to the No.1 bestselling lesbian romance, Finding You (Book 1 of The Vincenti Series

Thanks

Thanks to everyone who has read my debut novel,
Finding You, and then gone on to pick up this book.
Your support of my work is humbling and amazing.
I hope you enjoy this book even more than the first!

Thanks also to my partner, Murielle, for her unwavering
support and belief, and to our young children for not
hanging off my arm too much while I'm writing.

Finally, thanks to my beta readers.
Your contribution has been immense -
Bev (the Copper) and Rebecca.
You know who you are... thank you x

With love, Emma

Dedication

To all my readers and followers, I am indebted to you.

1.

'It doesn't matter how many times you tell me, Mother, I just don't remember her, alright. I don't remember your wedding, I have no idea who the fuck Henri is, and...' She paused as her father's image appeared in her mind's eye and her breath stuck in her throat.

'Language Lauren,' Valerie chastised, looking around to see if anyone else had overheard, even though they were the only two people in the room. The move was instinctive, conditioned, and even though she had mellowed significantly in the previous months since the death of her first husband and marriage to Henri, reactive.

'Don't you fucking dare,' Lauren spat through gritted teeth. Every ounce of her body wanted to launch itself at her mother, annihilate her, render her powerless, make her pay, but she couldn't move and the constriction was killing her. The choking sensation gripping her throat, the pressure compressing her head, so claustrophobic, and nothing about anything made any sense. Her world had spiralled out of control, and *she* didn't do *out of control.* 'For fuck sake stop hounding me.' Anger burned through her veins, the squeezing sensation in her brain and tightening in her gut, reaching an unbearable level. 'Leave me alone. Go home. I don't want you here.' There, she'd said it and with more control than she thought she had inside her. Years of wanting to be heard and the words that had escaped then, in that moment, summed up her relationship with her mother - Valerie Vincenti. Distant. Detached.

'Lauren, you don't mean it. You need help.' Valerie responded emphatically.

'Don't fucking tell me what I mean and what I need. You've controlled me my whole life in one way or another and it's got to stop. I'm thirty fucking six. I'm not your baby girl and it stops now.'

'What do you mean. I've always supported…'

'Mother.' Lauren interrupted forcefully, trying to raise herself in her bed, struggling with the pain and effort involved. Valerie moved to assist her and Lauren shrugged her off. 'You've supported me to the extent that it benefitted you and the family name. It's always been about appearances for you. I don't give a fuck what people think and I don't *need* anything, and especially not from you. Please leave, now.' Lauren's eyes focused on the door and her gaze never shifted until her mother had walked through it. She sunk heavily down into the bed, her body ached, her head spun, and her eyes closed to keep the burning sensation from releasing the suppressed tears. The black hole took her in again and this time she hoped she would stay there.

*

'Hey.'

Lauren's mouth twitched, her eyes fluttered, opened, her hazy gaze locating the sound coming from the side of the bed. *Was she dreaming?* She opened her eyes wider, blinking to clear her vision. She hadn't heard the door. 'Anna,' she mumbled.

'Hi.' Anna tried to smile, the skin on her face remaining taught, her eyes glassy, and supported by dark rings.

Lauren couldn't hold her gaze - the excruciating pain - and the instant she looked away the barrier between them grew, wider, taller, and deeper. It's density providing some distance from the pangs of guilt haunting Lauren, the space allowing for the anger to rise again. The anger gave her power, protected her. She felt stronger with it and levied it indiscriminately. 'Hi,' she said with the tone of an inconvenienced stranger.

The absence of any warmth, of any humanity, cut through Anna again. Her legs felt weary, her heart sore, her mind numb. She couldn't penetrate the walls Lauren seemed to have erected and was beginning to lose the will to try. The woman she knew, the one she had fallen in love with, had vanished in an instant. She didn't recognise the person now lying in front of her, though she agonised over the familiarity of the brown curls, tanned skin, high cheekbones and dark brown eyes that had once penetrated her soul with such desire. 'How are you today?' she asked, hoping, yet knowing the answer would be the same as the previous thirty-days, moving them no further forward.

'I've been better,' Lauren quipped sarcastically, staring towards the window.

Anna breathed deeply, working hard to bury the pain. Every ounce of her wanted to shout out, scream at Lauren to grow up and stop behaving like a petulant child. To tell her that she was pregnant with their child, to wake her up. But she couldn't. Every time she went to open her mouth, to let the pain out, to provide the truth, she stopped. The conflict cut her in two, but that pain was nothing compared to the hurt she felt at the vacant look in Lauren's eyes and the anger that filled the room every time she was in it. She sought solace in the fact that Lauren appeared to be angry with everyone, including her own mother. She only hoped it was a symptom of the problem rather than a permanent state. Though with every visit, any ray of hope was dwindling. The darkness had become consuming, claustrophobic, and she needed to extricate herself for the sake of them all. 'I'm going back to Paris,' she said, watching for Lauren's response. Finding none.

Lauren heard the words but nothing registered emotionally. There was only the perpetual tightness in her head, bulging with rage. Nothing that went on in the external world changed that fact. She stared at Anna, seeing the heartache, knowing she was the cause of it, unable to do anything to fix the situation between them. If she let that pain into her heart she would surely dive down the black hole and not come out. She didn't have the strength to deal with the truth right now. 'I'm sorry Anna. I need time,' she said, hoping her words might provide some comfort, yet unsure whether there was any truth in them. She had no idea what the future would bring, or even if there was a future.

*

Lisa approached the doorway with her arms outstretched as Anna staggered heavily through the front door, looking pale and lost, shaking her head slowly as their eyes met. 'I'm so sorry darling,' she whispered into her hair as she pulled her into the warm embrace. The inner strength her mum radiated felt comforting and she allowed herself to be held, rocked gently - allowed the tears to flow effortlessly. She sobbed silently into her mum's shoulder. Lisa stroked her hair, soothing, protecting, wanting to remove the suffering. 'Hey,' she said softly as Anna snuggled into her chest. Here Anna felt safe. Here she could breathe. The sobbing eased, replaced by the inner strength and comfort that had suffused her.

'I can't do it any more,' she said with finality.

'I know.' Lisa said, nodding with resignation. She and Vivian had been so happy to see their daughter in love. They had seen a future in Lauren, and the accident had blown that future apart. The transformation in Lauren had happened so quickly, and the devastation that caused had touched them all deeply. 'Come on. Let's get a cup of tea.' They wandered into the kitchen and Lisa put the kettle on, staring out the window as she worked. It was a bleak winter's day today, she mused, as dark clouds moved in with the gusting winds. The kettle's whistle pulled her out of her thoughts and she poured the hot water into the bone china teapot, pulling the hand-knitted cosy over the top. There was something comforting about the process of making proper tea. She placed the steaming pot on the table.

Anna watched her mum's movements, entranced by her own thoughts. 'I've tried to get through to her but she's so angry, and every day it's as if the barrier gets thicker, more impenetrable,' she said, her eyes seeking unconditional support from her mum. 'I don't have the strength to go in there again. She's not the person I fell in love with, and yet she is. It's all so... messed up.' Anna streamed her thoughts. Her mum nodded. 'There's no way I can talk to her about the baby,' she said with certainty. 'That would either tip her over the edge or she'd want to get back with me just for the sake of our child, and I can't do that. I don't want her to be with me out of some warped sense of honour. I want her to be in love with me again... and not so angry.' Anna's voice trailed off, her red-rimmed eyes glassed over again.

Lisa stepped towards her, wound a stray hair around her ear, thumbed away a tear, and cupped her face tenderly. 'I understand darling, and you know that whatever you decide we'll both support you. Vivian can help you if you choose a termination. Only you can decide, but never forget that we're here for you.' She held Anna's eyes with sincerity as she spoke. Anna nodded.

'I can't terminate, mum.' She held Lisa's gaze. Even though Anna had talked with them both about the possibility of terminating the baby in the early days after the accident, in just four-weeks Anna knew that was no longer an option for her. She already felt connected to the tiny embryos growing inside her, and in some bizarre way that also connected her to the woman she loved, and, she guessed, she would always love.

'I know. I just wanted you to know whatever you decide we'll be there for you. You can live here if you like, though I'm sure you'd rather be at your place. Viv's snoring is relentless.

Even the cat complains and seeks solace in the garden,' she jested in an attempt at lightening the mood slightly. Anna sniggered, took out a tissue from the box on the table, and blew her nose.

'I want to have this baby. Yet I also feel really bad that it's hers too. I mean it really is a bigger part of her than it is of me. They're her eggs. Jesus, what a mess.' Anna's eyes tracked her thoughts as she drifted.

'It is hard, and no one could have predicted this would happen. Yes, she is a big part of you, and in some ways, that is a wonderful gift. If she were herself, what would she want you to do?'

'Have the baby with her of course.'

'Exactly. You're enabling her genetic chain to be continued, the biological imperative remember,' she said with a wry smile. 'With her would be ideal, but right now that's not an option. But things can and will change.'

'You sound like mum,' Anna said, raising a brow. 'I know. You're right though. And there's always a chance that she'll remember at some point in the future.'

'Exactly, and if and when she does, maybe there'll be a future for you all, together. At least, I would hope for that.'

'Me too,' Anna said with a deep sigh.

'Now, drink your tea.' Lisa poured two cups and passed one across the table.

'Thanks mum.' Anna leaned across and pressed a kiss to her mum's cheek. 'I love you.'

'I love you too darling.'

'I'm going back to Paris next week as planned. I've got work to do there and I think it will help to get some space.' She spoke the words as if to cement her thoughts, for fear that she might change her mind if she didn't.

'Of course.'

'The thought of Lauren in the hospital just drives me to want to be with her, until I get there and face her anger and persistent rejection, then I can't wait to get the hell out. At least in Paris there's no temptation, and I need the space to move forward. I've got to create a life for this little one... or ones,' she added, holding her belly.

'I understand darling,' Lisa offered, cupping Anna's face, studying her intently for evidence of a lift in her spirits.

'You and mum have been great, as ever, but I need to let you get on with your lives too. You don't need me crashing your exciting retirement together,' Anna said, smiling, feeling a little lighter.

'Well you know you're welcome any time, and you'll need to think about birthing plans at some point,' she teased. 'You're welcome to stay here for the birth if you want, or we can come to you of course. I just thought I'd put that out there. No pressure.'

'Thanks.' Anna took her mum's hand and squeezed, comforted by the offer of assistance. Though she would prefer for Lauren to be there for the birth, her mums would come a close second in the running.

'You're welcome.' Lisa pulled her in and hugged her tightly, fighting the tears that pressed at the back of her eyes. She didn't want her daughter to see her upset. She needed to be strong for her, even though she felt anything but.

2.

Anna stepped out of the aircraft door into the slightly cooler air of the makeshift tunnel that led passengers into the arrivals hall. She hadn't really wanted to leave London. Being with her mums had felt safe. Consumed by her decision, she felt weary and anxious. Five weeks had passed since Lauren's crippling accident and although she was recovering slowly from the physical injuries she had sustained, there was still no sign of recovery of her memory.

Retrograde amnesia was so unpredictable and although there was every chance she would remember the forgotten aspects of her past at some point in time, when that point would be no one could predict. And there was always a chance that she would never remember. *What then?* Anna's heart sunk at the thought. Lauren's father's death, her mother's remarriage, her divorce from Rachel, and her new relationship with Anna - none of it remembered. Their decision to create a family, and Lauren's resignation from her London job, still nothing! All of it lost in some time warp, and worst still the look of confusion and distress on Lauren's face as she tried to process the missing information, ripped through Anna's heart. The images of each conversation with Lauren over the past weeks had played out repeatedly in her mind during the flight. No matter which angle she watched the movies from, her conclusion was the same: moving back to Paris and trying to create a life for her and the baby, or babies, was the right decision. It irked her, though, that some part of her disagreed with that decision and she didn't know how to deal with that.

She had visited the hospital every day in the early days after the accident but her presence seemed to cause Lauren even more confusion, and the constant rejection and anger had slowly destroyed her, so she had pulled back her visits to give Lauren the space and time she needed. The pain of watching her, now, ex lover's constant suffering was harder than returning home to Paris alone, or at least she had tried to convince herself of that fact. Until now! Faced with a cold Paris morning, a chill that was driven by more than the weather permeated to her bones. Shivering, she ambled aimlessly through the concourse, which was bustling with life, feeling nothing. She glanced around, looking for Eva's characteristic blonde spiky hair. She was grateful her best friend had been able to collect her. The thought of getting to the taxi rank, even though she was very familiar with its location and the regular drivers, felt like too much to handle. She needed the security and comfort of a trusted friend, hoped it would fill the emptiness and help to heal the wounds.

'Hey.' The familiar voice, arms waving, grabbed her attention and she fell into an enthusiastic full-on hug. 'We've been so worried about you.' Eva said, releasing the limp body slightly, so she could see into Anna's steel-blue eyes. The layers of black shadow sitting below the blue hollow stare caused Eva's stomach to flip. 'Anna… Anna…' Compassion oozed through Eva's voice as she pulled her dear friend into her arms again and held her close.

'Hi,' the timid voice responded.

'Come on. Let's get you home.' Eva picked up the abandoned bag in one hand and linked arms with the other to support and guide Anna to her parked car.

*

Jesus fucking Christ, Lauren cussed inwardly, letting out a frustrated groan, as Jean insisted she take three more steps. An excruciating burning pain coursed through her hip and down her left leg as she raised it the couple of inches off the ground, and her right shoulder still carried a dull ache, increasing the challenge of supporting her body weight as she re-learned the

9

process of walking, sitting, and moving. She glared at the physiotherapist's smiling face with contempt, even though she knew the situation was nothing to do with the poor woman who was just doing her job. Huffing and puffing from the strain as she finished the last step, wanting to double over, she was prevented from doing so by the upbeat words assaulting her ears.

'Stand up, open your lungs.' Jean modelled the expected behaviour enthusiastically as she spoke.

Fuck off, she wanted to say, anger brewing, boiling, beneath the fine veneer that constituted *her* protection from the outside world. Holding back, she followed the instructions swearing outwardly. 'Fuck. Fuck.' Jean ignored her remonstrations and continued to smile. The pain eased as she stood still, momentarily tricking her mind that this was all a dream - a really, really, bad dream.

'Well done Lauren. You're doing really well.' The chirpy voice, intending to inspire and motivate her, did the opposite, breaking into her illusion, dragging her back into the hideous truth of her current reality.

'Right.' She didn't hide the disgust she felt as she manoeuvred herself to sit in her wheelchair. The discomfort of sitting, marginally less than that of working out, allowed her to release the breath she had been holding. Suppressed frustration flowed out with the release and she sank heavily back into the seat, resigned momentarily to her fate. Her dull eyes tracked their route back to her private room, past the canteen, left at the main entrance and two flights up in the lift.

People stared. They didn't mean to. It's a perfectly natural human behaviour, to question, to find out the truth, she pondered. We're inquisitive beings and had the shoe been on the other foot, Lauren too would have looked on and wondered what had happened to the poor person - too young - slumped in the chair. Their questioning gazes went unanswered and Jean chatted, oblivious. Lauren had no idea about what, since her mind seemed permanently absorbed by the void - except when doing her physiotherapy, when she was totally consumed by the physical pain racking her body.

Her last memory before the accident, just before Christmas, had been a court case she had attended in the August. She had won the case and had felt elated for the client, who had been clearly taken advantage of by the organisation she worked for. It was a common problem: poorly administered HR practices, and she thrived on being the one to bring justice to the victims of such managerial incompetence. They had celebrated long and hard at the local bar, as was customary at McDermott, Knight and Davies. It was early February now and the only memories she had accrued in the last six weeks were hospital based, and the only feeling that seemed to dominate her waking hours was anger. She couldn't get close to that feeling of euphoria, even as she recalled the events as she remembered them back in August. The space between that memory and waking up in the ICU on December 24th was literally that. Nothing but a black hole, and she felt as deep and dark as the blank space that occupied her mind.

Even worse still, everything she had been told, by her mother, by Rachel, and by Anna over the last few weeks, made no sense to her whatsoever. *Grief*. That's what the counsellor had said. Apparently, she had a lot to process and readjust to. Her father had taken his life and her mother had remarried. *How the hell had that all happened in such a short space of time? And why was her mother trying to be so fucking helpful?* She knew she had badly over-reacted to her mother's presence. But the woman had a knack of winding her up, making her feel inadequate, making her feel like a child. And she didn't like that feeling. Lauren had always felt controlled by Valerie. That was one of the reasons she had decided to study in London and leave home as soon as she could. And whilst, since the accident, her mother seemed to be trying to make amends with her, she wasn't ready for that. She hated how her mother made her feel and she knew she had kicked out at her, viciously. With hindsight, since she sent Valerie packing, she felt bad, guilty, and ashamed. She knew Valerie was concerned and trying to help, yet there was more that didn't make sense. For some strange reason Valerie seemed very accepting of Anna, supportive of her in a way that she never had been with Rachel. In fact, her mother had always dismissed her relationships and certainly denied the fact that her daughter was a married lesbian. Yet here she was defending Anna's case and pleading Lauren to try to work it out with her. Even her apparent acceptance of her being in a lesbian relationship had become irritating it was so out of character. She had never demonstrated caring to her before. Remote and emotionally detached is what she remembered of her mother. She didn't recognise the new woman Valerie had become, and that was almost more disconcerting than her loss of memory.

'I really don't recognise Anna... at all,' she had said to Rachel, head in hands, rubbing her temples hard, as Rachel had tried to help her remember that they had agreed to get divorced and Anna was the new love of her life. 'Nothing.' She trawled her memories for just a hint of something familiar. 'Don't get me wrong, she's gorgeous, but she might as well be a stranger in a bar to me right now.'

'Do you remember where you met her?' Rachel had asked, searching for something to help.

'Nope. I can't even remember that my father died, for Christ sake,' Lauren had responded, fast becoming frustrated with both the conversation and her lack of recollection. All she had seen was the pain in the beautiful woman's steel-blue eyes as they had searched hers daily, for something... anything that would trigger remembrance of their short time together. Nothing.

When Rachel had phoned Lauren's boss early in the New Year to explain that she had been involved in an accident and wouldn't be in work for a while, it had come as a big surprise to her to find out that Lauren had walked out of her job the same day she had walked in front of the van. Lauren had looked at her in dismay, shrugging her shoulders at yet another event about which she had no recollection. 'Give it time,' Rachel had said, but she hadn't been convinced that time would solve how she was feeling. And now, apparently, she was also out of a job.

'Right, here we go.' Jean's chirpiness accompanied the squeaking of rubber wheels on the linoleum floor as she halted the chair next to Lauren's bed, facing into the room. Lauren was beginning to hate the sounds that had come to surround her over the past weeks. Hate them with a vengeance.

'Thanks.' She looked into the kind green eyes, trying to engage with their lightness, but a smile wouldn't come even if she felt like trying to raise one. She had no inclination to work too hard at trying either. What would be the point in that?

Jean smiled softly and squeezed her lightly on the shoulder. 'Remember to do your static exercises Lauren and I'll see you tomorrow,' she said, as she turned and left the room. 'And don't sit in that chair all day,' she nagged, as the door closed quietly behind her.

Lauren stared, as she did every day, at the clinical prison in which she had spent the last six-weeks. The monitors had been removed, thankfully. The low-seated armchair sporting a paisley pattern out of the 1950's looked as though it had been acquired from a charity shop and was uncomfortable to sit in. Perhaps that was done deliberately to make sure people didn't get comfortable and sit there all day, she reasoned. The walls were absent of any form of art, the dark and light blue blankets providing the only colour in the otherwise grey and off-white austere room. And the room was always too hot... or too cold if she opened the window. She sighed, trying to convince herself to accept her situation and move on, whilst another part of her brain fought against the idea, wanting to fill the gap that should have memories in it. Neither was winning the battle and she was feeling weary with oscillating between seeking answers and accepting her new world.

The red brick view from the tatty window and grey clouds overhead did nothing to lift her mood. She wanted out, but there was no way the Doctors would agree to her going back to Corsica yet, neither did she particularly want to spend time under her mother's control. But, she needed to find the missing memories and the best way to achieve that was going to be by retracing her steps, creating familiarity in the hope that something would trigger her brain to function properly again. She reached for the metal frame and eased herself out of the wheelchair, wincing as pain gripped her. Turning slowly, she pondered her choices - chair or bed? She sat herself in the paisley relic and reached for the Kindle that Rachel had bought her, hoping that immersing herself in a good book would allow her to escape the constant torment of her thoughts.

*

'Do you want to talk about it?' Eva asked, steering her way out of the airport and towards the motorway, sleet lashing against the windscreen.

'I'm not sure what to say or where to start,' Anna said, her eyes staring vacantly at the trickling water on the window and passing grey landscape, still unable to reconcile the turn of events over the past weeks.

'Mum wanted to come with me but I persuaded her against the idea. I didn't think you'd want her jabbering at you all the way home. I hope that's okay with you?' Eva said, filling the uneasy silence.

'Yeah... thanks.'

'Work's good,' Eva continued as she flicked the indicator to move into the outside lane to overtake a dawdling British registered campervan. 'Mum's got a couple of things lined up for you when you're ready. Seems family portraits are becoming popular,' she babbled, intent on talking.

Rowena had received two requests on recommendation from Valerie Vincenti, one of which was based in Corsica. A fact that Eva didn't think it appropriate to reveal at this point in time. The other potential client was based in Marseille, apparently an old friend and work colleague of Henri's, Valerie's new husband, and technically now Lauren's stepfather.

'That's good.' Anna mumbled, though Eva's words hadn't been able to penetrate her thoughts. Eva glanced across at her briefly. She cleared her throat and continued the drive in silence, keeping a watch on her through the corner of her eye. Anna's expression didn't change, her eyes remaining unfocused and distant. Only the familiar crunch of the gravel leading up to the barn eventually stirred her from her musing. 'Sorry, I must have got lost in thought,' she said, rubbing at tired eyes.

'A little,' Eva responded with a frown and pinched lips. She jumped out of the seat and opened the passenger door before Anna had unbuckled her seat belt. Grabbing a second bag from the back of the car she followed Anna, took the key from her shaking hand, and opened the door. Dropping the bags in the hallway she shot into the kitchen to ramp up the heating and put on the kettle. 'Sit down. What do you want to drink?'

'Camomile tea please. Top cupboard on the right.' Anna pointed as her eyes scanned the room. Memories of Lauren flooded her thoughts instantly. Here in this room, laughing, teasing, and that hideous time with Sophie trying to wriggle her way back into her life. She shuddered. Lauren had rescued her, held her, and loved her. That event had been a turning point in cementing their relationship. It had been the first time they had openly discussed their desire to have children. Lauren had defended her and then committed to creating a life with her. *Just a short time ago her relationship was exhilarating, and now this.* She slumped onto the high-stool, elbows resting on the kitchen island, head in hands. A dull ache filled her as she watched Eva make their tea, wishing it were Lauren. She wondered if the despair would ever leave.

'Here.' Eva passed her the steaming drink. Without thinking she pressed it to her lips and jumped as the sharp burn scorched her mouth.

'Shit!' She leapt up, sprinted across the room, and spat into the sink. 'Fuck, fuck, fuck,' she screamed, at the injustice. She wasn't sure if the tears preceded the tremors or vice versa. Either way there was no stopping the implosion that now consumed every part of her body. She slumped over the sink and dry wretched.

Eva stepped calmly across the room. The tender touch in the small of Anna's back added to her internal pain and suffering, as guilt and anger vied for a space to be released. She didn't deserve kindness and sympathy for deceiving a woman she loved out of her own flesh and blood. She felt exhausted and physically ill, wanting to be held and comforted, and yet also needing to be alone. Unable to reconcile her conflicting feelings she pulled herself up straight, turned, and allowed Eva's arms to envelope her.

'I know I'm not who you really want right now, but I'm here for you. I'll stay as long as you need,' Eva said as she pulled Anna into her chest, traced her face with her finger and gently rubbed the tears away. 'Hey… I've got you,' she said, placing a soft kiss on her forehead, holding her tightly as a second wave of sobs rose to the surface.

'I'm sorry,' Anna snivelled, pulling away to regain her composure.

'Hey, it's okay. I can't imagine what you're going through. I think you're entitled to cry you know.' She smiled

16

heanteningly, tucking an errant hair behind Anna's ear.

'I'm pregnant,' she blubbered.

'I suspected.'

'What am I going to do?'

'About what?'

'Everything?' Anna moved back to her seat, slumped onto the hard surface and sipped carefully at the cooling tea. She winced as the liquid found her sore mouth. 'The baby; Lauren, my life, our life as a family?' She hugged the cup in both hands even though she didn't feel cold.

'Honestly... I don't know. But nothing needs deciding right now and some things are a little out of your control.' Eva said.

'I know, and that's what's so fucking frustrating. She doesn't even know me and I'm carrying her baby... our baby, maybe more than one. I love her so much, and I hadn't planned on doing this,' she pointed at her belly, 'alone. I can't just walk away and spend the rest of my life wondering if she'll remember me - remember us.' Anna drifted off with her oscillating thoughts.

'Look, how about you unpack and take a rest while I go get us some food. I'll cook supper and we can chat for as long as you like. I've got no plans to leave. I can do any work I need to from my laptop. Deal?'

'Okay.'

'It will work out Anna,' Eva offered as she headed for the front door and jogged to her car.

I hope so, she thought as she followed her through to the hallway, grabbed her bag and climbed the stairs to her bedroom. The essence of Lauren's scent seemed to linger in the room and a white fluffy towel still lay where it had been dropped on that fateful morning that Anna had received the call. She stared out the window at the pounding rain.

17

They had been out there, exploring the first flurries of winter snow together. Anna had teased Lauren for her thrill at something that barely constituted snow, in Anna's mind. Her child-like excitement at the sight of the fine light powder, and insistence that they go and build a snowman, at first irritating, had eventually dragged Anna out of her stressed state. The initial flurries barely covered the ground, but within an hour the flakes had grown significantly and a coating of at least four-inches had descended. Giggling, they had thrown on their boots, coats and gloves and trudged out into the cold, like two kids on a mission. It had to look like *Olaf* Lauren had insisted. It was a matter of principle, with *Frozen* being one of her favourite movies of all time. The first push of the carrot to make his nose resulted in his head collapsing and it had taken three-attempts to get it firmly in place without his eyes drooping. Anna had felt high just watching Lauren's relentless enthusiasm. She had discovered a fun side previously hidden and had known then that Lauren would make a wonderful parent. And then they had had a snowball fight, when Lauren's competitive spirit showed another dimension of her character that bordered on scary. Anna had pleaded, whilst laughing so hard, for Lauren to stop the assault as snow found its way into her neckline and down her back. Lauren's glare had turned to lust in an instant as her lips, warm and wet, had crashed urgently onto Anna's. The passion between them had been fierce that day. Lauren's hand had quickly found the gap at Anna's waistline, she had pushed down into the warm wet area between her legs and thrust into her deeply in one swift movement. Anna could barely breathe as she tensed around Lauren's fingers, claiming her mouth with her own. 'I love you,' Lauren had said as she held Anna's steel-blue eyes, searching, probing. She, of course, had responded and kissed her tenderly before allowing herself to be helped up to her feet. They had showered together, made love slowly, tenderly, and mutually. Everything had been perfect. Too perfect! They had lit a log fire, toasted chestnuts and made mulled wine even though it had been a little too early for Christmas. They held each other closely through the night, and then Lauren had left for London, with a promise to be back soon.

Anna stared at the spot where the snowman had been erected. The grass was green now not white. The ground was wet not crisp. The sky was a dull grey not abundant with cleansing snow. So much looked different now. But the essence of Lauren remained. Anna curled up on top of her bed and pressed the pillow Lauren had used against her cheek. Taking in the soothing scent, she drifted with her memories.

3.

'Don't look at me like that,' Lauren said with a smirk.

'Well I don't know whether to be impressed that you stood up to your mother at last, or appalled at the fact that you reacted so badly when her intentions are in your best interests,' Rachel said. 'You basically sent her packing, just because she was trying to help you remember the last few months. Seems a bit harsh, though I better than most know how challenging she can be. You certainly picked your moment,' she admonished.

'Thanks for that.' Lauren said, looking mildly sheepish.

Today was a good day. Today she was feeling relatively calm and in the absence of anger, her rational mind was also acutely aware of her over-reaction to her mother. 'You need to forgive her Lou,' Rachel said, holding Lauren's gaze intently.

'How do I do that?'

'I don't know. That's for you to work out. But you need to remember that she's an old lady now. She's not going to change much and although she's controlling and dictatorial at times, she really loves you. She's your mother and it's just her way of protecting you.'

'Controlling my life is her way of protecting me? She's rejected me all my life. Corry was always her favourite and when she died I might as well have been Satan's child. She's hated the fact that I'm gay, until recently it seems. She barely tolerated you.'

'Thanks,' Rachel said with a smirk.

'It's true. She never accepted our relationship and only accepted you because of what you do. She respects you. That's different,' Lauren continued.

'I know. But that's just her stuff remember, not yours. It's her history and beliefs that she's living by. That doesn't mean she doesn't care about you. It just means she's got a different way of showing it. And it doesn't mean you have to agree with her either.' Rachel squeezed Lauren's hand. 'You need to learn to accept her and not take her too seriously.'

'Yeah, right. How do I do that?'

'Start by accepting her offer of help rather than rejecting her. You don't like being rejected, she won't either.'

'Fuck me. Since when did you become such a big fan of my mother?'

'Since I spent time with her watching you like a hawk. Since I saw her looking frail and vulnerable at the thought of the damage you had sustained. Since I watched her shed tears at your bedside, pleading your forgiveness, whilst you fell in and out of consciousness.' Lauren's eyes widened, her body stiffened and she withdrew from Rachel's hand. 'She's not a bad woman Lou and she's changed a lot since the death of your father. The trouble is, you don't remember and you're still living in the past. You're not giving her a chance.'

'I know, and it's killing me.'

'I know, baby. And I hate seeing you like this too.' Rachel waved a hand in her direction. 'And I don't just mean physically like this. I mean in your head. This isn't you. You've been so angry, and I get that. But...'

'But what?'

'I don't know. It's easy for me to say, sitting here. You need to move on. I know it's early days since the accident, but you need to let go of the past too. Cut your mother some slack and see what happens.' She shrugged realising the challenge might be too much too soon, but hoping Lauren's calm disposition might help her to be open to the suggestion. Lauren sighed and slumped back in the chair. 'Call her.'

Lauren mumbled. 'All right, I'll think about it.'

*

'Would you like a glass of wine?' Eva asked as she picked up the Merlot she had decanted an hour earlier. 'I know with being pregnant…' She stirred the sizzling beef casually with her free hand as she spoke.

'Yes.' Anna cut her off with determination. 'I'm sure a little wine won't do any more damage than my emotional state has this last few weeks. If this little one can hang on through that turmoil, he'll be fine with a little escapism.' She took the half-filled glass and took a delicate sip. The silky-smooth texture slid too easily down her throat. The instant hit weakened her legs and her head felt woozy.

'He?' Eva questioned with a smile as she swigged a healthy glug from her glass. Anna shrugged. 'Mmm… good choice Adams,' she commended herself before stirring the food again and taking another swig. 'Mmm… really good.'

'Yes, good choice Adams,' Anna teased lightly, in her mind hoping that she was only carrying one baby.

After unpacking, she had fallen asleep on her bed for an hour then spent the afternoon in the loft reacquainting herself with her work. One canvas remained carefully covered in the corner of the room. She had glanced at the cardboard packaging, knowing its contents, but had no desire to open it. She couldn't face looking at the picture she had created of Lauren. Couldn't deal with her heart breaking all over again. Instead, she had focused on immersing herself in a new abstract. Something fresh, through which she could lose herself and express herself simultaneously. She had hoped the therapeutic effects would kick in quickly and at some level they had.

Descending the stairs after three-hours of painting, to the spicy aromas, soft music and light-hearted Eva singing out of tune had given her cause to smile for the first time in a long time. She would worry about the future tomorrow. Tonight, she would do her best to unwind and chat, and Eva was the best person to have around for that.

'This tastes great,' Anna said, sounding surprised.

'You didn't realise I can cook, eh?' Eva laughed. 'How d' you think I survive on my own?'

'I guess I never really thought about it. You just don't strike me as...'

'What, domesticated?' Anna laughed as Eva pulled the hurt look.

'Dancing? Yes. Drinking. Definite yes. Domesticated... mmm... not so much.'

'Okay, so it doesn't come that naturally, but I do have a couple of dishes under my belt. You should try my Spag Bol. It has received rave reviews.'

'I look forward to that. What do you do, repeat the two meals in rotation?' Anna teased.

'Harsh. Anyway, moving on... do you have any plans?' Eva asked, tentatively.

Anna looked up and into space. 'I'm going to get stuck into work,' she said unconsciously resting a gentle hand on her womb as she spoke.

'How long's Lauren going to be in hospital?'

'I don't know. I think it's down to the physio to confirm that she can manage, with some assistance of course. Hopefully not too much longer.'

'So why did you leave now?'

'My being there wasn't helping. Lauren is very confused and gets frustrated easily. The stress wasn't helping me... or this little one, either.'

'So, she doesn't know you're pregnant?'

'No.' Anna held Eva's gaze looking for criticism, but found nothing but kindness and support. 'None of them know. Just you and my mums.' She put down the half-eaten fajita on her plate and sipped at the wine. 'I had thought of terminating you know.' Eva didn't respond. 'Still crosses my mind, from time to time,' she admitted. 'But deep down I know I can't do that.

This baby is more hers than it is mine. It's totally *of her*, her eggs were used.'

'I didn't know that,' Eva said, reaching out to hold Anna's hand. 'Give it time. This baby is as much a part of you as it is Lauren. It's yours and he... or she, needs you now more than ever.' Eva's eyes glassed over as she processed the pain on Anna's face.

'I know. Mum said the same thing. Do you think she'll ever remember me?' Anna pleaded for the confirmation that no one could provide.

'I don't know what she might remember, but that doesn't stop you learning to be together again, does it?'

'Maybe it's possible, but that's not going to happen right now. She doesn't want me around. It's too stressful for her and she needs to get physically better before she can begin to retrace her steps and try to remember anything.'

Eva nodded, glugged her wine, and squeezed Anna's hand. 'So what work are you going to get stuck into?' she asked, shifting the topic.

'No.' Anna said, pulling herself up straight, grabbing her food and taking a bite. 'Enough about me already, what have you been up to? Anyone special on the cards yet?'

Eva smiled wryly. This would be a short conversation. 'Just work and no there's no one, let alone anyone special.' But her eyes betrayed her words as she held Anna's inquisitive gaze.

Anna pushed her plate away and stood. Leaving the last remnants of wine in her glass, she nodded towards Eva. 'Fancy a movie?'

'Great idea,' Eva said, jumping out of her seat and moving to clear the plates.

'I'll do that in the morning,' Anna offered.

'It's okay, I've got it. Do you want a tea?' she asked, as she filled her glass with the last of the wine from the bottle.

'That would be lovely. Do you mind?'

'Nope. I'm good. Now, go relax.' She raised her eyes to the door and Anna followed the command willingly.

*

'Mother.' Lauren spoke softly into the silence.

'Lauren. I'm so happy you called. I'm really sorry that I upset you. I...'

'I'm sorry. You didn't deserve...' Lauren interrupted. It had taken every ounce of courage to pick up the phone and she needed to get the words out before she backed out.

'It's okay darling. I understand.' Valerie said, with genuine compassion. Lauren's shoulders dropped and her eyes watered as she stared into space, pressing the phone to her ear. 'How are you?' Valerie asked.

'Improving. Hopefully I can get out of here soon.'

'I hope so too.' Valerie paused, before continuing tentatively. 'Darling, I know you would rather go to your London home but you won't have anyone there to support you.' She waited for Lauren's response.

'I don't need support,' Lauren countered biting her lip, knowing that she would need some help, if only whilst settling in. She also knew her mother would go overboard with any assistance she procured, clamp her independence, and render her feeling incapable. She dreaded the thought of being vulnerable within her mother's clutches, but she was also aware that she needed to find a way to give her a chance to bridge the gap between them. And she had to work at that too.

'Yes. But that's not going to give you the exposure you need to events that might help with recovering your memory, darling. Remember what the Doctor said.' Valerie spoke softly making every effort not to come across too assertively.

Lauren knew she was right and she did remember what the Doctor had said. The triggers, if there were any, were most likely to come from familiarity. She had spent most of the three-months before the accident in Corsica, with brief visits to her office in London, and a great deal of change seemed to have taken place within a short space of time. Maybe it would help being at her family home where there was more chance of triggering those memories. If only for her mother to keep reminding her of the conversations they had been through in the last three-months. Right now though, even Valerie didn't feel that familiar, Lauren worried to herself.

'Okay,' she conceded. 'If and when they let me out of this place, I'll come back to Corsica for a short while.'

'Of course they will let you out, soon I hope. I'll see if Henri can pull some strings...' she started, stopping at the realisation that she might be overstepping the delicate line they were treading together.

Henri, Lauren dwelled on the unfamiliar name of her father's replacement in her mother's life. It felt alien to her. 'Henri. Right.'

'Keep doing your exercises darling,' Valerie said encouragingly and as a signal to end the call. 'I've got to go as we have a dinner tonight with some of Henri's family.'

Valerie had stayed with Lauren after hospitalisation across the Christmas holidays, until it was clear that her physical recovery was simply a matter of time. Since her return to Corsica she had planned a number of events to make up for the inevitable cancellation of Christmas.

'Yes,' was the only word that came to Lauren, as she searched for some hint of a memory of her new relatives. Nothing came. 'Mother?'

'Yes darling?'

'Can you send me some pictures please? Who knows, maybe it will help?'

'Of course darling. I'll get some out to you tomorrow. Now take care. Remember, I love you.'

The words stung, raising old wounds. She held her breath, processed her commitment to building the bridges between them, and then slowly released the compressed air. 'I love you too,' she mumbled. Lauren felt the burning behind her eyes before the line went dead. As much as her relationship with her mother had been strained for so many years she could remember, she couldn't help that she still craved to feel loved by her.

As she placed her new phone on the side table, a light knock preceded the opening of her room door and Rachel's heels clipped across the floor at pace; stunting the release of the building tears and causing Lauren's head to thump with the subsequent pressure.

'Hi.' Rachel leant in and kissed her on the cheek, ruffling her hair in a way that she had never remembered her doing before. Lauren looked at her quizzically. 'You okay?' she asked, noting the glassy eyes.

'Yeah, I'm fine. Just spoken with mother.'

'Ah. How is Valerie?'

'She's fine. I've said I'll go there when I get discharged.'

'Good.' Rachel said with a confirming nod of her head.

'Anyway, how are you? You seem... different. And I don't mean different just because I can't remember anything,' Lauren added. 'I mean different, different.' She tilted her head as if assessing her ex for clues as to the light-hearted tactility she had just been subjected to.

'I'm happy and having a good day,' Rachel buzzed with an uncharacteristically gooey look on her face.

'Bully for you,' Lauren scathed. She didn't like the persistent anger that she projected on anyone and everyone, especially when they seemed happy, but she had no means of stopping it. 'Sorry. I'm being a dick,' she pleaded as her eyes held the sparkle in Rachel's. 'So, what's got you so chirped up?'

27

'I'm not sure I should tell you. Whether it will help you move on or not?'

'Try me. At the moment I really don't give a shit.' Lauren spat. 'Sorry. I'm just so fucking angry. I don't mean to take it out on you.'

'Hey... it's okay Lou. I get it.'

'Please tell me. Maybe it will add a light to the dark tunnel I'm in,' she said, with more than a hint of sarcasm.

'I went on a date last night and she's great.'

'Oh.' Lauren's gaze bypassed Rachel and fixated on a spot on the wall over her right shoulder. She didn't know how to process the information she had just been given. She knew she should be happy for her ex, but in her mind they were still together even though she knew they weren't.

'Sorry, I shouldn't have said anything.' Rachel said, noting Lauren's response and averted her eyes as she thought of a change of topic.

'No, it's okay. I just need to adjust. I'm happy for you... really,' she said, less convincingly than intended. 'Who is she? What does she do? Where did you meet?'

'Her name's Mia and she's a teacher. Primary school. We met at a bar last weekend and agreed to meet up last night. She's funny, smart and adorable.' Rachel couldn't keep the beaming smile from her face as she recounted the details of her new love.

Lauren had never seen her look like that in all the time they were together. 'Wow...'

'Yes.' Rachel caught her eyes. 'Sorry, I hope this isn't too hard for you to hear.'

'Umm... no. I... err... I'm not sure what to think... or say,' she confessed. 'You look really happy. In fact, I've never seen you look so... made up. I'm surprised, but I don't feel any resentment. Good on you.' Lauren's smile increased as she adjusted to the news.

'Anyway, I bought you these.' Rachel handed over the box of mixed Ferrero Rocher chocolates she had been clinging to. 'I know you like the coconut ones and I thought you might need sweetening up after my news,' she said with a slight twitch of her mouth and shrug of shoulders.

'Thanks.' Lauren slapped her on the arm as she took the box. 'You didn't need to, but since you did, do you want one?'

'Fuck it, let's!' Rachel's carefree attitude piqued Lauren's interest as they dived into the box and savoured the soft chocolate and crunchy texture.

'Mmm… scrummy. I haven't had anything sweet for what feels like forever. Can you feel that rush? Weh hey…' Endorphins flooded Lauren's brain, instantly lightening her mood.

'Not quite the same rush you seem to have. I hope you don't come down as quickly,' Rachel said, with some concern as she took in Lauren's elevated state.

'Ah, fuck it. I need this right now. I'll worry about the downer later and just eat more chocolate if it gets too bad.' Lauren sniggered like the child she had regressed into. 'So, tell me more about…'

'Mia,' Rachel finished for her and her eyes glazed over as she drifted off to the previous evening.

'Have you slept with her?' Lauren asked directly. Rachel jumped, thrust out of her reverie by the question.

'No….' she defended. 'It's not like that. I mean, it's not that I… we, don't want to. She's different. Special. There's no rush and we've just been having fun and I haven't known her long,' she babbled.

'Where's she from?'

'She's from Brighton but her mother's Spanish and father's English. She's got that Spanish passion and intensity and…'

'Catholic?' Lauren interjected.

'Yes, she is, but not practicing.'

'Well I guess that would be a bit tricky being gay, eh? How are her parents about her sexuality?'

'They're aware...'

'Uh hum... meaning?'

'They're okay with it, but she's not that open. Her closest friends know, but she keeps her private life private, especially because she teaches little ones.'

'Mm hmm, a bit tricky then?' Lauren asked, remembering clearly the time she and Rachel had got together and how important it had been for them to be overtly *out* for the purpose of her career. How times had changed, she mused, watching Rachel in adoration.

'We're not in a rush,' she said picking at a rough fingernail before biting off the offending piece.

'Hey, I'm really pleased for you and I hope it all works out. She sounds fab and I look forward to meeting her when I get out of this God forsaken place.' Lauren reached forward and took the hand out of Rachel's mouth, squeezing it as she held the worried eyes with her own, before popping another chocolate into her own mouth.

'I do hope so. I've never felt like this before,' Rachel admitted coyly. Her eyes watered and she sighed, brushing her thumbs over Lauren's tanned hand as a wave of guilt passed through her at the honesty of her revelation.

'It will.' Lauren nodded convincingly. A fleeting image of Anna passed through her mind, causing her heart to stop momentarily, as she acknowledged that she had probably felt this way about her too, before the accident. The sugar wrestled with her internal reality to keep her spirits high. As Rachel made her exit, the sugar lost the battle and Lauren drifted into an even darker interior world.

4

Lauren reached across to the bedside table, picked up and opened the envelope the nurse had left for her. She wasn't expecting mail. She was curious. She pulled out a hand painted card of two people standing, holding hands, facing out over the river Seine and looking down toward the Eiffel Tower. The sun was setting and the Tower was lit up like a Christmas tree. Even though she couldn't see the faces of the two women in the picture she could tell they were in love. Their bodies complimented each other effortlessly. Their heads rested at the same angle, and there was something about the way they held hands - gentle and connected. Something about the small details seemed significant. Lauren studied the card for a long time before opening it. The message inside read...

You'll always be my Valentine, Love Anna x

She closed the card quickly finding the words disconcerting, curiosity forcing her to trace over the images of the two women with her finger. They were happy, in love even. The card was an excellent piece of art, she thought with a wry smile. She placed the card upright on the table and picked up her Kindle. The physio would be along shortly and she was hoping it would be her last session before being released from hospital. She had pushed the point and, even though they would have liked her to stay a bit longer, she had convinced them that she would have the necessary support at home. Her mother had arranged for a personal nurse and physiotherapist to take care of her, even though she insisted she didn't need a nurse. She was returning to Corsica with more than an ounce of trepidation, but she was also pleased to be getting out of the hospital that had been her home for far too long.

The knock at the door interrupted her reading. She plopped the reader onto her lap and looked up. Rachel galloped through the door wielding a large holdall bag and sporting an even bigger grin. 'I got the bits you asked for. It's all in there. Are you sure you're going to be okay... in Corsica I mean? I could spend some time with you if you want to stay in London for a while?' Rachel offered.

'Thanks, I have debated the idea, but I don't have the energy right now to fight mother, and as you said I need to give her a chance.' She smirked, taking the bag and dropping it on the floor next to her bed.

'Yes, I did say that didn't I?' Rachel winced in response, holding both hands up.

'Anyway, you're chirpy. I take it one lady named Mia is the result of your overwhelmingly happy face?'

'Ahhh... I think I'm in love,' she swooned before stopping suddenly. 'It's not that I didn't love you,' she said, defensively. Lauren grinned at her panicked retreat.

'Hey, it's fine. We're both big girls and anyway, I divorced you... remember. Yes, apparently you do! Which, by the way, we do need to finalise.'

Rachel beamed and pulled Lauren into her chest for a hug, releasing her just as quickly when Lauren winced and groaned with pain. 'Oops, sorry,' she apologised, looking Lauren up and down for any evidence of damage. 'I'll sort out the paperwork so you don't need to worry about anything,' she confirmed.

'Sure. Anyway, tell me more. How is your gorgeous Mia?'

'She's wonderful. She's so... cute, in a hot way... and naïve, in a good way, so everything feels fresh and fun. I feel more alive and free than I've ever felt. I'm even thinking of giving up politics.'

'Fuck! You're kidding me. I'm shocked. What has this woman done to you?' She teased, looking Rachel up and down. 'It suits you though,' she complimented finally, an air of serious acknowledgement passing between them.

'Thank you, I think it does. Now, we just need to get you sorted,' she said, pointing a determined finger at Lauren's chest.

Lauren sighed, averting her gaze, disconnecting momentarily. 'Well hopefully going home will help.'

'Lovely card.' Rachel said noticing the image on the table. 'Did you go there together? So romantic.'

Lauren looked at the card, searching for the answer. 'I guess we must have. How did you know it was from her?'

'I didn't, but there's no mistaking that's you and Anna. Did she paint it?'

'Yes.'

'She's good. I might have to commission her at some point.' Rachel picked up the card and studied it further. 'Really good.'

'Yes she is,' Lauren whispered.

A knock and the door opened, simultaneously. 'Are you ready Lauren?' Jean chirped.

'Right, I'd better be off,' Rachel announced. She leaned in and hugged Lauren firmly before kissing her on the cheek. 'I'll see you tomorrow about eight-thirty,' she said as she passed Jean, beamed a smile, and shut the door behind her.

'So… I understand you're planning on leaving us tomorrow?' Jean asked, rhetorically, as she glanced at the holdall sprawled on the floor.

'Sure am. I'm going home to Corsica.'

'Well there's nothing like sunshine and warmth to help with the healing process,' Jean remarked without judgement.

'True. I'll have plenty of help, and a physio,' she confirmed. 'Though I doubt they'll give me as hard a time as you do,' she grinned as Jean removed the wheelchair from the bedside and placed a frame in front of Lauren.

'Good, so you'll be ready to walk to the gym today then?' She winked as she stood back and watched Lauren move herself slowly into the hold of the frame. 'Right, follow me. Easy does it. We're not at the races today.' She placed a tender touch on Lauren's good shoulder before stepping off to open the door for her patient. Lauren was sweating before they reached the gym, but determined. She was going home.

*

'Right. So, you'll be there to pick her up at 4.30pm?' Antoine nodded as Valerie flapped around restating the plans that they had gone over many times in the previous twenty-four hours. You didn't get in the way of a Vincenti with a plan, and especially Valerie Vincenti, he had learned over the years, initially working with Petru Vincenti at the vineyard, and subsequently living as his lover. Even though Valerie wasn't technically a Vincenti, she might as well have been born one. She exhibited all the same attributes and had shared a life with Petru for nearly forty years. He watched patiently as she continued to flap. Henri sat in the background, observing his wife from time-to-time over the top of his newspaper.

'The nurse will arrive first thing. She is going to take the room at the back. The physio will come over at 6.30 on Friday for an initial assessment and then she'll tell us the plan for her rehabilitation. I haven't arranged anything for her mental health. What do you think Henri?' She spun around to seek his counsel.

Henri looked up from the newspaper he had been trying to read. 'I think you need to ask Lauren what she thinks she needs. Maybe working with someone will help her deal with how she's feeling, but the recovery of her memory is most likely to happen as a result of familiarity....'

'Good, I'll arrange something with Lauren then,' she interrupted, cutting him off. 'Damn! What about climbing the stairs? Is she going to be able to get up the stairs or do we need to get a lift installed... or one of those stair lifts?'

'I don't know darling,' he said calmly. 'I'm sure the physio will be able to assess that, and they'll want her to do as much as she can to live normally. If she needs something we can get it sorted. In the meantime, we can make a bed up in the study, which has the bathroom right next to it.'

'Yes, yes.' Valerie flustered around the room, reiterating the plan. Antoine and Henri shrugged at each other. Waiting for the next set of orders, Henri's eyes were drawn back to the paper in his hand.

'Right, so you've got the pick-up time, Antione?'

'Yes Valerie,' Antione said, more firmly. He had work to be getting on with and needed to get back to the vineyard. 'Will that be all ma'am,' he teased with a mischievous smile, hoping to ease the rising tension.

Valerie stopped pacing and breathed deeply. 'Thank you... both. I just want things to be perfect for her.' She looked from one man to the other, an almost broken woman. Both men fidgeted uncomfortably, recognising the uncharacteristic vulnerability in Valerie and unsure how to deal with it.

Antoine stepped up to her and pulled her into his arms. 'She will be fine. Lauren is a strong woman. She takes after you remember.' He released his hold and took her chin in his hand, lifting her eyes to meet his. 'She will be fine and so will Anna. This will pass and we will all be here to help them both.' He kissed her affectionately on the nose, squeezed her arms, and headed for the door.

Henri replaced him and held his wife close. She succumbed to the embrace and sniffled into his shoulder. 'Sshhh... it's okay darling. Whatever she needs we can provide and she will get better. It's just a matter of time. We need a plan and you are the best person for that.' He kissed her on the top of her head as they swayed together.

'I don't want to let her down again,' Valerie whispered. I haven't been there when she's needed me most, and I'm ashamed of myself for that,' she confessed.

'Don't be too hard on yourself darling,' Henri said softly.

'I won't, but I can't lose her again. I need you to know this. When Corry died I closed myself off to Lauren. Petru withdrew into himself and as you know, he and Antoine had each other by then. But Corry's death drove Petru into that silly affair. An affair that cost him his life in the end,' she continued stoically. 'When Lauren told us she was a lesbian it was the final straw. I blamed Petru and I cut Lauren off. I couldn't accept her that way. It was against everything I had ever stood for. My husband being gay was devastating enough, but we had an arrangement that worked for us all. I couldn't face Lauren's openness and I was cruel.'

'Darling,' Henri tried to interrupt.

'No, it's a fact. I treated her badly. I became cold towards her. Detached. She felt it and I've watched her pain for years. Pain that I've caused, in my ignorance and pride,' she admonished herself with a shake of her head. 'When Lauren told me to leave the hospital, she was right to do so. I thought I'd lost her forever and the idea of that killed me inside, here.' She pulled away and placed her hand on her heart, her eyes searching Henri's for his response. The kindness she found caused the tears to fall effortlessly onto her cheeks.

'We all have a past Valerie. And it's not always something to be proud of. The best we can do is to learn from our mistakes and hope that our children don't repeat our errors. We're all human beings, drawn by thrills, controlled by our fears. It's a wonder we do as well as we do,' he said, kissing away the tears on her cheeks. 'I love you. I have done since I've known you, and that's a long time now. Petru and Antoine were lucky to find each other, and we have been lucky to find each other. Lauren and Anna have found each other too and I'm sure, with time, they'll pick up where they left off,' he said confidently.

'I hope so,' Valerie whispered. 'I do hope so.'

By the afternoon, Henri had been on to a lift installation company in Ajaccio. The earliest they could install anything was the following week. He had booked them in just in case it would be needed and they had spent the rest of the day rearranging the rooms. Lauren's bedroom had been transported, almost in its entirety, to the study. Curtains and screens had been erected to hide the bookshelves, to make it feel cosier and less like a workspace. Valerie had even sprayed some of Lauren's perfume in the room hoping it would help her feel at home. Lauren's cosmetics, shower gel, shampoo and conditioner, and bath towels had been placed in the downstairs bathroom, which was now considered out of bounds to anyone other than Lauren and her nurse.

Antoine had stayed away. He would be in Ajaccio for the pick up at 4.30, and he would keep a track of the flight's progress until she landed. In truth, he would be as happy to see Lauren back home as Valerie was. He had enjoyed their time together before the accident and hoped to be able to pick up where they left off. He was convinced the vines would cast their magic.

5.

'Will you come with me?'

'Are you sure?'

'Yes. I don't think I can do this on my own.' Anna picked up her handbag and Eva's car keys from the table, handing the keys to Eva with doe eyes. 'Please?' she begged.

'Okay.' Eva said, melting under the heat of Anna's pleading gaze, grabbing for her jacket. 'Do you know where the clinic is? Got the postcode?' she asked, as they took their seats in the car.

'Yes.' Anna scanned the paperwork in her hand and read off the postcode before sitting back in the leather seat and breathing deeply. The butterflies in her stomach knotted and her heart raced. She hadn't expected to be in this position, and certainly not with Eva by her side. But, she felt reassured with her support, albeit still anxious. She reached across and squeezed her arm. 'Thank you for coming with me, I really didn't want to go through this alone.'

'That's okay.' Anna's steel-blue eyes, the dark rim highlighting their depth, caught Eva's breath. 'I'd do anything for you Anna,' she said. She flustered as she tried to put the key in the ignition, embarrassed at her confession, confirmation that she meant what she had said. 'Right, let's get going,' she mumbled, hoping Anna wouldn't notice the rise in colour of her cheeks. Giving her attention to the road ahead she cleared her throat and eased the car into gear, the gravel crunching heavily under the slowly rotating wheels. 'Music?' she asked, reaching for the radio before an answer came, hoping the distraction would ease the tension she felt building.

'Sure.' Anna looked at her phone, as she had done every day since sending the card, hoping she might have received a message from Lauren, hoping she had received the card. Praying that the image might mean something to her. Nothing. They travelled in independent silence to the clinic. Anna stared vacantly at the light covering of snow on the landscape, reminded of days past. Things would have been so different with Lauren. The sharp blue sky and wispy clouds gave a stationary appearance, with the movement of the car, and pulled her deeper into trance. It seemed to have an energising effect on the cold winter's day. She felt it: the lightness, the freedom. Absorbing herself in it, to distract from the anxiety building inside her, she tried to relax. When they arrived at the clinic, the shaking that had started in her stomach was showing in her hands.

'Are you okay?' Eva asked with concern.

'No, not really,' she said.

Eva took her hands, rubbed a thumb softly across her knuckles and held her eyes. 'Hey. I'm here for you. We'll do this together okay.'

'What if there's a problem?' Anna voiced her concerns.

'Then we'll deal with it.' Eva said, shrugging involuntarily, her confident smile working hard to reassure Anna even though she didn't have a clue what she would do if there were a problem. The thought hadn't really crossed her mind.

Anna forced a smile and squeezed Eva's hand. 'Come on, let's go in,' she said, as she opened the car door. Eva nodded, releasing her hand.

The building looked small and dingy from the outside, the inside though was pristine and decorated simply. Posters and information sheets decorated the walls, a water cooler sat at one end of the waiting room. Three-doors, which appeared to be clinic rooms, fed off the main corridor. They stepped up to the reception window hand in hand. The receptionist glanced down at them, from one to the other, her eyes passing judgementally across their linked hands. 'Can I help you?' she said, reluctantly.

'Ms Taylor-Cartwright is here for a scan,' Eva said assertively, continuing to hold Anna's hand and squeezing tightly.

The woman's eyes veered towards the computer screen in front of her. She tapped the keys, waited, and then looked up at Anna. 'Right. You're booked in. Please take a seat through there, the technician will call you when she's ready.' She indicated with her eyes toward what appeared to be the main waiting area.

'Thank you. Have a nice day,' Eva said, slightly facetiously. Smiling, she turned and led Anna into the room, taking the two seats by the window, opposite a single woman reading a magazine. 'Would you like some water?' she asked.

'Yes please.' Anna smiled, the tension palpable. Sitting back into the chair, she glanced around the room. One other couple sat holding hands in a halo of love and anticipation. An image of Lauren came to mind briefly as she watched them, causing her body to react, taking her by surprise. She looked up as Eva handed her a bottle of water. It wasn't the same. It was very different from how she had planned the experience of her first scan. 'Thanks,' she said, taking the bottle from Eva.

'You're welcome,' she said, picking up a birthing magazine from the low table. She sat next to Anna, nudging her in the side. 'You okay?'

'Sure,' Anna responded, unconvincingly.

Eva opened the magazine randomly as she watched Anna. Her eyes popped out of her head as she caught sight of a woman in a birthing position, with the head of the baby crowned. 'Holy fuck,' she said, louder than she intended. Pairs of eyes locked onto her. 'Sorry,' she apologised sheepishly to the room, closing the magazine and wincing at Anna who was stifling a much-needed giggle.

'Ms Taylor-Cartwright?' The technician looked up from her clipboard to identify the person responding to the name she had just called. Anna stood instantly and pulled Eva to her feet.

'You sure you want me to go in there with you?' she asked queasily.

'I need you with me Eva.' Anna said, fighting the vulnerability she felt weakening her legs and causing her heart to race.

'Right.' Eva said. Her hands were beginning to sweat and her heart thumped in her chest.

'That's me,' Anna said, looking at the nurse who smiled warmly at them both, easing Anna's tension. She breathed out deeply.

Eva, noticing the small muscles around Anna's mouth twitching, realised she too felt nervous, and put her arm around her. She needed to be supportive, not wimp out at the first sign of a needle, she admonished.

'Hello, I'm Regina. I'm your technician today. Please, come this way,' she said, as she opened the door for them to enter the clinic room. A bed with a strip of blue paper towel, a monitor with ultrasound equipment attached to it, and a computer sat on the desk in the room. There was an armchair next to the bed facing the monitor.

Her eyes sparkled, Eva noticed, relieved that the technician's attitude was more inclusive than the receptionist's, and briefly curious as to her sexuality. Her gaydar hadn't gone off, but then she hadn't been thinking about that at the time, she mused.

'Have you done this before?' Regina asked.

'No.' Anna answered, nodding as she spoke. Eva blushed, thrust out of her reverie, and also found herself nodding unconsciously at the question.

'That's fine. So, you're the one having the scan.' Regina looked to Anna for further confirmation.

'Yes.'

'Please make yourself comfortable on the bed, loosen your jeans and relax. I'm going to put some gel on your belly and then this,' she said, holding up the ultrasound scanner. 'It will be cold,' she said, as she pointed the large phallus menacingly, squirting the gel onto Anna's sensitive skin. She shuddered at the slight chill.

The technician pressed a few buttons on her computer as she plopped the instrument firmly onto Anna's lower belly and wriggled it around. She clearly knew what she was looking for. Anna prayed. She had an idea of what to expect, having seen the scans during her earlier, failed attempts at AI, and couldn't cope with the idea of not seeing a heart beat. Eva's jaw dropped and her eyes doubled in size as she tried to make sense of the black and white fuzzy image on the screen.

'So, this is an early scan,' Regina commented but continued before Anna confirmed. 'You say you are about seven weeks pregnant, so we are looking for a small kidney bean shape and a heartbeat...' Anna's anxiety sky-rocketed as the technician pressed and rolled the scanner. 'There we go.' Anna released the breath she had been holding, her gut lurched then fizzed, and a wave of pure relief washed over her. Immediately, the anxiety had turned to excitement and she felt lighter.

The pulsing light flashed quickly in front of their eyes. Both women stared open mouthed before broad grins crept across their faces. The technician wiggled the scanner and the flickering light disappeared. With further movement, it appeared back on the screen. Anna's heart skipped, jumped, dropped, flipped and tears flowed uncontrollably as the first signs of her baby registered in her mind. One baby. Sobbing, she glanced at Eva who also had tears running down her face and snot beginning to dribble from her nose. Eva wiped her sleeve across her face and continued to stare in awe.

'Congratulations both of you,' Regina said.

Anna looked at Eva, tears turning into a giggle. Her heart raced. She didn't want the technician to ever turn the monitor off and she had no inclination to correct her assumption about the two of them. 'Can I have a picture?' she asked.

'Of course.' She wiped Anna's lower belly, then the end of the phallus and placed it back in its holder. She pressed a few more buttons and the printer spurted out a number of images. She looked them up and down and handed over three-copies of a black and white image. The bean shape and tiny fleck of white light was barely visible, but it was enough of a confirmation that Anna was carrying one baby, and that that baby's heart was pumping. It was the only result that mattered. Anna held up the images, her hands shaking. Eva wrapped an arm around her shoulder and pulled her in for a hug, equally entranced by the tiny spec of white inside the kidney bean.

'Thank you so much,' Anna beamed at Regina who was smiling contentedly.

'You're welcome. Have a good day,' she said, as she got up from her chair and opened the door for them to leave. Eva linked arms with Anna and they practically skipped out of the building.

Nothing could wipe the grin off their faces as they talked incessantly about the tiny bean that was so full of life already. 'Thank you for being there with me.' Anna said softly, as the familiar crunch of gravel brought them home.

'I feel privileged,' Eva said soberly, as she pulled the car to a halt. She looked intently at Anna, her heart racing, and heat surged through her body. 'I feel like I know that little guy already,' she joked, as her eyes lowered to Anna's belly. 'I might need to celebrate this momentous occasion,' she stated, nodding to herself as she stepped out of the car. 'But you my friend are on tea.' She winked at Anna who still had her hand unconsciously resting on her growing baby.

'Ah hmm...' Anna had slipped into dreamland and missed the last sentence. Her phone pinged, drawing her attention instantly. Eva averted her eyes and headed for the front door.

Thank you for the card. It's beautiful. Lauren

Anna's stomach rose and rammed the back of her throat. She read and reread the message as she staggered into the barn, unsure what she should be feeling, but realising that what she was feeling was far from the state of positive elation she had journeyed home in with Eva. Incensed, she stared at the screen trying to rationalise the situation. She had hoped to hear from Lauren, but not like this. *Was this as good is it could be?* Her disappointment at the lack of affection or connection irked her, as much, if not more than, the contents of message itself. She was itching to share the good news with Lauren, but, how could she? She didn't want to cause her any further distress. Even though Eva had been there for her, Lauren was the one who should have been there. A sudden surge of anger invaded her senses and she slammed her phone on the kitchen table.

'Everything okay?' Eva asked as she poured the hot water onto the teabag. Anna growled, uncharacteristically. Eva turned, brows raised. Confused. 'What's up?'

'A text from Lauren.'

'That's great news, surely?' Eva questioned, feeling disappointed for a different reason.

'It should be,' Anna responded. 'I know I should be pleased... and I am glad she's responded. It's just...' She looked to the ceiling, lost for the right words.

'Just what?' Eva took a healthy slug of the wine she had just poured.

'The formality of it... I might as well be a stranger... Fuck it, I am a stranger to her.' She thrashed a hand towards the phone on the table. 'Sorry, I'm being emotional and irrational,' she admitted with a deep breath.

'Hey… go easy on yourself. It's early days. Give it time,' Eva said softly, taking another long swig. 'We need to work out a plan,' she said, thinking aloud, as she poured a second glass of wine. She had slugged half the glass in one hit, trying to dampen her own troublesome feelings, before she passed Anna her tea.

6.

'Hello, Rita Pasqual I assume.' Valerie approached the slightly built woman to greet her. 'You come highly recommended,' she said as she assessed the nurse, moving to shake her hand with authority. It was 2pm. Valerie had insisted Lauren's private nurse arrive in good time to settle into her room before Lauren arrived at the house.

'Hello Mrs Vincenti. It's a pleasure to meet you.' The young nurse smiled and submitted to the overly firm grip. The tension in Valerie's body was palpable and an indication of the level of concern this woman had for her daughter's welfare. Perfectly natural, but from what she could tell from the report of her daughter's injuries this all seemed like an overreaction. Rita wasn't convinced that her services were really necessary, but good money was being paid and it was not her place to judge her client's decisions. She had made a lot of money over the years as a private nurse working with wealthy and desperately insecure clients.

'Call me Valerie, please. I'll show you to your room. This way,' she said, turning briskly and stepping into the house.

Rita nodded. 'Of course,' she said respectfully, extending her pace to keep up with her spritely host. She smiled inwardly. This was going to be an interesting gig, she mused.

Valerie opened the door to the small room adjoining the study. Sparsely decorated, a double bed with a bedside table and lamp, sofa, television, and coffee making facilities - it resembled a hotel room; one that a businessman might use. It was clean, warm and private. Perfect. 'You can use the bathroom next door, which will be closed to anyone other than you and Lauren,' Valerie explained, pointing in the direction of the facilities.

'Thank you. This is perfect.' The room backed onto the side of the garden through a windowed door. Sun provided light

46

and heat, giving an airy and warm feeling to the room. Rita placed her bag at the foot of the bed and paced around the room. Looking out across the southeast façade she was drawn to the snow caped mountains across the valley. Born in the Auvergne region of central France, the combination of mountains and forestation reminded her of home. The wistful thought tugged at her chest. She hadn't visited Auvergne for more than fifteen-years. She spun around to face Valerie. 'Thank you,' she said, focusing her attention on her host.

'I'll leave you to unpack and freshen up. Please feel free to explore the house, and make yourself at home. There's coffee in the dining room, a bar in the living room and the chef is always on hand in the kitchen should you need anything.'

'Thank you. You're very kind,' she offered.

Valerie nodded briefly at the compliment. 'Lauren will arrive here early evening. Her flight arrives at 4.30. I'm afraid she's not entirely on board with having a nurse, yet.' Valerie confessed with a coy smile. Rita raised her eyebrows in question, waiting for Valerie to continue. 'Whilst I would normally expect you to help her settle in, I'm sure she'll want to do that herself.' Valerie grimaced at the thought. 'Perhaps we could meet in the living room at about 6.30? I'll introduce you to her then, and we can take it from there.'

'Yes of course.' Rita recognised the request as the command it was. In truth, she couldn't wait to meet Lauren and get a better understanding of what would be required of her over the coming weeks.

*

Lauren cussed loudly. Irritated. Her injuries, her vulnerability and her dependence on others for simple everyday tasks, irked her. Pain was one thing, needing others hurt far more deeply. I can't even get a fucking sock on, she mumbled to herself, flinging the offending article across the room just as her door opened.

'You look like thunder, what's up?' Rachel asked, raising her eyebrows as her eyes tracked Lauren's stare at the lonesome sock, which was hanging off the orange lid of the waste bin. 'I'm guessing you need that?' she said, pointing towards the bin with a wry smile.

'Fucking fuck,' Lauren swore again, fighting against the pressure that was building behind her eyes.

'I got it,' Rachel said, diving and wrestling with the sock in an attempt to lighten the mood she had walked into. 'Come on, let me help?' She reached for Lauren's bare left foot before she could reject the offer. 'I know it galls you to need help, but you're going to need to be a bit patient Lou.' She pulled the sock onto a stubborn foot and kissed the top of Lauren's head. 'So, when can we leave?'

'As soon as I'm dressed! I was hoping to be ready before now, but...'

'That's okay. There's plenty of time. You've already been discharged then?' she asked.

Lauren held up the large carrier bag with her paperwork and the drugs that she needed for the next month. 'Yep. All done.' She grimaced at the contents. 'These will need to go in the hold though. I was just about to...' Rachel took the bag of drugs and pressed it into the holdall on the bed.

'Come on then. What you waiting for?' Lauren slid her good foot into the slipper-like trainer on the floor and swore again as she tried to put the shoe on her left foot and failed. Rachel rested on her knees, eased her foot into place, patted her legs and held out a hand.

'It's okay, it's easier to get up on my own, thanks.' She looked up at Rachel. The sadness embedded overtly in her features couldn't penetrate the happiness in Rachel's face. She reached for the metal frame, leaned heavily on it, and rose slowly to her feet. Standing to adjust her balance, she breathed to release the air held in her lungs. The effort was excruciating, but getting home would make the pain worth it… for now, she thought. 'Right, let's go.'

Rachel picked up the suitcase with agility that annoyed Lauren. Her eyes scanned the austere room one last time, searching. Nothing left behind. Nothing to be missed either. She turned slowly, moved the frame forward, stepped, and repeated the process. The painfully slow progress shifted into a rhythmical gliding movement at some point in the short distance to Rachel's car. The pain of her vulnerability was easily forgotten as fresh air brushed her face and the sense of impending freedom dawned. She breathed deeply, stared briefly at the grey cloud-filled sky, and eased herself into the front passenger seat. It felt different being on the outside, she thought. Immediately thrust out of her reverie with the pain that shot through her left side as she moved to sit, she groaned. Rachel threw the frame and bag into the boot and leapt into the driver seat, exhilarated.

'Will you stop leaping around. You make me feel like a fucking invalid,' Lauren barked.

'Aha… Well here's the truth baby. You are! But only temporarily remember.' She nudged Lauren in the arm, pressed the start button, and moved the automatic into drive. Her desire to accelerate was brought to an instant halt by the slow-moving London traffic. Lauren tried to hold her body weight to reduce the pain, eventually settling into the least painful position she could find. Releasing a deep breath, trying to relax her body, her eyes wandered between the passing cars, the sky, the buildings, and Rachel's mouth, which was moving in time to the sounds coming from the radio. She felt a strange sense of achievement being out of the hospital, as if there really was a future out here for her. At the same time she felt completely lost and alone. The woman sitting beside her was her ex and she was clearly in love with someone else. That felt odd. An image of the Eiffel Tower card flicked across her mind and a twitch of a smile crossed her face. That felt odd too.

'You can just drop me off at departures,' Lauren tried to insist, as Rachel pulled into a busy Gatwick airport.

Rachel glared. 'Don't be an ass... you ass. You're in no fit state to get yourself and your bag into that building. I'm parking up and going to help you to Customer Services. Then they'll make sure you get checked in and to your gate on time, which also means you can't escape,' she teased. 'It's not all bad. You get to ride on one of those buggies that bleep constantly... like an old person,' she laughed.

Lauren slapped her in the arm and laughed, resigned to the plan but still insisting that she make her way to Customer Services under her own steam. 'Do old people bleep then?' she asked.

It took them ten-minutes to get into the departures hall from the car park and Lauren had taken on a shade of white not normally seen in one with her skin pigment. Her eyes had receded even further into her skull, her body was tense, and beads of sweat were forming across her brow. Stubbornness was costing her, Rachel thought, but she didn't interject. She skipped up to the Customer Service desk, introduced Lauren, and handed over the booking paperwork to the dyed blonde hair with a plastic smile and bright red lipstick attending the desk.

'Fancy a coffee?' Rachel asked, as the clerk handed back the processed paperwork.

'No, it's okay. You can get off now. I'll get a drink when I'm through security.'

'If you're sure?'

'Of course.' She looked with sincerity, took Rachel's hand and squeezed tightly. 'Seriously. Thank you. I'm not sure what I would've done without you the last few weeks.' She felt as exhausted as she looked pale.

Rachel stepped closer and pulled her into a tender embrace, rocking her back and forth gently. 'You are welcome baby. Now, take it easy, get well, and I'll come out and visit as soon as I can,' she whispered. The warm breath on Lauren's ear felt comforting and she fought to hold back the tears.

Eventually they released each other as a piercing beeping sound interrupted their personal space. Lauren looked round to see the buggy with its large, squeaky, rubber wheels - driven by an elderly looking man. Her eyes locked back onto Rachel's and they chuckled loudly. Rachel threw Lauren's bag into the back of the cart and Lauren eased herself into the back seat with her frame. 'Keep in touch,' she said grabbing Rachel's hand just as the cart sprung forward.

Rachel blew a kiss and waved as Lauren squeaked and bleeped her way across the hall, to be escorted through check in and then security. A wave of sadness brushed through her before her phone pinged and she shifted back into the world of her new love, Mia.

*

Anna slumped into Rowena's office, unsure of why she had agreed to pay her a visit. Eva followed her through the door and headed straight for the coffee machine. She hadn't bought croissants this time, but a box of donuts sat begging on the low table, each with different coloured icing and some with multi-coloured sprinkles. Rowena's podgy hand was already wrapped around a half-eaten, pink iced and sprinkled bun that she appeared to be devouring. 'Mmm... these are scrummy,' she mumbled through the masticated dough, pink sugar icing decorating her upper lip, raising the donut into the air at them.

Anna flopped into the couch and Eva handed her a glass of water before grabbing a chocolate iced donut and taking a mammoth bite. 'Mmm... sugar. Just what I need.'

'How are you darling?' Rowena asked, full of concern.

'I'm okay... surviving I guess.' Anna sipped at the water and placed her glass on the table, selecting a simple white iced donut from the box and taking a mouse-sized nibble. The sugar caused her mouth to salivate and she munched her way through the sticky bun before the others had finished theirs.

'Do you feel ready to take on another project?' Rowena asked tentatively over the top of her red-rimmed reading glasses.

'I think so. I mean... working helps me to not dwell on what's happened. I can't force the situation with Lauren. I've just got to keep in touch with her, hopefully see her from time to time, and hope we can get back to where we were before the accident,' she rambled, saying more than she intended.

Rowena stared sadly at her protégé. She wouldn't have felt any differently had it been Eva in this situation. The small eyes, peering through plump cheeks, wetted. 'I'm so sorry Anna. If there's anything I can do to help?'

'Thanks.' Anna straightened her spine and tried to refocus. 'So, tell me more about this project.'

'Okay.' Rowena downed the last of her donut and picked out a chocolate-topped one, walked to her desk, squeezed into her director's chair and clicked on the screen. 'So, this is a little different than your normal genre, but as you know you came recommended to the client and they are paying handsomely, not that you particularly care about that bit - but I do.' She looked up, frowned, and grinned at Anna. 'They want you to do a pet portrait.'

'What?' Anna burst out laughing. 'I don't do pets.'

'I did tell them that this wasn't your thing as such, but they insisted. They want you. They've seen your Vincenti portrait.' Anna shuddered involuntarily at the mention of Lauren's surname. 'They want you, and who am I to deny them your talent. Think of this as a new venture,' Rowena said with a shrug, grinning from ear-to-ear at the look on Anna's face.

'What pets do they have?' she asked feigning interest.

'Three-dogs, two cats... and I think they mentioned rabbits, or was it gerbils? Some form of rodent. There isn't a snake though.'

'Well thank fuck for that,' Anna interrupted. Eva sniggered. Anna glared at her and she quickly filled her mouth with another donut, popping another pod in the coffee machine. She turned away to concentrate on making the coffee.

'And I think they have tortoises too. Very popular in Corsica you know...' She lowered her eyes intently. 'Think of it as an *extended family* portrait,' she said, holding back a hearty laugh.

'Really,' Anna frowned, looking at her mentor helplessly.

'Come on, where's your sense of adventure?'

Anna sighed. 'I'll think about it.' she said, holding her head in her hands knowing she would most likely concede, and possibly against her better judgement, in this instance.

'Oh, and the good news is that the client wants you to visit as soon as you can. They live a stone's throw from the Vincenti's, apparently. I hope that's not going to be a problem?' Rowena asked, staring at Anna, watching for her reaction.

'No, I'm not doing it,' Anna said, too quickly for Rowena to take her seriously.

'I'll chat to you later in the week. Just give it some thought... please.' Anna's response had been expected but Rowena also knew that her protégé rarely refused an opportunity, especially where an interesting challenge was involved. Maybe this was one step too far though, she thought wistfully.

'I need to go into town,' Anna said changing the topic suddenly. 'Do you want to come?' She looked across to Eva who had a small cup poised at her lips.

She lowered the drink and glanced at Rowena. 'I need to catch up with mum but we can meet for lunch then shoot back to yours early afternoon if that works?'

'Sure. I'll leave you to it then.' Turning she paced out of the office, her heart thumping through her chest, the sugar putting a spring in her step, images of Lauren chasing her thoughts. She was sweating by the time she hit the street.

'Is she really okay?' Rowena asked after the door had shut.

Eva shrugged. 'She's getting there.' Her eyes glazed over as she spoke.

'Anything I should know about?' Rowena pried.

Eva held her mum's glare. 'No,' she said, less than convincingly.

'Hmmm...' Rowena continued to stare to the point Eva thought she might be reading her mind. She hoped she wasn't.

Eva dropped her eyes to her coffee, brought the cup to her mouth and sipped deliberately, trying to clear her head of any thoughts her mother might pick up on. 'Honestly. There's nothing. She's been working. I've been there for company and she's had brief contact with Lauren, who still can't remember her. It's heart breaking and I feel for her.'

'It is,' was all Rowena said, but the way she looked at her told her that Anna was not available. The only thing missing were the words, *don't you dare mess with her!*

*

Anna ambled along the bank of the Seine, wrapped snugly against the winter chill. The air was cold but thankfully there was no breeze. Frosty mornings made way to clear blue

54

skies these days, but even then, the temperature barely shifted above eight-degrees. Today was a lot colder than that. She watched her breath merge into space, the water constantly moving, the BATOBUS sailing down to the Institute Du Monde Arabe, leaving the Eiffel Tower's dominant presence occupying the near distance. She could see their bench. They had sat there, huddled together, comforted by each other. It seemed light years away, yet only a few painful weeks separated then from now.

She stopped at the frost-covered bench seat, rubbed her hand across its surface. Was it a vain attempt to clear a space to sit, or something else? Sitting anyway, her thick coat affording sufficient protection from the frozen wood, she leaned back into the hard surface and stared out over the water. Perhaps she was secretly hoping to connect with Lauren by being here. She didn't know her reason for coming - she hadn't planned to, she had just been drawn to walk this way. When she had asked Eva to join her, she had intended to wander around the shopping precinct, immerse herself in retail therapy. There were no Christmas lights on the Eiffel Tower, she noted, just its steel structure reaching up into the clouds. A ladder to nowhere, she mused. Her nose tingled, exposed to the elements.

She hadn't realised how long she had been sat, the ping of a text message jolting her out of the daydream. She shivered involuntarily as she reached her phone out of her coat pocket and the reality of how cold she had become hit her senses. Her jaw shuddered uncontrollably as her eyes scanned the screen.

Ready for lunch when you are x

It wasn't the person she was thinking about, hoping to hear from. She smiled at the message though, thankful for Eva's support and her carefree nature. She was easy to be around and right now she needed the company.

On my way, be there in 15 x

Taking one last look out across the river she lifted and orientated her phone, steadied her shaking hand, and pressed the button. Day or night the Eiffel Tower always looked stunning, and with a hint of steam rising gently off the river from the sun's contrasting warmth, the haunting scene made for a great picture. A keepsake. She clicked on the image, pressed the message tab, clicked on the contact details, and typed...

Thinking of you x

Pressing the send button, she watched as 'message sent' appeared on the screen. Pocketing her phone, she walked at pace back to Rowena's office with a hopeful smile on her face. Maybe she should take the project? Maybe she should push harder for Lauren to remember her? *But what if...*

*

Lauren eased her way down the steps of the aircraft and stood on the tarmac. A wheelchair awaited her and she sat tentatively, feeling thoroughly miserable. The flight to Paris had been physical torture and the flight on to Ajaccio had been further torture, even with the assistance of very compassionate ground staff and crew. Popping pills hadn't helped and over the course of the last few hours she had seriously questioned her rationale for agreeing to her mother's proposition. Had she stayed at her London house she would be settled in by now and the journey would have been much less painful. As it was she ached from head to toe, had sharp pains shooting through her hip and leg, and she still had a nearly two-hour car journey in front of her. The only upside was that her mother had agreed not to come to the airport to meet her.

She smiled as she caught sight of Antoine waving at her through the thick windowpane looking out onto the tarmac. His broad smile softened Lauren instantly and she raised her eyebrows towards him, in mock disgust at her debilitated state.

She was still angry with herself for walking out in front of the transit van and it might take some time for her to get over her idiocy. But she looked forward to having time with Antoine on the journey home. They had a lot to catch up on... or so it seemed.

Antoine walked through to meet her in the baggage claim area. Lauren stumbled as she stood to greet him. Dismissing the wheelchair, she grabbed her frame for support. He looked her up and down shaking his head, but his eyes were filled with compassion and love. 'You've looked better,' he said as he held her tentatively. 'Oh my,' he sighed.

'My bag,' Lauren interrupted his appraisal as her eye caught sight of the moving blue holdall and she flapped at it with urgency.

Antoine released her, dived for the conveyor belt and grabbed the bag. 'Let's get you home,' he said with smiling eyes. Lauren nodded, and turning her frame in the direction of the exit made the slow walk to the car.

The journey was relatively comfortable, the seats of the car being far more supportive than those of the aeroplane. Antoine talked easily, appraised her of the vineyard and their preparations for the upcoming season. Lauren had nodded in what she hoped were the right places and smiled when Antoine looked in her direction.

Her phone had been buzzing repeatedly in her pocket as it adjusted to being on French territory. She looked at the screen and her eyes were immediately drawn to a message from Anna. She hadn't told Anna she was leaving for Corsica. She didn't know whether she should feel bad about that, but the anxiety that instantly hit her gut told her she did anyway. Opening the message, she stared at the image. It was very different from the painted card she had received. Still haunting. Beautiful. The absence of the lovers left an emptiness that touched her, and her eyes burned without logical reason. Her fingers danced over the keyboard...

Beautiful picture. How are you?

She hovered over the send button unsure whether she was ready to open up a real conversation with Anna. Antoine braked suddenly, at nothing in particular, and Lauren's hovering finger tapped the send button. She looked up at him questioningly, his eyes fixed firmly on the road, his mouth sporting a huge grin. 'Everything okay?' he asked, knowing the answer.

She frowned. 'How's mother?' she asked, changing the subject as she pocketed her phone.

'Valerie is well... very pleased that you will be home so that she can have you taken care of. She has everything in hand of course.'

'That's what worries me.' Lauren raised her brow.

'Ah, yes. She can be very determined no?' Lauren tilted her head. 'Henri too is very well.'

'Yes, I keep forgetting she has another husband. So surreal,' she shook her head, her eyes scanning the landscape.

Antoine rested his hand lightly on her thigh. 'This accident is a very sad thing Lauren. You have such a beautiful and powerful mind. That you cannot remember the last few months is a tragedy. So much has happened. So much love too.' He shook his head mirroring Lauren.

'I know. I feel very confused. Scared. It's like I've got to go through all the bad bits again without having the good times of the last few months to draw energy from.' Holding her head, she rubbed at her temples.

'Anna?'

'Yes, Anna in particular.'

'What do you feel when you see her?' he asked directly.

'Nothing.'

'Nothing at all?'

She sighed and turned to face Antoine, assessing him for a few moments. 'Well... no... not really nothing. To be honest, I'm not sure what I feel - confused most of the time. I feel like I should know her... like I should respond to her... but then something deep inside stops me.'

'What scares you Lauren?'

'That's a good question. My therapist asked me that question a number of times.'

'And how did you answer?'

'I didn't. I haven't worked that out yet.'

'All that matters is love Lauren. We can overcome all our fears when we love, and have the love of, someone special. Love changes everything.' Lauren twitched involuntarily. His words rang true. 'Let's start from the very beginning. When you arrived here for your father's funeral...'

By the time they reached home, Antoine had given his interpretation of events over the previous months, especially focusing on her father and his relationship, and her mother's marriage, trying to bring her slowly up to date. Lauren had just continued to nod at appropriate moments and smile when Antoine smiled. Nothing he had said felt familiar, but then it didn't feel completely alien either. Perhaps because she had been told the stories by Valerie at the hospital.

*

'How shall I respond?' Anna thrust her phone across the table at Eva so she could read the message she had just received from Lauren.

Anna's excitement was good to see. Eva's heart raced as she read the message... and not in a good way. Clearly Lauren wanted to engage with Anna and that would most likely erect a barrier between the two of them. She would be watching from the outside again, whilst wanting to protect her best friend from yet another heartbreak. 'What do you want to say?' Eva said, more dismissively than intended, as she handed back the phone and looked at the menu.

'I need your help here. I don't want to scare her away.' Anna pleaded.

'So, talk to her about your work... your pet project?' She winced. 'That's safe territory,' she said, giving her attention to the food and drink options on the menu. 'What are you having?'

'I'm not that hungry?'

'You need to eat properly remember,' Eva said looking toward Anna's belly.

'I know. Okay. You choose.'

'You okay with the wild boar?'

'Sure.'

Eva nodded and a waiter appeared. 'Two wild boar specials please. I'll have a half-carafe of red wine and can we have a bottle of water please.' The waiter nodded and took their menus, returning within moments with their drinks in hand. 'Do you want to see her?'

'Yes... well... yes and then no.'

'Confusing!'

'Yes it is. I love her so much that it hurts to face her: to face her rejection of me. I know she doesn't mean to hurt me. But it's excruciating. She looks right through me and it kills me every time. The last week I've spent with you I've started to relax a bit and sort of find myself again. Then when I think about the baby, I feel really guilty. She should be a part of this and I want her to be, but I'm so scared of how she will react when she finds out. I'm just too freaked out by it all. I need time to adjust.'

'I can understand that... and for what it's worth I've enjoyed your company this last week too.' Eva smiled weakly. Anna fiddled with the phone in her hand as Eva poured her a glass of water and took a long slug of her wine. 'Are you going to take the pet project?' she asked with a wry smile.

Anna looked up at the change of subject, giving the question a moment's thought. 'Yes, I think I will. I'll only need to visit for a long weekend and can do the main work from home, which suits me just fine. It could be a fun challenge. What do you think?'

Eva held Anna's eyes softly, surprised to be asked for her opinion. 'I think you should do whatever you feel is right for you?'

'Profound words,' Anna teased. Eva shrugged her shoulders and slugged her wine.

Two plates of wild boar stew appeared. They both breathed in the rich aroma. 'Mmm…' they said simultaneously and smiled.

'This looks great,' Eva said before picking up her fork and tucking in. Anna watched her, momentarily, enjoying the simple food, before she too attacked the dish with gusto.

'It's very good,' Anna said, wiping a chunk of baguette around the plate to collect the remaining gravy.

'You've done well for someone who wasn't hungry,' Eva jested, finishing her second glass of wine with ease. She watched, enamoured by Anna's obvious enjoyment of the meal. 'That was excellent… coffee?' she asked, as Anna rested her cutlery on the empty plate.

'Not for me, but you go ahead.'

'No, it's okay. I need to get back to the office, anyway, for an hour or so. What are your plans?' Eva asked as she summoned the waiter for the bill.

'I'm going to walk off this lunch and take more photos. I can meet you back at the office for about four if that works?'

'Sure. I'll get this.' Eva pulled out her credit card handing it to the waiter before Anna could object. 'What are you staring at?' she asked coyly.

'Sorry. I was just watching you. You're really sweet. Thank you for being such a brilliant friend,' Anna said, reaching across and planting a soft kiss on her cheek. Heat flushed Eva's face and she fiddled with her wallet to distract herself from the touch that had sent fire through her veins.

*

Lauren moved painfully slowly to extricate herself from the car. Her mother, standing at the entrance to the house, hands over her mouth and wide eyed, told her all she needed to know about the mess she had made of herself. She was exhausted and in excruciating pain. 'Hello mother,' she said, wincing, and breathing heavily.

'Oh my God, look at you.' Valerie rushed forward wanting to help, not knowing how, her arms flapping in empty space.

'I'll be fine mother. Stop fussing please. Just let me get there in my own time.'

'Right, right.' Valerie backed off apologetically, watching closely, unconsciously biting at the index finger on her right hand as Lauren stepped cautiously, following the frame. Antoine grabbed Lauren's bag, skipped in front of her and into the house.

'How are you feeling darling?' Valerie asked. Lauren glared. 'Sorry, I shouldn't have interrupted your concentration. Can I get you anything?'

Lauren stopped. She was sweating at the exertion. Holding her mother's gaze, she sighed. 'Thank you. A glass of water would be great. You go ahead. I'll get there.' She nodded toward the door and Valerie set off at pace. 'And mother...' Valerie stopped, looked back. 'Please try not to fuss. I'll be fine, honestly.'

'Yes darling, of course.' Valerie hadn't heard a word since the request for water. She needed to be *doing* not *watching*.

Lauren took a deep breath as she stood in the doorway. Looking back over her shoulder, the eucalyptus tree stood quite still. Statuesque, it dominated the horizon from this vantage point. Her eyes traced down its silver skin to its base and off to the right. A white rose sat atop the rough soil. She couldn't read the headstone from here but she knew it was her father's grave. She would go down there later, she promised.

'I've put you in the study for now,' Valerie said, glass of water in hand, disturbing Lauren from her trance. 'When you're feeling stronger we can move you back upstairs, or we can get a stair-lift fitted. Henri's been checking out the details. We can get one next week if you think it would help for you to be in your own room. I've had your bed...'

'Mother...' Lauren's tone was softer than she felt.

'Sorry... I'm babbling again aren't I?' Valerie raised her brows at herself and marched back into the house, still carrying Lauren's water. Lauren followed steadily behind and into her new, temporary, bedroom.

Her eyes appraised the room, a smile making its way onto her face. 'This will be great. Thank you for doing all of this,' she indicated with her eyes. 'I need to rest for a bit if that's okay?' she held her Mother's eyes with appreciation.

'Of course darling.' Valerie placed the water on the bedside table, cupped Lauren's face, kissed her forehead, and made her way to the door. 'I'll introduce you to Rita later.'

'Rita?'

'Your nurse.'

'Oh, right.' Lauren could feel her blood pumping and fought against the rising anger.

'Get some rest.' Valerie shut the door softly.

Lauren lowered herself onto her bed. Groaning she pulled her legs up and laid out flat, sighing deeply with the effort. The room spun until eventually she succumbed and her weight sunk heavily into the mattress, everything in front of her eyes becoming still. The constant buzzing sound that had accompanied her through two flights and the car journey home slowly receded. Her eyes closed and she noticed her breathing had softened. Lavender... and some other indefinable scent drifted into her awareness.

The door clicked softly. A light flowery aroma with a hint of vanilla teased at her senses, urging her to wake. Gentle warmth spread through her body easing into tense muscles, softening, massaging, enlivening. Embracing the sensations, they seemed to soothe away the pain. Reaching across the bed an arm slipped around the soft warm scent. A hand traced the curves, up and down, the body melding effortlessly with the touch of tender fingers. The two bodies move synchronously, hot breath stinging tender skin, goose bumps racing. A glimpse. Steel-blue. Lauren's eyes opened in a flash and her arm thrashed across the bed causing a sharp pain to rip through her shoulder. *Fuck* she murmured to herself, pulling her arm back and rubbing at the throbbing joint. She lay with her eyes open for a few moments adjusting to her surroundings, unsure of how much time had passed. Yawning she stretched, testing her injured leg's response. It screamed. Nothing new. The sky outside the window was dark. The room was dark too, but for the low table light. She sat up, sipped at the water and stared at the starlit sky, adjusting her senses. Grabbing her frame, she walked slowly towards the slither of light surrounding the door.

Opening the door, she nearly jumped out of her skin. A familiar essence of vanilla hit her and the face that had just scared the shit out of her was unfamiliar. 'I'm so sorry. I didn't mean to make you jump,' the voice said.

Lauren caught her breath and steadied herself with the frame. She was breathing quickly and still shaking from the shock. 'Erm.'

'Sorry, I'm Rita. Your mother contracted me to look after you. I...'

'I don't need a nurse,' Lauren said gruffly, trying to manoeuver her way through the doorway and down the corridor toward the living room. 'Mother,' she shouted. Rita flinched then smiled, intrigued, as she watched the stubborn woman struggle.

'Ah here you are at last. Did you have a good rest darling?' Valerie said, rising out of her chair as Lauren fought her way into the room, swearing as the frame leg battled with the doorframe.

Red faced, she stood up fully from the frame. 'I do not need a nurse,' she pronounced. Henri turned from his seat to face her, peering over his glasses, before standing and moving in to greet Lauren.

'Hello Lauren,' he said softly. 'I'm Henri.' Holding out his hand, Lauren just glared with contempt.

'Henri,' she said, finally nodding towards him in acknowledgement, ignoring his hand, grabbing her frame, still seething. 'Mother?'

'Darling, I know you don't need a nurse, but at least Rita can be here just in case you need any other help. It can't be easy getting washed and dressed.' She looked Lauren up and down with disdain as if to say... 'like that'.

'I am perfectly capable of washing and...' An image of her sock sat on the orange-lid bin from earlier that day flicked across her mind and she stopped. 'You'd better have a few good books with you?' she growled at a subservient looking Rita who virtually bowed as the words flew at her.

'Can I get you a drink?' Valerie asked, stepping toward the bar.

'Whiskey please...'

'I don't think that's a good idea,' Rita bravely interjected. 'The blood thinning drugs?' she reminded.

'I know.' Lauren smirked. 'With ice please,' she said, glaring at Valerie as if challenging her to give her anything but what she had asked for.

Valerie handed her a small tumbler of the gold coloured liquid with two large ice cubes. Rita frowned and held up her hands in defeat. Valerie shrugged and waved off the criticism. Lauren sipped at the drink and coughed as her throat burned. It had been a long time since her last drink but she welcomed the flaming sensation. She needed the escape.

'Feel better for that?' Valerie asked derisively, though not wishing to provoke her daughter who seemed intent on making life difficult for them all. Lauren raised her glass in a toast. 'Right.' Valerie ignored the insolent gesture and spoke as if calling them all to order. 'Shall we eat?'

'I thought you'd never ask,' Lauren jibed, setting off for the dining room door.

'I've delayed the physio meeting until tomorrow,' Valerie said, as she stepped past Lauren, who just huffed in response as she took her seat at the table.

'I'll have a glass of that red please,' Lauren said lifting her glass to meet the bottle her mother was passing around the table. She smiled inwardly at the glare from Rita's hazel coloured eyes across the table. Her face pinched, sharpening her already fine-features, and as she swished her dark brown hair it fell back neatly, exactly where it started. Lauren couldn't help but wonder what was the point of that swish? At least she was good looking, she thought, as their eyes met with fiery intensity. Lauren smiled. Rita scowled.

7

I'm okay. I really miss you and wish we could spend time together.

Anna looked at the words again. Too honest she thought. Something didn't feel right. She wanted to spend time with Lauren, but she felt like she was being needy, and she didn't want it to come across that way. She sighed deeply, scrubbed out the last sentence, and thought again. She had been pondering a response ever since receiving Lauren's message over a week ago and part of her worried that already Lauren might think she didn't care. Of course, nothing could be further from the truth. She had intended to respond immediately she received the message, but her initial feelings had been of irritation. Although Lauren had responded quickly to her original text this time, the formality of her words caused a shift in Anna. She wanted more from Lauren. She needed more than one line that could have been destined for a colleague she hadn't seen in a while, not to a lover.

She had decided to calm down before responding and then had gotten wrapped up in her work. Whenever she had thought about responding something had stopped her. She didn't want to feel manipulated, and the randomness of Lauren's communication made her feel that way. Lauren had reacted to Anna's texts and she was sure that, if she hadn't been the one instigating communication between them, Lauren would probably not bother. She was tempted to try out her theory, not respond and see what happened, but she worried that would get her no-where. She deleted some of the words.

I'm okay.

That's not enough.

I'm okay, busy. Going back to Corsica next week for a project, thanks to your mother's recommendation. How are you?

Eva had suggested she talk about work so that might do it. She hovered a finger over the send button, running the words through her head, not wanting to be misinterpreted in any way.

'Supper's ready?' Eva shouted up the stairs. She flinched and pocketed her phone like a child caught cheating, before she realised she wasn't doing anything wrong. Pulling her phone out, she clicked the send button before she could think any more about it and breathed a sigh of relief.

'Something smells good,' she said as she descended the stairs. 'This would be the second dish on your extensive menu then?' Anna teased as she plodded into the kitchen, wiping at tired eyes.

'Actually, I've been studying a cookbook and come up with something new.' Eva gulped as she looked up from stirring the pot. Anna looked radiant, even in baggy jeans and sweatshirt, and sporting red eyes with black rings under them. She looked tired, but more than that. Her hair looked as though she had just run her fingers through it, slightly awry and with more than a hint of sensuality. Eva pondered whether the sexual aura she was experiencing was the impact of Anna's pregnancy and dismissed the idea with a deep breath and a large glug of wine.

'Ooo, look at you! What delights await us tonight then Ms Hélène Darroze?' Anna teased in reference to the famous French chef, leaning over her shoulder, sniffing at the bubbling concoction, trying to make out its contents. Eva froze at the close contact then stirred the pot vigorously.

'It's chicken a la something. Not too spicy, creamy with mushrooms and baby onions... with rice,' she said in a slightly higher voice than normal.

'Well it smells delish.' Anna kissed her on the cheek and squeezed an arm around her shoulder. 'I'm going to really enjoy this.' She grabbed a glass and filled it with water from a bottle in the fridge before sitting at the kitchen island.

Eva shuddered and released the breath she had been holding, still aware of the scent of Anna clinging to the collar on her shirt. She took another large slug of wine from her glass, tipped the remainder into the cooking pot, stirred the rice, and refilled her glass. 'How was your day?' she asked, attempting to regain her composure.

'Good. I told your mum I'd do the pet project,' she watched for Eva's response. None came. 'Got some painting done... and...'

'And what?' Eva took another slug of wine, hoping the impact would dumb down her senses.

'I just text Lauren,' she winced slightly as she spoke.

'Oh.' Eva's stomach dropped. 'That's good, right?' she offered, knowing that encouraging Anna to pursue her relationship with Lauren was the best and most honourable course of action, despite her body disagreeing with her logic. She stirred frantically, eyes firmly on the bubbling pot.

'I hope so,' Anna said, weakly.

Eva tried to clear the lump in her throat that seemed to be trying to choke her. Her stomach constricted and she began to cough. Reaching for her drink she took another slug.

'You okay?' Anna leapt to her feet, cradling Eva's head, not sure whether she should thump her in the back or not.

'Sorry.' Cough, cough. 'I'm okay.' Cough, cough. She was getting redder with each cough. Anna thumped her in the back anyway.

'Ouch. Jesus Anna.'

'Sorry... I'm sorry. You looked like you were about to choke.'

'I was choking. I'd just got through the worst bit. Now I have a broken rib.' Anna rubbed at Eva's back softly, causing heat to shoot through her.

'I'm so sorry.'

'It's okay,' Eva said, taking Anna's hand and squeezing

it. 'Thanks for caring enough to try and save my life,' she said, smiling wryly.

'Can I get you some water?' Anna asked as Eva spluttered again.

'No. Honestly, I'm fine.' Holding up her hand to prevent a further slap she slurped her wine. The spluttering stopped. 'See, all gone. Right let's eat,' she said turning to the food on the stove and breathing deeply, her body throbbing with desire. She would go and get laid while Anna was in Corsica, she mused. Come to think of it she probably should go back and live in her own apartment and wondered whether Anna would be okay with that? She knew *she* wouldn't. 'So… text… Lauren. You seem unsure,' she said, reflecting the conversation they had started.

'It's taken me a day and a half to find the right words and even now I'm not sure I pitched it right.'

'You make it sound as though you're trying to set up a date.'

'It feels like that. No, actually it feels a lot worse than that. We had something really special together and then… boom. It's gone in the blink of an eye.' Anna's eyes glazed as she drifted into the painful reflection.

'She's still the same person though, surely.'

'Maybe. I'm not so sure. She seemed angrier and detached, and she'd never been like that when we were together.'

'Is that to do with her injuries? I mean, do you think she's been affected, in her brain?' Eva asked tentatively.

'I don't know whether the emotional stuff will be permanent or not. I can understand her being pissed as a result of the accident, but the idea that it might be permanent, that scares me. I'm not sure I could live with someone who is angry most of the time. Sophie was aggressive and angry and look how that turned out!'

'Is she having therapy? Lauren that is.'

'I don't know. She doesn't communicate. When I left we agreed to take a break so she could recover without the increased stress my presence seemed to cause.' Anna's eyes watered as she spoke. 'We've only just started to engage by text, in a limited way, which is why I want to get it right. No pressure!' she said, wistfully.

Eva could feel the internal fight thrashing between her logical mind and her passionate heart. She knew the right thing was to support Anna in her quest to win Lauren's heart again and in doing so her own would be crushed, finally. Unrequited love hurt. 'So what did you say to her?'

'I said I had taken on the pet project in Corsica thanks to her mother's recommendation and asked if she was well.'

'Seems simple enough.' Eva shrugged nonchalantly as the steel-blue eyes on her sought approval. Anna's need cut through Eva, tapped a part of her she hadn't known existed until her recent wake up call. She wanted to wrap her up, hold her, comfort her, sleep next to her, touch her with tenderness - make love to her. Most of all she wanted to make love to her. Her clammy hands gripped her glass and she held the wine in her mouth, sensing every aspect of it on her tongue, in a vain attempt to distract her thoughts. 'Has she responded?'

'No. But she may be in treatment or something.' Anna searched for a reason, even though she had only sent the message an hour ago. In her mind Lauren's recent history of poor communication needed a rational explanation.

Eva reached across and took Anna's hands in her own. Their eyes locked together with tenderness, and Eva broke the gaze lest she might reveal her deeper desires. Anna flushed at the intimate contact and cleared her throat. 'I'm sure things will work out between you both,' Eva said softly. 'I think you're in danger of overthinking the whole thing and holding back when you should be going to get what you want.' Saying the words that would take Anna away from her was killing her, but she was gaining momentum for doing the right thing by her friend. 'I think you should put yourself out there and give her every reason to remember you. Do the things you used to do together. Something will click. You need to be together. You're soul mates. Don't let her anger and moods stop you Anna. They may just be temporary and you would kick yourself to let a good thing pass you by. In fact, I would kick you,' she smiled wryly and Anna squeezed her hands with a slight smile rising across her face.

'Thank you. I love you,' she said, leaning across the space and kissing Eva on the cheek.

Eva cleared her throat again and took another swig of her wine. Her head was spinning but it wasn't due solely to the alcohol. She had a greater capacity for that than she did for coping with erotic sensations. She needed to get laid, and quickly. 'When are you thinking of going to Corsica?' she asked.

'Later next week, just for a few days, then I'll come back here to work on the canvas.' Anna stood and moved to put the kettle on. 'Coffee?'

'No thanks. I think I'll stick to the wine, or something stronger,' Eva said as she finished the last of the bottle in one swig. Not that alcohol normally did anything to dampen her arousal once it was awakened, but she needed to try something.

8.

Lauren's eyes watched Rita intently as she moved around her bedroom. Auburn streaks shone in her dark brown wavy hair, probably a natural feature of the sun. Her fine features belied her physical strength. Her hands worked quickly, with tenderness and assuredness. She was struck by the generally quiet demeanour, beneath which lay a confident maturity. Wise. She knew when to speak and when to hold back, even if she had strong views. In the short time she had assisted Lauren, and in spite of Lauren's initial reticence towards her, she had earned her respect through her professionalism. Lauren hated to admit it, but her mother had been right about her need for assistance and she had made a good choice in Rita.

'Right, let's get you dressed. You have physio. Lucia is already here. I heard her talking with your mother,' she smirked. Knowing how to get Lauren's attention had come easily to Rita, having mastered the art of manipulation at an early age. As the oldest of five-children, all girls, and with an ailing mother throughout her childhood, she had needed to learn how to handle their moods and tantrums. She had become an excellent peacekeeper. It was a game she was good at and she revelled in her ability to win people over.

Lauren raised her eyebrows as Rita smiled at her conspiratorially, nodding towards the voices behind the closed door. She still took care as she eased herself out of bed, but walking had become more comfortable over the past week, with her shoulder feeling stronger by the day. She had discarded her frame for a single walking stick as soon as she had reached home and tried not to use it when moving around the house. Reaching for the baggy t-shirt and bra Rita had placed on her bed, she threw off her nightshirt without a care for Rita's presence. She fiddled to get her underwear over her healing leg, cussing at the

73

restricted mobility in her hip. Rita stood silently and watched as Lauren winced trying to put on her socks and jogging bottoms.

'Can I help?' she offered softly. Lauren looked up, welcomed the genuine compassion and nodded. She watched silently as the strong hands worked effortlessly and respectfully, doing only that which was necessary for Lauren to remain as independent as possible. 'There we go.' Rita smiled and touched Lauren lightly on the thigh as she stood.

Lauren could feel the heat creep into her cheeks and hoped Rita hadn't noticed. Something about the nurse touched her. She stirred something in Lauren that made her feel... feel what? Just feel. She couldn't explain it, but it felt better than the previous weeks of hollow darkness. She wanted to hold onto the light feeling for a while longer. 'How did you get into nursing?' she asked.

Rita seemed momentarily taken aback by the unexpected question and her eyes lost focus as she looked into space. In the two weeks she had helped Lauren, their conversations had revolved around evading Lauren's mother. They hadn't talked about her and that was the way she liked it. She was happy to find out all about her clients, but her own life was usually off-limits. It enabled her to maintain her professional boundaries, and avoid a topic that still caused her pain. Yet, the genuine interest she had spotted in Lauren's eyes left her wanting to share her story.

'I watched my mother die at the hands of medical incompetence and vowed I could do better,' she said as matter of fact as she could muster, though her face held the remnants of the scars of that time.

'Oh...' Lauren said, her eyes softening, holding nothing but compassion. 'I'm really sorry,' she said with genuine tenderness, hating the thought that Rita, who was such a kind person, would have suffered. Hating that Rita's mother had suffered too.

Rita's eyes darkened as they held Lauren's gaze, and she looked momentarily paralysed. 'It was a long time ago now,' she said softly, before brushing off her grief and getting back to work. She folded a jumper and placed it at the bottom of Lauren's bed before turning and heading towards the door. 'I'll tell them you're on your way?' she said, her voice shaky.

'Okay,' Lauren said, almost at a whisper. She immediately felt Rita's absence as the door closed behind her. Something about the astute, compassionate woman made her want to spend more time with her. She wanted to know the pain that caused those beautiful eyes to darken and maintain a barrier to something deeper. The thought of finding out more about the dark, secretive nurse caused Lauren's body to light up in a way that she didn't remember experiencing in a long time. Rita had been imprinted in her mind's eye, and she had no desire or inclination to remove the image, preferring instead to immerse herself in the associated sensual feelings that were beginning to infiltrate her body.

Lauren made her way slowly down the stairs taking care to place each foot as previously instructed. She tried to tune in to the thought of physio and failed as her attention was drawn to Rita's voice, now confident in its tone, coming from the kitchen. Lauren's lower stomach flipped and her mouth dried. There was something about that voice.

'Ah, there you are,' Lucia said, exiting the kitchen with two glasses of water. 'Rita tells me you're pretty much dressing yourself, which is great.' Lauren blushed and Lucia continued. 'So, shall we get going?' she said, marching off. She entered the study, that had been converted into a mini-gym the minute Lauren had been fit enough to move back into her bedroom, and held the door open for Lauren. 'Okay,' Lucia commented, as if she had more to say, as she watched Lauren's movement. She was walking quite well without the cane, albeit deliberately and with a great deal of focus. 'You need to be careful. I know you want to get better quickly, and you are. But we can't afford an accident on that hip and leg and I don't want you developing a limp because you're doing too much,' she said. 'Your weight distribution is a bit skewed,' she confirmed, eyeing Lauren's gait closely.

'Right.' Lauren nodded in affirmation of the strict instruction that she knew was valid. The stronger she felt the more she pushed it too far. Yesterday her body had ached and shooting pains had torpedoed down her leg after she decided to use the stairs for a self-designed workout. Going up and down them just ten-times had wiped her out and she had pushed it to twenty. It had irritated her that she would have normally been able to run up and down those same stairs all day long without feeling a thing. Instead she had tossed and turned all night with the spasms in her leg and hip. She hadn't been able to get comfortable and Rita had come to investigate after she had called out in pain, providing her with pills and water and gently massaging the tension out of her shoulders and back. She still felt stiff, though the pain had reduced significantly. 'I did too much yesterday,' she confessed, wincing.

'Okay. I had something specific planned for you today, but looking at you I think we'll do something else,' she said handing Lauren a glass of water and sipping her own before placing it on the desk.

'Sure. Sorry.' Lauren whimpered, taking a sip from her glass.

*

Lauren stepped out onto the frosty grass and wandered down towards the eucalyptus tree. She had promised to visit her father's grave sooner, but nearly three weeks seemed to have flown by, consumed by surviving her mother and progressing through physio. Her recovery was going well Lucia had insisted, even though pain still plagued her hip and leg at times, and she had learned her lesson from pushing too hard. She liked Lucia's attitude and character, which was far more imposing than her height of five-foot two-inches. She was always enthusiastic, always supportive, and Lauren wondered if she was naturally exuberant or just reserved her high-spirited enthusiasm for her clients. She couldn't envision herself feeling that chirpy about anything and questioned whether she might be depressed. Except for when she was in Rita's company - when she could forget everything - she seemed unable to shake the hollow feeling that haunted her for more than a few minutes. Then that inner darkness descended again. She dismissed the idea. Vincenti's didn't do depression, she admonished, as the grass crackled under each step.

Receiving the text from Anna had thrown her. She had noticed her hands shaking, as she held the phone to read the message. Her intense and growing feelings for Rita had warred with something she couldn't name as she processed the fact that Anna would be visiting Corsica. She hadn't known what to say so had simply responded with... *That sounds great*. Guilt had tormented her. She should have told Anna about her move back to Corsica. She hadn't though, and now Anna was going to be visiting one of her mother's friends. *Did her mother know about the visit?* She could see the neighbour's house from beside the tree and cringed. *What would she say when she saw Anna?* Their paths would be sure to cross in the next couple of days. Lauren's throat constricted and butterflies thrashed around her stomach looking for an exit. The Eiffel Tower image flashed across her mind. *Lovers? And Rita?*

She breathed deeply in an effort to control the internal flailing sensation that was gripping her, and leaned against the tree's silver skin to take the weight off her shaking legs. Giving her attention to the light breeze that whistled across the valley, bringing a chill, refreshing after the warmth of the house, she felt almost grounded in its familiarity. Her eyes cast out over the valley as she reflected on the reality that her father lay beneath her feet. Her breathing calmed. She looked down at the white glistening earth. *What happened papa?* The words echoed around her mind. *I feel so lost papa.* Tears burned at the back of her eyes. She had read and reread the letters he had written, tracing the ink with her finger. He had taken his own life to avoid the shame of having contracted HIV through a brief affair, to preserve the family name over and above his life with Antoine, Valerie and her. *What was the true cost of maintaining appearances?* She had cried all over again. The roses - there were two now she noted, lying across each other - had wilted, burned by the frost. A sudden sense of déjà vu came and went in an instant.

'Hello Lauren.' Antoine's soft, confident voice brought a tight smile to her face. 'Chilly eh?' He rubbed his arms around his body, hopping from foot to foot.

Lauren hadn't thought it that cold. 'Beautiful though,' she said, scanning the silver-blue sky, wispy clouds seeming to sprout from the distant tips of the snow-clad mountains. 'I bet the skiing's good? We should go sometime,' she said earnestly.

'Sure.' Antoine looked her up and down, raising his eyebrows at her walking stick. 'Maybe next season eh?' he grinned. Wrapping an arm around her he pulled her into his chest. 'This was your father's favourite place you know? He used to spend hours sitting here just staring out over the valley. You can see a good part of the vineyard from here, down there,' he pointed. 'When he wasn't at the vineyard he watched over it like a guardian of the souls of the vines. And now, I guess, he watches it from up there.' He scanned the expansive sky.

'I feel really lost,' Lauren blurted. Something about Antoine's calm disposition made her want to talk to him.

'Do you want to talk about it?'

'I don't know where to start. It's like there's this big black hole that I've fallen down. Alice, but not so Wonderland.

I'm scared, but half the time I don't know what about. I seem to have missed so much in such a short space of time. I think I might remember stuff, but then I wonder if it's just because I've been told. It's confusing and irritating. And now...' Lauren went silent and stiffened in Antoine's arms.

'And now?'

'Anna's coming to Corsica tomorrow. She's been commissioned by the Dubois'.' She pointed to the large property sitting further up the hill even though Antoine knew to whom she was referring.

'Ah. I see.' Antoine paused as if considering his next words carefully. 'I lost your father for a time,' he ventured, cautiously. 'He was still present physically, but mentally and emotionally he belonged to someone else. It nearly killed me. To have had to stand back and watch, wait, and hope that at some point he would come out of his *black hole* and see the light again. It was very difficult for me. What we had I know I will never have with anyone else. We were special together and I will miss him until I die. But, for a time it was really hard to believe we had a future, and at points I feared he would never come back to me.' Lauren noted the sadness in his eyes as he revisited that time in his memories. 'Love prevails Lauren. You must have faith in that. This is hard for you both I'm sure. Just try to be honest and talk to her about how you feel, your fears, your concerns. You never know, you may be able to work it out together?' He shrugged, pulled back, a little worried that he had said too much already.

'I didn't know.' Lauren said, entranced by Antoine's openness.

'Through our pain we grew. We became stronger together after that time,' he continued. 'Inseparable... until this, of course.' He pointed to the ground. 'The roses keep us connected, I like to think,' he said, with a wry smile.

Lauren rubbed her hand up and down his arm. 'I'm not sure I'm ready yet. I can't face Anna right now. I find it hard to talk to her. It's as though if I talk to her I might rekindle something I can't sustain with her. I would let her down again. Break her heart again. And whether I know her or not, I can't do that to her, or anyone. I haven't even told mother she's coming either. Please don't say anything,' she begged. Antoine nodded.

'In good time Lauren, all in good time,' he said philosophically. 'Your mother knows she's coming. She and Claudia will have spoken about it, I can guarantee.'

'Why hasn't she said anything to me?' Lauren asked, confused.

'I think she's giving you space and time. She loves you and doesn't want to lose you, and she knows you feel controlled by her. She's trying Lauren, you need to know that.'

'I…' she started.

'I know things have been tense between the two of you, but that is all in the past. She has always been a challenging woman, but her heart is big and you are her life now.'

'She has Henri.'

'Ah yes, of course. Henri is a great companion for Valerie and vice versa. But she kept Petru's name when she remarried for a reason. She's a Vincenti through and through, and you are her only surviving daughter. You are a Vincenti. Blood and family loyalty are important to her and she will not give up on that until she is taken from this world.' Antoine shook his head in thought. 'You and she are very similar in many ways, but you also have your father's passion for love. Valerie has always kept her cards a little closer to her chest and she doesn't show her love as easily. Like you, she doesn't trust her heart because she fears it will be broken. But in truth, your heart will not lie to you Lauren. And you must follow your heart. Don't let your fears stop you… and they will try,' he finished. Lauren bowed her head and leaned into Antoine's shoulder.

'Thank you,' she said after a pause. 'I still cannot face Anna tomorrow,' she said. Antoine remained silent for a time.

'Would you like to come to the vineyard today?' he asked. 'I'd like to show you around.'

'Again...' Lauren admonished herself, her brows rising in mock annoyance.

'Many visits to the vines can never be enough.' He moved to link his arm through hers then stopped as she lifted up her cane and batted him out of the way. 'I can see I need to keep a wide birth. You wield that stick like your mother,' he teased.

'She doesn't use a stick,' Lauren retorted.

'I know, but if she did that's exactly how she would wield it.' They chuckled, and walked side by side up to the house.

*

Anna carefully folded three white shirts, a pair of dark blue jeans, her burgundy red waistcoat and dark blue Aran wool knitted sweater, packing them with precision into her cabin bag. She would add her toiletries in the morning after her shower. Her clothes to wear were already laid out on the chair in her room. She was ready to go, but the fizzing that persisted in her stomach left her unsettled. After three-mornings of sickness she was feeling drained and had started to question whether travelling was such a good idea. The text from Lauren had been far from encouraging, expecting a more expansive conversation to flow between them, the persistent disappointment was disheartening. The distance between them seemed to be growing, and insurmountable. Sighing deeply, she closed the bag and wandered downstairs to a new aroma wafting from the kitchen.

'Hey, I thought you might like something simple tonight,' Eva said, taking a healthy swig of wine. 'What with the sickness and all.'

'Thanks. What have we got?'

'Steak and chips. I've made a pepper sauce but you might not fancy that. It's got cream in it. There's peas, and mushrooms if you want?' Eva looked for Anna's response. 'I figured the protein would be good for you,' she continued. 'And since you can't stand the smell of fish or the sight of chicken, our options are becoming limited.' She smiled, happy with her foresight.

Anna cringed and suddenly turned pale at the words *fish* and *chicken* and Eva wondered if just saying the word might make Anna sick. 'Good call. Steak sounds doable. No mushrooms though. I think that could be a step too far... the texture...' She grimaced and shuddered.

'So, you ready?' Eva stared at Anna.

'I think so,' she said, though lacking conviction.

'You'll be fine. It's only a few days.' Eva stepped towards her and brushed her hair gently to the side of her face, holding her eyes with kindness.

Anna melted into the soft touch and her eyes started to close as she inhaled the scent hitting her nostrils. 'You smell of frying,' she sniggered and pulled back.

Eva jumped back, sniffed her hand, laughed and shrugged. 'The trials and tribulations of being a head chef, eh?' she joked. 'It's not exactly sexy, is it?' She blushed at her comment.

'It's certainly not *Nine and a Half Weeks*, that's for sure. Food is always made out to be so sensuous - so seductive - in the movies, but then they're not slapping a steak at each other, are they?' Anna laughed at her vision.

Eva choked on her wine. 'Beat the meat,' she laughed loudly. 'Maybe we've been watching the wrong movies,' she choked again with laughter. Something she seemed to be doing a lot around Anna the last couple of weeks and she was even, secretly, enjoying it. Anna's haughty laugh filled the kitchen and Eva watched her with joy in her heart. She loved the happy, fun Anna. Eva flipped the steaks... 'I'm gonna beat your meat,' she sang, wiggling her hips provocatively, wine in hand. Anna watched the light-hearted display with amusement, and her mind drifted.

Eva set the plates down on the surface, grabbed her wine and the sauce, huffing as she sat. 'This is perfect,' Anna said, with no signs of retching Eva noted.

'Tastes great,' Eva said chewing on a big chunk of meat doused in the pepper sauce, evidence remaining in the corner of her mouth. Anna giggled and pointed at the errant food, which Eva's tongue sought out and gathered into her mouth. 'Thanks.'

They ate in comfortable silence.

'I've been thinking.' Eva said, the serious tone catching Anna's attention.

She lowered her knife and fork to her plate. 'Sounds serious?' Anna queried.

Eva's eyes searched for the right words over Anna's right shoulder, instead catching the inspirational quote attached to the magnet board on the wall. *"Step out of the history that is holding you back. Step into the new story you are willing to create." - Oprah Winfrey.* I didn't realise you were an Oprah fan?' she said, frowning.

'Is that the thinking that caused you to look so serious... and stop me eating?' Anna admonished lightly.

'Sorry... no. I got distracted. Urmm... I was going to say.' Eva looked down at her plate before raising her head to hold Anna's eyes. The way Anna looked at her made her mouth go dry.

'Still waiting to eat.' She looked intently. 'Whatever it is can't be that bad, surely. Why are you shaking? Is everything okay?' Anna was starting to worry at the uncharacteristic vulnerability on display.

'Everything's fine. I was just wondering if I should move back to my flat now? Only if you're feeling up to being here on your own when you get back from Corsica?' Anna's eyes dropped to her plate, her face paled and she breathed deeply. 'I mean, it's not that I want to particularly, it's just that I don't want to get in your way,' Eva continued.

'Thank God. I thought there was something seriously wrong with you for a moment.' She relaxed her posture and reached for Eva's hand, rubbing her thumb over the soft skin. 'Look. I've loved having you here I'm not going to deny it. I've had fun and I feel safe with you around. I'm not sure how I would have coped on my own this last few weeks. But I realise you also have a life and I don't want to keep you from that either. I'm sure I'll be fine when I get back from Corsica, and it's not like we're a million miles away from each other. So, as long as you promise to come over, cook me supper... and let me eat it,' she teased. Eva smiled reluctantly.

'Deal,' Eva nodded as she spoke, enjoying the soft pressure on her hand. This was exactly why she needed some space from Anna. The boundaries between them were already blurring and she was beginning not to trust herself to keep on the right side of the line.

'Good. Now finish your steak before it gets cold.' Anna glanced at the half-eaten steak as she released Eva's hand and grabbed her knife and fork. Eva picked up her glass, swirled the wine before downing it in one in an attempt to erase the tingling sensations in her body.

'I'll shoot off after you leave tomorrow then. Keep in touch though eh?' Her eyes burned, but her resolve wouldn't allow the tears to escape.

'Of course! I'll pester you every day for sure.' Anna teased. 'You have a key so you're more than welcome anytime.' Eva watched Anna as she finished the last of her meal - the way she chewed, sipped at her water, wiped her mouth with a piece of kitchen roll. The way her eyelids fluttered slightly when in deep thought, the shades of blue her eyes achieved depending on the light and what she was feeling. Her heart stopped as it dawned on her that she would really miss not being with Anna. Really miss her.

9.

Anna stepped onto Corsican soil, walked the familiar route from the tarmac into the arrivals lounge, ignoring baggage reclaim, and headed for the sign held aloft with her name on it. A tall Italian looking man, tanned rugged features, swept back black hair and light brown eyes; lingered in the lounge area, attached to the sign. She nodded as she approached him, held out her hand, and introduced herself. His smile revealed a shining row of white and his eyes sparkled. He could have been a model Anna thought. The musky scent that surrounded him added to his alluring confidence.

'Hi, I'm Georgio Carbone. Claudia is my mother.' He shook her hand firmly, dipping his head, holding her gaze. 'I understand you are a very good artist,' he said over his shoulder as he took Anna's bag and strode out towards the car park.

'Thank you. I'm passionate about my work,' Anna responded with a light blush, struggling to keep pace with him.

'Well my mother and Madame Vincenti seem to think you are a rare talent,' he said smiling infectiously. The image of Valerie Vincenti caused Anna to stop breathing momentarily. Even though she had promised herself to keep in touch with Lauren's mother, she hadn't kept that promise. She liked the somewhat cantankerous old woman and had enjoyed the interactions she had had with her. She certainly had a passion for art, and especially hers it seemed. Anna's stomach skipped at the thought that their paths might cross during her visit, unsure whether that would be a good or bad thing. Feeling guilty for failing in her promise. Catching her breath, she focused her attention on the stunning landscape and tried to relax.

The familiarity of the route provided some comfort as they navigated the mountainous terrain and forest-lined winding roads to the Sartène, its sandy-granite soil dominating the winter landscape, rising out of the fast flowing Rizzanese.

Images of Lauren flashed through Anna's mind. Remembering the first time she had made this journey without realising the woman who had commissioned her was the mother of the woman she had fallen in love with. The intensity of feeling that had nearly floored her as Lauren had walked into the dining room, with Rachel - her partner - one step behind her. The guilt overridden by the pure lust... and love she had felt. Still felt. A wave of intense grief pounded at the back of her eyes as she wondered what Lauren was doing and how well she was recovering. She had managed not to think too hard about it over the last few days, immersing herself in her work and Eva's company. She had been protected. Now, she felt strangely vulnerable and out of sorts.

'It's beautiful isn't it, even in winter?' he said, pointing to the snow-capped mountains.

'It is quite spectacular.' Anna said, wriggling in her seat.

'You seem... unsettled?' he asked with genuine concern. Anna was briefly reminded of the kindness of Antoine and wondered if it was a Corsican male trait. She smiled at the idea.

'I have fond memories that...' she trailed off.

'Lauren's accident?' he asked, knowing the answer. Anna turned sharply to face him. 'It's a small place and everyone is up on everyone else's business, even though the façade might suggest otherwise,' he said, smiling honestly. 'I don't mean to pry.'

Anna sighed with the realisation that her situation wasn't something she was going to easily be able to ignore. 'So, your mother knows too?'

'Of course. She and Valerie are lifelong friends. Lauren and I played together as young children.' He shrugged as if it would be the most natural thing in the world for his mother to know. 'I'm sure she'll be glad to see you.'

'Valerie... Is she intending to visit your mother while I'm here?'

'Probably, and especially if Lauren comes around to say hi... She can't leave her...'

'Lauren.' Anna gasped as her stomach lurched. 'Lauren is here?'

'Sure. She came home a few weeks ago now. Apparently, her mother had strong words with the hospital on the basis that she could provide more than adequately for Lauren's needs at home. She has a nurse and physio looking after her. Seems it's been good for her too as she's walking mostly without an aid now.

A surge of emotion fired through Anna. She wretched in her throat and held her breath to prevent the bile from reaching her mouth. The bitter taste still hit the back of her tongue. Her heart thumped through her chest, her head exploded with hurt. *How could she not tell me she was being moved to Corsica?*

'You didn't know, did you?' Georgio said in an apologetic whisper. Anna shook her head in silence. Voicing her thoughts would result in an expression of emotion that she didn't feel ready to share with this stranger. 'I'm really sorry. I can relate to your pain. My father had Alzheimer's. It is very hard when someone loses their mind and can't remember you. I used to sit and watch him wasting away in the chair, hoping he might for one small second recognise me, that we might capture a few moments of the memories we shared before he died. They never came and even though he has passed away now, my memories of that time still cause great pain.' His honest eyes held Anna's momentarily before moving back to the road. Anna's mouth opened but no words came out. She shut it again and they continued the journey in silence, Anna unable to prevent images and thoughts of Lauren from consuming her.

By the time they had reached the Carbone residence, the large family home set in the rising hills, sitting just above the Vincenti estate, the anger had receded, replaced by deep sadness. She had debated asking Georgio to take her back to

Ajaccio. She would find somewhere to stay until her return flight, or even find an earlier one. But she also wanted to face Lauren; thump her in the chest, slap some sense into her. Completely irrational thoughts when all she really wanted was for Lauren to recognise her. To be able to pick up where they left off before Christmas. She tried to take comfort in the fact that being at home might help her recover her memory, but the reality of Lauren not even letting her know she had moved back home hurt deeply. What chance did they have of getting their life back on track if Lauren struggled to communicate openly with her? Her hand rubbed absentmindedly at the twinge in her womb.

'Welcome. How lovely to see you again.' Claudia greeted her with the same bright white smile as her son, pulling her into the present moment. She too had a rugged appearance, rarely seen in paler skinned women. Her tanned skin, weathered over the years, held wisdom, and the soft brown eyes caressed her with gentle affection as her arms swung confidently around Anna. 'I'm so glad you could come. I couldn't help myself once I'd seen the portrait you did for Valerie. It's exquisite.'

They had only met fleetingly at Valerie's wedding and Anna could barely remember Claudia, having been introduced to so many people throughout the day. She was taken aback at the fervent greeting, as if she were an old, long lost friend returning from an arduous trip. A high pitched, persistent, barking sound coming from somewhere inside the house assaulted her ears. Claudia's kind eyes blended with excitement providing a powerful cocktail of enthusiastic empathy, even in the absence of words. Anna was reminded of the eager welcome Valerie had given her when she had first shown up at her house. 'Thank you. It's a pleasure Mrs...'

'Claudia. Please. No formalities. Can't stand the pretence. We all pee the same way darling, so let's not lose sight of the fact that we are all human, eh?' she said, waving Anna to follow her into the house. Georgio sniggered, two paces behind, Anna's bag in his hand. 'Right. I've had the spare room made up. We don't have the space here that Valerie has, but I'm sure you'll be comfortable. If there's anything you need just ask. I'll let you freshen up in your room and then perhaps we could have a drink before lunch?' she said, pointing to a room down a short corridor. 'I've got loads of photos to go through with you and of course you'll need to meet them all. I'm so excited.' She rubbed her hands together vigorously as Georgio moved past her and headed up the stairs with her bag.

'Follow me,' he said, just as Claudia opened the door to the kitchen and a squealing, bounding black puppy skidded and leapt across the floor.

'Ahhh.' Anna dropped to her knees and was immediately accosted by the small bundle of energy. 'Is he a Labrador?' she asked quizzically looking the puppy up and down.

'Artois off.' Claudia bellowed. The dog cowered for a millisecond before continuing to bounce and climb onto Anna's lap, lapping with his overactive tongue. Having succeeded he nuzzled intently at her hand, huffed at his owner, and wiggled his clipped tail on Anna's thigh, pleased with his success. 'I'm sorry...' Claudia said with raised brows.

'It's fine, honestly. He's so cute.' Anna stroked his head and he settled his chin on her lap.

'And he knows it. This is Artois. He's a Cane Corso. He was born just before Christmas. He's the last of the litter to find a home. We have his parents too, they're called Stella and Peroni.' She shrugged. 'He clearly likes you. He doesn't normally settle in someone's lap,' she said, watching the dog as his eyes closed in contentment.

'Well Mr Artois,' Anna said as she ruffled his neck. 'You are one cute boy.' He snorted, flicked his eyes open, bounced up and scooted back into the kitchen at the sound of a cat flap. 'So much for loyalty eh?' Anna laughed.

'That'll be Edith.' Anna raised a confused eyebrow. 'One of our cats. She teases him relentlessly and he loves it. Typical male-female relationship,' she smirked. 'He'll never win, but he'll keep trying.'

'Ha ha,' Georgio sniggered. 'Welcome to the madhouse! Shall I show you to your room?'

'Thanks.' The loud hissing and whine of a clearly pissed off cat drew her eyes as she headed up the stairs. Claudia raced into the kitchen, arms flailing.

'Artois! Get off.' She bellowed shutting the door behind her.

*

Anna could see the top of part of the Vincenti mansion just down the slope from the bedroom window. The Carbone house was a simple farmhouse by comparison, and even with its five-bedrooms and three-bathrooms it was barely a shadow of the neighbouring property. She could just about see the top of the eucalyptus tree. There wasn't any movement that she could discern through the dense forestation that created privacy and distance between the two properties. Her body tensed and her stomach lurched in anticipation as she watched, wondering how she would react to Lauren when their paths crossed. Should she make a point of visiting her? If she thought about it too hard she still felt angry, rejected by the lack of communication, and wanted to run back to Paris. Hard as she tried to rationalise that Lauren must have had good reason not to tell her about her move back home, she couldn't think of anything beyond the fact that the omission sent a message of lack of interest.

The bedroom was sparsely decorated with a mahogany wood, hand crafted, dressing table and matching double bed frame. The bed was covered in a stone coloured throw. The walls were also of a stone colour, probably in an attempt to draw in the light, with delicate, hand painted flowers and foliage breaking up the monotony and adding subtle colour to the otherwise bland looking room. The curtains were also simple in design, matching the dark furniture, and rarely used, preference being given to the external shutters. With all its austerity, however, it still felt homely and warm, in a way that seemed absent from the Vincenti property, despite its grandness and potential. Anna sighed as she stepped away from the window, released the hold she had around her lower body, and walked towards the door.

The sound of a familiar voice stopped her in her tracks as she opened the solid wooden door. Hearty laughter. Her stomach jumped and sent a wave of tingling discomfort throughout her body. Her legs tried to buckle and she caught hold of the stair banister for support. She couldn't hear Lauren's slightly husky voice, but Valerie's timbre was unmistakeable. She stood trying to breathe for what felt like an eternity, through tight chest and a dry mouth, expecting to hear Lauren's voice at any moment. Breathing deeply and forcing herself to stand tall, a high-pitched yapping sound pulled her from a near panic attack, as her attention was drawn to the small black puppy who had clearly come out to greet their newly arrived visitors. Slowly she descended the stairs, her heart thumping so hard in her chest it must be visible from the outside.

'Ah, there you are,' Claudia greeted her, claiming her like a daughter as she stepped into the small foyer.

'Anna. How lovely to see you again,' Valerie said, stepping towards her with open arms, hugging her closely as she had done at the hospital. Nothing seemed to have changed between them, she mused. 'It really is lovely to see you again darling.' She pulled Anna in for another hug before holding her out in front of her for assessment. 'We've missed you.' She kissed her fondly on each cheek. 'You look... well.' Her eyes revealed something Anna couldn't define, as she felt her shoulders being squeezed lightly before Valerie released her fully.

Anna faltered. 'It's lovely to see you again too.' Her stomach flipped as she questioned whether she should have been more proactive in keeping in touch with Lauren's mother. In truth, she didn't know how they had got to this place of lack of communication and she felt bad for the fact that Valerie seemed as clueless as she felt about Lauren's behaviour. 'Is… Is Lauren here?' she stammered.

'No darling she isn't. She went to Ajaccio for a couple of days to visit her friends. You remember Carla and Francesca?' Anna's heart sank along with her shoulders. She didn't know whether she felt relieved or disappointed. Probably both. 'I assume by your question that she didn't tell you?' Valerie asked, tension rising in her voice.

'Umm, no,' was all that Anna could say without breaking down in front of the two women.

'She'll be back on Wednesday. I assumed she would have told you and that you would be catching up before you leave. When are you leaving?' she asked.

'Wednesday?' Anna said soberly, as her eyes lowered to the floor and locked onto a very excited puppy bouncing around her legs. Even his lively innocence couldn't lift her spirits though. 'And yes, she did know I was coming and no she hasn't been very communicative,' Anna added, feeling the fury ignite in her head.

'I'm so sorry Anna. I've been trying to let her have her own space, to make the right choices but clearly she's incapable.' Valerie said, indignant at her daughter's behaviour. 'That's it. I'm going to insist she goes to see someone about her mental health. I have tried to persuade her to see someone but she's refused. She's clearly not right and I'm not happy with the fact that she has treated you like this. And whilst I have every sympathy for the fact that she's had a rough time of it, if she continues down this road she's on, God only knows where she'll

93

end up.' Valerie's hand moved up, down and then across shoulder to shoulder and she kissed her fingers at her reference to the almighty. 'I think she's still in denial,' she said, thrashing her arms for dramatic effect as she spoke with intense passion. 'You need to keep in touch with me darling. We need to help her to see sense. I mean it's nearly four-months since the accident. Physically she's better but mentally she doesn't seem to have shifted at all... She didn't tell me you were coming, Claudia did. I assumed you and she were in touch, though now I think about it every time I've asked her how you are she's been pretty evasive in her response. Damn. I should have guessed something was up. This isn't right...' Valerie continued to rant. Anna and Claudia watched, nodding in the right places, Anna feeling drained and detached, unable to reconcile the fact that Lauren had chosen this particular time to visit Carla and Francesca and to actively avoid her.

'Well hopefully she'll speak to Carla while she's there. She's a psychiatrist after all.' Anna said.

'I damn well hope so,' Valerie said. 'Or she'll have me to answer to when she get's back here on Wednesday.' Valerie stopped pacing up and down, beginning to pant from the exertion, her eyes wild with fury.

'Let's have that drink?' Claudia offered as she linked arms with her old friend, softening the mood slightly, directing them into the dining room. 'I'm sure Lauren has a lot going on for her right now. She'll come to her senses. Champagne darling?' she asked, hoping to distract Valerie from her continued ranting.

'I'll have water please, or juice,' Anna said. Valerie stared at her, looking her up and down, and nodded knowingly.

'Does she know?' Valerie blurted, with renewed frustration in her tone.

Anna stammered. All eyes were on her, including Artois', whose bottom was also wagging in anticipation. Claudia

94

looked confused at the question as she handed Valerie her drink. 'No. I haven't told her yet.' Anna said lowering her gaze. 'I didn't want to make matters worse and when I left London she had pretty much made it clear to me that I caused her more stress than happiness. Since then we've hardly communicated. There hasn't been a right time. So, I...'

'Haven't told who what?' Claudia interrupted.

'Anna's pregnant.' Valerie held Anna's eyes with a mix of sternness and compassion. 'I'm right aren't I?'

'Yes.' Anna whispered, wanting to look away but unable.

'Oh my God. That's such wonderful news,' Claudia chirped, clapping her hands together, missing the full extent of the situation.

'And Lauren doesn't know?'

'Holy shit,' Claudia blurted, as her mind caught up with reality.

'Yes, holy shit.' Valerie reiterated, swearing out of character, taking a long swig of her drink and coughing as too many bubbles smacked at the back of her throat.

'Please don't tell her. Please.' Anna begged both women. 'I need to find the right time to tell her... Please. It needs to come from me, no one else.'

'This is just not right,' Valerie lamented. She started to pace again. 'We need to help Lauren somehow.'

'I'm not sure how anyone can help if she won't communicate. Maybe a professional can help her. Since coming home does she have any recollection of events before the accident?' Anna asked.

'I don't think much has changed.' Valerie shrugged as if defeated. 'I mean we keep reminding her of the things she's missed, looking through photo albums, talking through events. She even went around the vineyard with Antoine again the other day. He's going over the same ground he did before

95

Christmas, but it all seems new to her. Even though she's seen pictures nothing seems to register in her eyes. The only person she seems to respond to at the moment is her nurse.' Valerie continued to articulate her streaming thoughts. 'She needs professional help though, you're right.'

'Her nurse?' Anna queried.

'I hired a private nurse and physiotherapist for her. She seems to get on with them both but has formed a closer bond with Rita. On the one hand that's a good thing. Maybe I need to get Rita involved. See if she can help Lauren to open up.'

'That may work. I don't think I've got anything to lose right now.' Anna looked deflated as she spoke. She drifted into thought, wondering what Lauren was doing and whether Carla would be able to help her. She had liked Carla and Francesca and both women had warmed to her too. They had even talked about Anna giving birth in Corsica. Francesca had offered herself as their private neonatal nurse and Anna had taken that offer seriously, though she had expected Lauren to be by her side at that point, of course. She grabbed her phone from her pocket, tapped and pressed the send button without further thought.

Give my regards to Carla and Francesca!

Anger bolted through her like lightening striking a lone tree, burning it from the inside out. She couldn't hold back the tears any longer. Sinking into the chair she sobbed uncontrollably. Weeks of rejection by Lauren, and an inability to connect with the woman she loved, now left her bleeding through the tiny ducts leading from her soul.

Claudia bent down in front of her and wrapped her in a warm embrace. 'There there,' she whispered. Anna sobbed into her shoulder. Valerie joined them and pressed a gentle hand on Anna's head. Artois whimpered and cowered trying to inch his way between the women's bodies and onto Anna's lap. He huffed as he settled into his target and nuzzled at her shaking hand. Anna stroked his head and snuggled into his body heat.

She smiled wanly at the huge doe eyes staring up at her, sniffled and wiped at her eyes and nose.

*

Lauren picked up her phone and paled at the message. Anna was clearly angry. 'You okay?' Rita asked.

'Ever crushed someone's world and felt unable to stop yourself from destroying everything?'

'I'm not sure I understand,' Rita said, studying Lauren for clues. 'I used to get frustrated at forgetting something really simple, like where I put my keys,' she tried to explain.

'Having no memory of a phase of my life is killing me, and then I'm killing Anna too. It's a double fucking slaughter and I can't work out how to stop myself from continuing to inflict the pain.'

'Okay, now I'm really confused. I assume... Anna... she is, was, your lover?'

'Yes. We were lovers before the accident, but I only met her recently and I have no memory of her or us. I've been told about the things that have happened over the last few months, but none of it makes any sense to me. I might as well just have flown in from outer space. All I feel is confused, very angry, and pressurised. And yet, I know there's some truth in what everyone has told me. I have this.' She held out the small box. 'It was in my pocket at the time of the accident. I was lucky it didn't get damaged or lost. I haven't spoken to anyone about it, but it must have been bought for Anna. I must have chosen it specifically for her.' Rita took the box carefully, holding Lauren's pained expression. 'Open it.' Lauren indicated with her hand towards the elegant padded box.

Rita gently eased the sprung lid revealing a large round blue diamond set in an elegant white gold band. 'Wow... That looks...'

'Expensive.'

'Amazing, I was going to say. It's very, very beautiful. You must really love her?' Rita looked for affirmation in Lauren's eyes. The dullness she found there caused her chest to tighten.

'I must have.' Lauren said, but her eyes had glazed over before she spoke. The waiter appeared and Rita ordered the house specials and a bottle of house Rosé.

'So, why are we here?' Rita asked tentatively. She had wondered why Lauren had decided to spend time in Ajaccio at very short notice. Although they had built a close relationship over the past weeks, Lauren still held her cards close to her chest. It was Rita's job to assist her not to quiz her about her motivations or decisions.

Lauren held her hazel eyes. 'Anna is here.'

Rita automatically looked over her shoulder and scanned the restaurant. 'Where?'

'In Corsica.' Lauren smiled weakly. 'She's been commissioned by our neighbour to paint a portrait and has come over for a few days to meet with Claudia. The house up on the hill,' Lauren continued, orientating Rita.

'So why are you here? Don't you want to see her?' Rita looked even more confused.

'I knew she was coming and I didn't respond to her text. I hadn't told her that I'm back in Corsica. I didn't tell anyone about her visit either, though I'm sure Claudia will have told mother. That's why this decision was short notice. I couldn't face a potential grilling from my mother and I can't face Anna like this. This ring... makes it even worse. What does that say about me? Don't answer that,' she said in the same breath. 'I even told my mother that I had plans to meet with friends here. I can't face them either at the moment.' She held her head in her hands and thumped at her temples. Rita's face reddened with the awareness that she had been dragged into a lie. She had inadvertently become an accomplice.

'I cannot lie for you Lauren. I would rather lose my job than cover up something that will get us both into trouble. I value my reputation.'

'I know. I'm sorry. This is all going so terribly wrong. I feel like I'm on some giant roller coaster about to go over the edge without that harness thing they wear over their shoulders to keep them in their seat. I'm about to be flung out of the chair at high speed and there's nothing I can do about it. You're the only person I feel I can talk to. Mother wants me to have therapy but I don't feel ready for that, even though I can feel myself self-destructing. I feel screwed whichever way I turn.'

'I'm not sure how I can help.' Rita looked at the ring in the box and then at Lauren. 'Do you still love her?' She passed the box back across the table.

Lauren stared at the sparkling blue diamond briefly before snapping the box shut and pocketing it. She sighed deeply, searching for a feeling. 'Right now I feel nothing but pain when I think about her, or see her picture. Yes, she's very pretty. She's gorgeous in fact and I'm attracted to her physically, as I am to other gorgeous women. But I would have expected something deeper than just sexual attraction and certainly not this pain.'

'I'm not qualified to deal with your mind Lauren.' Rita leaned back in her seat unsure of how deep Lauren was intending to go in her introspection.

'I know, and I don't mean to put any pressure on you to solve my problems. Can I talk to you though? Share my thoughts... maybe you can just apply some logic to my fucked-up brain and ask me dumb questions or something? Isn't that what counselling is about?' Rita sniggered inwardly at her dismissive summation of the profession. As much as she was annoyed to be put in this position, there was something about Lauren that was deeply endearing. She cared for her more than she should a client, and she could see how easy it would have been for Anna to fall in love with her. Lauren's vulnerability not only added to her allure, but it also generated a desire to protect and defend her, even though her behaviour towards Anna was not really defendable by Rita's standards.

'You seem indifferent to counselling?'

'Well...' Lauren winced. The waiter arrived, saving her from explaining herself, and poured them both a glass of wine. Lauren picked up her glass immediately and took a healthy slurp enjoying the chill in her mouth and the almost immediate numbing effect on her mind.

'Okay, I'll listen to you. But if you get too deep I'm going to have to recommend you see someone else. You're pushing my professional boundaries here, remember.'

'I know... thank you, and thanks for coming with me.'

'Your mother wouldn't have let you come if I hadn't agreed to baby sit you, even though you and I both know you really don't need my help.'

'She wouldn't have let either of us come if I had told her Anna was arriving,' Lauren said dryly. 'If she knew she didn't say anything.' Lauren said reflectively. Something seemed amiss. Her mother must have known that Anna was arriving. Claudia would have mentioned it. The fact that Valerie had not challenged her about her absence during Anna's visit irked her. Normally she would have ranted at her for such behaviour. There was something disconcerting about the lack of interjection from her mother. She must have known, Lauren mused repeatedly, heat rising in her chest.

'You are so in the shit when you get home.'

'I know.'

'And how do you think Anna's feeling right now?'

'I know. Please, that's not the sort of counselling I was thinking about. I already feel like a complete fucking shit. I've never felt this bad. I've never treated anyone like this before.'

'Sorry, I didn't mean to...'

'You're right though. That's the whole point. I should at least be trying to talk to her. Trying to get back to where we were. I'm not even sure what's stopping me,' Lauren interrupted.

'Fear?'

'Of what?'

'I don't know. I'm not the screwed up one here.' Rita shrugged. 'Seriously, what are you afraid of Lauren?' Lauren twisted the glass on the table with vigour. She knew the question was valid. What little counselling she had before she left the hospital drove at the same point and she hadn't had an answer then either. The arrival of steaming plates of food disrupted her thoughts. Something about the aroma struck a cord and she breathed in the homely scent, a prickling sensation tingling down her spine as the food hit her taste buds. 'This is good,' she said tucking into the stew.

'It's very good. So, what are your plans while we're here? Are we going to meet your friends?' Rita asked as she tucked into the food.

'I guess it would help if there were some element of truth in my disappearance, then you won't have to lie to my mother. I can see if they're around one night for supper. Otherwise, just escaping from my mother for a few days makes the trip worth it for me.'

'Your mother is a good woman Lauren. She means well and she cares deeply for you. She's just a bit old school... traditional.' The words tweaked at the back of Lauren's neck.

Traditional. She played the word over in her head, sipped more wine and carried on eating. 'I've booked a hotel locally,' she said as she wiped the last piece of bread around her plate. 'Sorry, did you want that?' she asked, looking at Rita who was staring at her oddly.

'You seem different already,' she commented.

'Must be the wine,' Lauren said, dismissing the truth. She did feel a bit lighter. Maybe talking was exactly what she needed to do, she pondered. 'And the company of course,' she smiled wryly.

'Ah, yes. Of course. I should have twigged... it's all in the vines around here,' Rita mumbled, unconvinced but smiling. It was a step in the right direction for Lauren she hoped.

'If we get to meet my friends can you please not mention the fact that Anna is here? Please?' Lauren begged.

Rita nodded reluctantly. 'Now text Anna and apologise for not being there,' she insisted, prodding at Lauren's phone on the table.

Lauren picked up the phone hesitantly and slowly typed out her message.

I will do. Sorry I'm not there.

*

'I've managed to get an earlier flight,' Anna announced to Claudia at breakfast. 'I hope you don't mind. We can get the rest of the shots done this morning and I'll leave later today. I have some great action shots to work from already.'

She smiled to herself as she recalled the fiasco getting the two, dark grey, French Lops in any position to be photographed together, not aided by Artois who had taken a shine to Anna and wouldn't leave her side from the moment he caught sight of her. Desmond the larger of the two bunnies and three times the size of Artois, after padding his back foot rapidly, to which Artois just tilted his head and wriggled his back end in excitement, had chased the puppy around the garden, eventually taking a chunk out of the poor chap. Anna had looked on in horror, whilst Claudia had laughed at their antics. 'They'll sort themselves out,' she had said. 'And my money's on the rabbits.' Anna's instinct had been to remove Artois and protect him. Instead she had pointed her camera and flicked away, happily distracted by creating art.

'I understand,' Claudia said, pressing a hand on Anna's shoulder as she walked across the kitchen to put on the coffee machine.

'I need to go home and see how I feel about things when I'm there. It's hard for me to be objective here. Too many memories.' Anna reflected on Lauren's recent text. A wall had been erected and she didn't have the first idea of how to scale it... or even if it was worth scaling anymore.

'I can appreciate that. I'm so grateful for you coming, and taking on the commission, but I wish it had been a more pleasant experience for you,' she said, reaching for the coffee and pouring them both a cup.

'Me too. I just hope Valerie doesn't get involved. Their relationship was strained before. I wouldn't want Lauren to feel pressured or I may lose her completely. I just hope I haven't already,' she mused, casually stroking a sleeping Artois who had settled himself on her lap.

'Well he's certainly going to miss you. You've made a big impression in a short time. Artois half-opened his eyes, wriggled and re-settled. Anna smiled as she ran her fingers down his soft black mane, gently massaging the loose flesh lying beneath.

'I'm going to miss him too,' she said, as she picked up her phone and typed out a message.

I'm coming home tomorrow. Can you pick me up from the airport? 12.30 If not I'll taxi. Thx

Sure. Everything ok? x

The response came instantly and Anna smiled, genuinely relieved. She needed to talk to Eva.

You're up early! ☺
Just getting in! x
Haha. Good night out? x
Crap! x

Oh! Want to chat? x
Later. You okay? x
Pretty shitty! x
Want to chat? x
Later x
See you 1230 tomorrow then. Take care x
You too x

10.

'So… You want to talk about it?' Eva asked, dumping Anna's case in the foyer and heading for the kitchen. 'Drink?' she asked as she pulled a coke from the fridge.

'Water. Thanks.'

The pick-up and journey home had been taken in an uncomfortable silence and Eva didn't know how much longer she could take the strain. It was clear things hadn't gone well, and from the monosyllabic responses Anna had given, it seemed that Lauren had evaded her during her visit, and without due explanation. They were back to square one, if not even worse.

Eva reached for a tall glass and filled it with cold tap water. Pulling the ring on her Coke can she took a long glug of the fizzing liquid before handing the water to Anna who had already slumped in the stool, head in hands, elbows resting on the table's surface.

Eva's heart sank. Standing by her side she rubbed her hand tenderly up and down Anna's back. 'Is there anything I can do to help?' she asked between gulps from the can.

Anna began to shake. Tears streamed down pale cheeks and blotchy eyes looked woefully at Eva, screaming silently for help. Eva put the can down and pulled her close. Anna's head rested against her stomach and with a soothing touch she brushed her fingers through the damp hair straggling her face.

'I'm sick of feeling like this. I've cried more than I've laughed in the last three months and that isn't what I wanted for my baby,' she blurted. 'I can't do this anymore. I've got to forget about Lauren and move on,' she continued, and immediately broke into uncontrollable sobs.

Allowing the wave of sadness to run its course, Eva stood silently. Pain wracked her body as she could only watch Anna's suffering. Ten minutes later, she felt as exhausted as Anna looked.

Slowly Anna pulled back and sipped at the water. Eva studied her, assessing whether it was safe to leave her side. Having determined it was, she threw the can into the bin, pulled out a wine glass and dived into the fridge. Anna began to giggle as she sniffled. 'You always do that?' she said.

'What?'

'Hit the wine. I don't blame you mind. I must be a nightmare to be around...'

'Whoa, stop right there. You are not a nightmare to be around. On the contrary, I love being with you. I love you remember. It kills me to see you so upset and know there's nothing I can do about it, and for that reason I need a drink.'

'Believe me, I'd be joining you if it wasn't for this,' she pointed towards her belly. 'I think pregnancy has saved me. I would have gotten smashed every night since the accident otherwise.'

'What are you going to do?'

'Nothing. I have to put the past behind me now and move on. I can't do the waiting game anymore. It's just too painful. Hoping that she might remember me... remember us... I just can't keep it up. And I'm feeling more and more tired. The emotional turmoil can't be fair to this little one either.'

'Hey, go easy on yourself remember. That little guy's going to have to survive a tougher world out here, so he, or she, is as safe as houses tucked up in there.' She nodded towards Anna. 'You're doing a great job, so stop beating up on yourself.'

'I've got to step off this merry-go-round though and move forward.' She hesitated, looking directly at Eva. 'Would you stay with me for a bit longer? I mean, I...'

'Of course,' Eva interrupted her and beamed a smile. 'For as long as you want. I'll be here for you, okay. Please don't worry. Just give yourself the time you need and start to enjoy your pregnancy. It's such a special time.'

'Say's… I've had fifteen-kids… Ms Adams,' she teased lightly.

'I've been reading up on things, okay,' Eva cowered defensively, slurping her wine. She reminded Anna of Artois at that moment, causing a soft smile to rise to her face.

'What?'

'Nothing. You just do a really cute *'I've been mortally wounded look'* with those eyes of yours, and it reminded me of a most gorgeous puppy I met in Corsica called Artois. One of my client's pets,' she clarified.

'You calling me a dog?' Eva teased back. 'Want me to lick you all over?' The words were out before any thought had been processed and she immediately blushed. Anna burst out laughing.

'I've missed this,' she said. 'You make me laugh a lot and right now that's got to be a good thing.' Anna stepped out of the chair and pressed a kiss on Eva's cheek. 'I'm going to unpack and then stare at a blank canvas and see what happens.'

'I'll sort something out for supper. Any ideas?'

'Nope. You decide. Not fish or chicken, and I'd rather not see or smell anything that's raw.' She cupped a hand and held it to Eva's face. 'Thanks,' she said with sincerity.

'You're welcome,' Eva croaked, still recovering from the licking images trailing across her mind. 'Supper about 8?'

'Sounds great.' Anna bounded up the stairs, and clicked the door shut. Eva breathed out deeply releasing the tension she had been holding before grabbing her keys and heading for her car.

11

'How about cinema later?' Eva asked from her bedroom as she squeezed her skinny jeans up over her hips.

'Hmmm, not sure.' Anna responded from her room. 'I think I fancy a quiet evening in.' Eva had been trying to get her out of the house since she returned from Corsica, but tiredness with the pregnancy was hitting her hard by early evening, and the thought of travelling into Paris and sitting in uncomfortable seats didn't feel all that appealing.

'How about a movie in front of the fire then?' Eva shouted through her t-shirt as she lifted it over her head.

'Sounding better.' Anna nodded to herself, searching for her red-leather boots under her bed, huffing as she stretched to reach them. 'Come here,' she mumbled.

'You want something?' Eva asked, standing in the bedroom doorway, smiling at the sight of Anna's raised bottom.

Anna jumped and bumped her head on the bedframe. 'Shit,' she said, rubbing furiously. 'I was talking to the boots.'

Eva sniggered as she moved forward and held out her hand. 'You okay?' she asked, pulling her to her feet.

'I wasn't expecting you to be there,' she said pointing to the doorway.

'Well some of us don't take forever to dress,' she said with a smirk. 'Anyway, what you do have on so far looks great,' she teased, as she eyed Anna from her feet upwards, her bare legs meeting a loose fitting white shirt hanging open. Even though she was three-months pregnant she wasn't showing, her natural curves easily accommodating the early stages of the baby's development. Her skin had a shine to it, soft and alluring, and her eyes sparkled. Eva's mouth parched as she glanced from her cleavage to her shapely lips. Fidgeting, she lowered her eyes. 'You want me to crawl under the bed and get them?' she asked.

'Would you mind?' Anna asked giving her a doe-eyed look, seemingly oblivious to Eva's moderate discomfort at her semi-dressed state.

'Sure.' She dived under the bed, thankful for the brief respite from the tantalising view.

Rising with a smile and pair of boots in hand she handed them over. Anna brushed at her shoulders. 'Dust,' she said. The light touch burnt a hole and goose bumps shot down Eva's back. She shuddered involuntarily. 'You okay?' Anna asked.

'Sure,' Eva managed, backing out of arms reach and towards the bedroom door. 'I'll go and put some coffee on,' she stammered. She had cleared the stairs before Anna could respond. Anna's curiosity piqued at Eva's strange response as she continued to dress.

*

'What do you think?' Anna asked as they exited the gallery.

'I think it's an amazing opportunity. I mean, to have your work shown at the Musée d'Art Moderne, that's brilliant. You're a star,' she beamed nudging Anna in the arm as they walked.

'But I'll be heavily pregnant by then,' Anna said with a concerned look.

'You've got me and mum. We can help you. Look, you don't need to decide just yet, but it's a great opportunity for visibility.'

'But I'm not sure what to show.' Anna said, uncharacteristically insecure and seeming to block the idea of accepting the offer.

'It's not like you to shy away from an opportunity,' Eva commented. 'What's up? What are you worried about?' she asked, probing.

'I don't know. I guess I'm concerned that it won't be good enough,' she said, shrugging her shoulders, eyebrows raised.

'They must think so, otherwise they wouldn't have offered,' Eva said.

'Your mum can be very persuasive.' Anna responded.

'Mmm!' Eva winced at the idea of her mum going to bat on Anna's behalf. 'She can be passionate about her protégé for sure, but it's still their decision to make, and they wouldn't show something that's crap. They wouldn't offer it to you if you weren't good enough,' she said, to nail the point.

'I know, I know. You're right. I'm just feeling emotional and not thinking logically,' she said soberly, leaning into Eva's side. Eva put an arm around her and pulled her snuggly as they walked in step.

'You're being a typical artist,' she said, squeezing Anna and causing them both to stagger. 'Creating a drama out of a non-event,' she said, releasing her hold a little so they could regain their step. 'Please don't be one of those talented individuals who needs to wait until they're dead to achieve fame. That's so out dated,' she finished. 'Now let's get home for our movie night. I was thinking spaghetti with a light tomato sauce,' she said, looking for Anna's response. She grimaced.

'I was thinking something meatier. I'm in need of iron.'

'Well you can't have liver, apparently.' Eva said, confirming the knowledge she had gleaned through her extensive research.

'Makes you wonder how pregnant women survived before discovering all the do's and don'ts of current theories,' she said, nodding with disdain. 'I really fancy liver and onions,' she said licking her lips. Eva frowned. 'In fact, the more I think about it, the more I think I might have a craving for it,' she said with a smile developing on her lips. 'Mmm, liver and onions in an onion gravy with potatoes.' Anna looked at Eva whose mouth rested open. 'What?' she asked.

'You can't have liver?' Eva insisted.

'Oh yes I can, and we will,' she said as she freed herself from Eva's hold and marched up the street with a sense of conviction. Eva followed, trying to get Anna to change her mind. By the time they reached the supermarket, she had failed. Eva adored this side of Anna. She just wished she had been as convinced about showing her work as she was eating something that wasn't recommended during pregnancy. Anna's only response was that she thought it was all a load of crap and she'd follow her instincts about what she needed and wanted to eat. Eva felt unable to argue the point, but still uncomfortable at Anna eating the liver. She would make sure it was cremated, she thought. 'And I'll cook it,' Anna said, as if reading Eva's mind. Eva shrugged in defeat and headed for the wine aisle.

'Hey look,' Anna said as they passed the DVD shelf on the way to the wine. *'Blue is the Warmest Colour.'* She said pointing at the movie. 'It's only ten-Euros and I haven't got a copy. How about we watch that tonight. It's ages since I saw it at the cinema. Have you seen it?' she asked, as Eva noted the front cover and nodded her head.

'I saw it when it came out. It's really good, but long,' she said, adding a little resistance because of her concern as to whether she could sit through the explicit sexual scenes with Anna sat next to her. It was provocative, and at points bordering pornographic and she knew she would struggle to control her feelings under the pressure.

'Go on. It'll be fun. You always see movies differently the second time around,' Anna insisted. Eva swallowed hard.

'Okay,' she said, blowing air out of her mouth in an overly controlled manner. She turned and continued towards the wine. Anna popped the movie into their basket and giggled excitedly. Selecting two-bottles of Merlot, Eva placed them into the basket and took it from Anna.

'Thirsty?' she asked with a grin.

'I figure it's going to be a long night. That movie's at least four-hours,' she said, raising her eyebrows, sporting a new shade of red cheeks.

'It's so not that long. It's just over three-hours and we can always watch it over a couple of evenings,' Anna offered as a compromise.

Eva shuddered internally at the idea. Prolonging the pain of lust she was inevitably going to feel watching the movie was an even worse plan. She'd just drink, a lot, and at the tricky points distract her mind with work, or something else she mused, even though she had no idea what the something else might be.

*

Anna poured herself half a glass of the decanted red wine and began chopping the onions. The potatoes were already on the boil, the steam creating a pattern on the backsplash of the cooker. Anna watched it rise up and trickle down, distracted from her task.

'Right. Fire's on and I'm ready for a drink,' Eva said, bounding into the kitchen and grabbing the glass Anna had put out for her. She filled it just short of the brim and downed a third of it so the wine sat at a more refined level in the glass.

'You heathen,' Anna teased.

'What can I say. I'm thirsty and just saving time.' She shrugged and sipped more elegantly at her drink. 'It's good,' she said, as if to herself, looking at the red liquid.

Anna looked towards her untouched glass as she picked up another onion. 'Good,' she said.

'I see you're having one.' Eva said, nodding towards the glass.

'Just that little bit and don't you go downing it all too quickly or you'll sleep through the movie.' She smiled, shaking her head at Eva who had already finished her first glass and was in the process of filling a second. At least she had the awareness to look sheepishly at Anna's mild reprimand.

'I'll go and get it loaded,' she said. 'Shall we eat in front of it?' she asked, hoping the food would be an added distraction.

'Sure.' A sizzle emanated from the pan as Anna threw in the chopped onions, turning away from the cooker as she sneezed. 'Onions' she explained.

'Ah yes. I always cry.'

'I always sneeze,' Anna confirmed.

'Good to know,' Eva joked as her back disappeared from view.

Removing the potatoes from the stove, Anna sieved them and quickly flash fried the thin slices of liver over the onions, adding the stock for the gravy. Plating the two meals she carried them both in one hand, her glass in the other, into the living room. The heat from the fire and crackling of wood felt cosy. She placed her glass and the two plates on the coffee table in front of the couch. 'Mustard?' she asked.

'Sure, I'll get it.' Eva bounced up, waving at Anna to sit as she headed for the kitchen, returning with their cutlery and the mustard. 'Smells great,' she said as she sat. 'Right, you ready?' she asked as she pointed the remote control menacingly at the wide screen. Anna nodded, grabbed her plate and attacked the food with urgency.

'Oh my God, this is divine,' Anna said halfway through the meal. She hadn't looked up since starting on the food. Eva had barely started, having sat watching Anna, amused at the intensity of focus being applied to the liver and onions. 'I think I just had my first real craving,' she said, looking up, finally taking a breath.

'Certainly, seems to have hit the spot,' Eva said with a wry smile. 'It's good to see you enjoying your food though.' She had given up on nagging Anna about the fact that liver wasn't recommended for pregnant women.

'Yum. I really needed that,' Anna said, licking her lips, placing the empty plate on the table. She reclined into the seat and released a loud belch. 'Oops, sorry,' she exclaimed, holding her hand to her mouth. 'That just slipped out without notice.'

Eva laughed. 'Must have been good,' she said, tucking into the last of her food before joining Anna, relaxing into the couch watching the screen through half-lidded eyes.

Eva could feel the tension rising in her body as the film progressed. They had sat in silence since eating, but Anna's subtle shift in breathing caused Eva to glance sideways towards her. Eva released the breath she had been holding and her shoulders dropped an inch. Anna's eyes were shut and she was snuffling like a child. Eva turned her head and watched for a while, a warm smile on her face. She leaned forward and poured herself another glass of wine before settling back into the sofa. It felt altogether different, and more tolerable watching the movie whilst Anna slept. It didn't feel as intimate and Eva could enjoy it a little more, even though her mind still strayed to the woman sat next to her.

At one-point Anna had shifted and rested her head against Eva's arm and she had frozen. Heat flooded her veins, creating an instant pulsing sensation between her legs, and her heart raced. She had breathed deeply saying the, *'we're just good friends'*, mantra repeatedly until the throbbing had subsided. She had switched the movie off then and sat in silence, increasing her sight as her eyes adjusted to the darkness, giving her attention to the dying embers in the fire. When Anna had stirred again she had woken her and helped her

114

up to her bedroom, kissed her softly on the cheek before returning to her own room and pressing her back against the closed door whilst she tried to regain her composure. Getting laid hadn't worked, she had mused as she tossed and turned, alone in her bed.

12

Anna stared at the blank canvas, as she had done every day since arriving back from Corsica. She had never experienced a block of this magnitude before. She'd had moments of indecision of course, but those had passed quickly and with a few movements of the brush she had been on her way again. This feeling had a density to it, weighing her down, holding her in place, restricting her movement... restricting the flow. The ideas for the picture she'd had in Corsica, as she had captured the pets' playful antics on her camera, seemed to lack something, but she couldn't pinpoint what. A month had passed since her visit and she was still no further forward. The sketches hadn't translated well to the canvas and it wasn't that they weren't right. It was more that she wasn't right. The depth and insight that normally flowed through had dried up. What little she had tried to create had felt forced, artificially constructed, and ended up in the bin by the end of the day. Standing, she stretched, feeling the growing bump already impeding her posture, and stared out over the green expanse of land. Spring was showing its face with delicate buds forming on the trees, snowdrops sitting proudly and even daffodils beginning to bloom, though it was still chilly most days and today the clouds threatened rain.

A sweeping image of Lauren brought a deep sigh. Residual sadness had come to her from time to time since arriving back from Corsica but she had rationalised the situation every time and the emotions had shifted quickly. She was doing fine and really enjoying Eva's company. More than, she mused. An image of spikey blonde hair and big submissive eyes popped into her mind and she imagined pulling her close, kissing her passionately, taking control. The image shifted and she was being thrust up against the wall in her kitchen and fucked hard. She tried to shake off the movie, something about it feeling a little odd, but it kept running, scene after scene until her body ached with desire. A buzzing sound wiped the movie in her mind instantly. She was physically shaking as she picked up her phone.

How's work going?

Heat flushed her cheeks as she responded to the object of her guilty pleasure.

Not great!

She waited, watching the screen, butterflies flipping in her stomach, her heart racing with the anticipation.

Need some inspiration?

Something like that ☺

Fancy a walk?

Good idea

Let's go

Anna slipped her phone into her back pocket and raced down the stairs, a beaming smile on her face. Eva walked out from the living room tussling her hair, rubbing her eyes and yawning.

'Did I wake you?' Anna teased, still looking flushed.

'No, just bored ridged and I can't look at the screen any longer. Fresh air will be good.'

'It's starting to drizzle,' Anna said, putting on her walking boots. Eva stared out the window, assessing the grey expanse overhead.

'Looks like it might blow over,' she shrugged, grabbing her coat, and throwing Anna's across to her.

'Yeah right... we'll see,' Anna squinted, but didn't really care if they got rained on. The shower might douse the rising heat, she smiled to herself, unconvinced.

They meandered the muddy tree-lined paths and hiked across open fields, a light spray bathing their faces, a comfortable silence between them. Winter was officially at an end. The new growth breaking into life seemed stronger, more determined from the ground, than it had appeared from the attic window. The sprouting leaves looked greener and more luscious, and birds were singing from the branches and hedgerows. There was robustness to nature that gave confidence in the cycle of life, where rebirth would always happen, since nature would take care of that, effortlessly.

Anna breathed in deeply, enjoying the cold air hitting her nostrils, already feeling more energised than she had done sat in front of the canvas in her studio. 'You never did tell me about your crappy weekend,' she said as it dawned on her that their conversations since she had returned from Corsica had revolved around her situation with Lauren or her struggles with work.

Eva buried her hands deeper into her jeans pockets. 'Not much to tell really.'

'What happened? Some girl break your heart?' she pressed, suddenly more interested in Eva's love life, a buzzing sensation sitting in her solar plexus as she watched for Eva's response.

Eva blushed lightly and mindlessly kicked at a stick on the ground, nearly tripping over, as the stick failed to move and she was thrust forward. 'Fuck.'

Anna burst into laughter as Eva stumbled, bracing the fall with outstretched hands. Standing with raised palms and a glint in her eye she chased towards Anna. 'No... no,' Anna screeched.

Anna tried to flee, flapping her hands as Eva reached for her face. 'I hear mudpacks are good for the skin,' she chuckled as she grabbed Anna round the middle, flipped her round and plastered the wet, grey, sticky substance to her cheeks.

Anna squealed. 'I don't believe you did that,' she said, indignant but giggling as she planted her hands in the sticky wet mud. Her eyes pierced through Eva, as she launched towards her with a pace she didn't even know she possessed. Ducking and diving to avoid being caught, choking with laughter, Eva eventually stopped, doubled over, and puffed hard. Anna dived onto her back, collapsing them both to the ground. Eva bucked suddenly and flipped Anna onto her back, holding her hands at bay. The fire in her eyes flamed, weakening Eva's grip, and Anna immediately flipped her onto her back. Sitting astride Eva with muddy palms threatening her face, she stopped suddenly. Eva's eyes, dark with desire, her resistance sapped, her vulnerability inviting Anna to take her, Anna bent forward and claimed her lips with burning passion. Eva groaned at the contact and opened willingly to the kiss. Deepening the kiss their teeth clashed and tongues danced. Pulling back they gasped for breath, locked eyes, and then their mouths clashed again. Eva's hands secured Anna's head, fingers grabbing her hair, holding her close - possessing her. Anna melted into the contact she craved.

Anna pulled out of the kiss and her steel-blue eyes bored into Eva momentarily before she broke the trance between them. 'You're filthy.'

'Oh yeah. You seem to like it dirty?' Eva teased, as her brows rose and lips pursed. Anna smiled as she stood, holding out a hand to help Eva to her feet. By the time they were facing each other seriousness had descended on Anna, and her eyes reflected sadness. Eva's heart pounded through her chest as she realised what she really wanted wasn't truly attainable. 'Hey, no sweat, right?' She threatened a muddy hand at Anna in an effort to lighten the mood. Anna leaned in and pressed a soft kiss to her lips before taking her by the hand. They walked home in heavy rain, in silence, looking like two camouflaged soldiers who had been on an exercise skirmishing through the woods.

'That's better.' Anna sighed as she padded into the dining room, fresh from her shower, still rubbing at wet hair. Eva's eyes wandered the baggy, dark grey bottoms and large red t-shirt hanging loosely over the slightly rounded bump. Her mouth parched at the sight and her skin reddened.

She had dived into the house and scampered to her room before Anna had even removed her shoes, mumbling about getting cleaned up. Quickly showered she had returned to the kitchen and poured herself a large glass of wine. She was on her second already and everything that held her eyes seemed to have a soft haze about it. She couldn't deny the kiss they had shared. Her body was still screaming at the after-effects. 'Hi,' she rasped through a tight throat. 'You look…'

'I'm sorry.' Anna interrupted with a sense of urgency. 'I'm sorry… I… kissed you.' The towel hung around Anna's neck and all Eva wanted to do was grab either side and pull Anna into a deep kiss. Her heart ached at Anna's words.

'I'm not sorry. But it's okay, I understand.' Eva's eyes searched her glass as she swirled the last of her wine. Suppressing the vivid sensation of Anna's lips on hers, she swigged the drink and stood. 'Can I get you anything?' she said, the awkwardness sitting heavily between them. She stepped to move past Anna who reached out to stop her.

Eva's eyes burned emerald green, questioning Anna's intent. She answered as she moved into the space between them and claimed Eva's lips with a tender, lingering kiss. Heat flared through Eva who groaned, yielding to the delicate, yet electric, touch. 'Oh fuck, Anna,' she moaned, barely audible, recounting her desires. She pulled back from the kiss, forehead still touching Anna's, 'Are you sure?' she asked. 'I'm not sure I'll be able to stop if you take this any further right now.'

Anna could feel Eva shaking as she spoke. Her hand tilted Eva's chin upwards, locking their eyes. 'You have beautiful eyes,' she said, placing a kiss to each lid. 'And you are very considerate, kind and caring,' Anna kissed her on the nose. 'And… I desperately want you to fuck…' Before the words were out, Eva's lips clashed with hers and their tongues moved urgently together. Eva pulled Anna firmly into her body, stopping instantly as she bumped into the bump. She tried to pull back but Anna held her firmly. 'Baby's fine.' They collided again, overtaken by arousal. Eva's hand slipped under Anna's t-shirt, moved swiftly up her body and cupped her breast, her thumb trailing across an erect nipple, a groan emanating from Eva as she connected with the soft, delicate flesh. Anna gasped and guided Eva back to the couch. 'Fuck me Eva,' she pleaded. Eva pressed a hand into the baggy pants, smiled inwardly at the absence of underwear, and instantly found the wet heat between Anna's legs. They fell into the couch and Anna opened further. She had to work hard not to slam her legs shut as Eva entered her seamlessly with three-fingers. 'Fuck,' she screamed as fire shot through her. Eva thrust again, deeper, as a surge of adrenaline took control of her desires. Consumed by lust, she continued to penetrate Anna, deeper, wider, responding to her screams, following the rhythm of their movement together. Eva's body moved between Anna's legs, forcing her to stay wide for her as she delved again into the moist, soft, cavernous space, driving the tremors as she curved her fingers to work Anna's G-spot. Anna thrashed, tensed, quieted, and squeezed her legs tight around Eva as her body jerked out of control and she released a final scream. 'Oh my fucking God.' Eva stilled herself, her dark eyes locked onto Anna, her fingers clamped in place, while Anna rode the waves of ecstasy as they shuddered through her body. As the tremors abated Anna started to giggle and caught Eva's intense glare. She cupped Eva's cheek with her hands and rose up to meet her bruised lips, holding the kiss tenderly, and pulling Eva down to rest on top of her. 'Thank you,' she said. Eva could hear her thumping heart as she rested her head on Anna's chest, unable to process the last few hours.

*

Anna woke to the smell of bacon and coffee wafting into her room. She lay awake assessing her feelings, looking for a negative response to the events that had resulted in her having sex with Eva the previous evening. She felt warm, comforted, and was surprised when she tested herself further by drawing on an image of Lauren. She felt no sense of guilt or anxiety. Nothing. Satisfied with her analysis, she smiled, pulled herself out of bed and grabbed her dressing gown from the chair by her bed. Plodding down the stairs, she took in the aromas emanating from the kitchen and her stomach grumbled.

She had not returned the sexual favour yesterday and felt somewhat guilty that she should have at least offered to pleasure Eva. They had made supper and simply snuggled up on the couch together watching a movie until Eva had woken her after a time and urged her to go to bed. Eva had made no move to go to her room, instead leaving her at the top of the stairs with a chaste kiss on the cheek before heading to her own bedroom. At the time Anna had welcomed the space in her bed, collapsed and hardly moved all night. Now, she wondered whether Eva was offended by the direction their relationship had taken and entered the kitchen with mild trepidation.

Her concerns faded as Eva turned from the stove and beamed a warm smile. Her emerald green eyes penetrated Anna, sending a tingling sensation down her spine. Eva looked even younger today, with her fresh face, spikey blonde hair and abundance of energy. She danced around the kitchen laying out the food, juice, and cutlery. 'Morning,' she said. 'Sleep well?'

'Very well thank you.' Anna said with a coy smile. 'How about you?'

'Yeah good,' Eva lied. She had tossed and turned all night trying to assess the implications of the turn they had taken, worried they had crossed a line they shouldn't, even though she had been wanting to, and willing to, for some time. She dashed to the hob and grabbed the eggs, tipped them onto a serving plate and placed it onto the island.

'Wow, this looks amazing, and I'm starving,' Anna said as her eyes feasted on the spread in front of her.

'I didn't know what you'd fancy so I did a bit of a lot of things and you can pick what you want?' Eva babbled.

Anna reached up and cupped her cheek with a hand. 'Thank you, this looks great. You look great,' she added, her eyes scanning Eva's athletic form, seductively. She leaned in and pressed a soft kiss to her lips before releasing her. 'Let's eat.'

Eva jumped into her seat and started to pile food onto her plate, licking her lips as her mouth salivated. 'Ah,' she said, suddenly leaping out of her seat, grabbing two mugs from the rack and pouring their coffee. 'Milk's in there and sugar, there,' she pointed even though both items were obvious. Anna watched and smiled lovingly. 'So what's your plan for the day?' Eva asked, through a mouthful of egg and toast.

'I'm going to paint this morning and see how it flows,' she said with a tilt of her head.

'Are you feeling more inspired?' Eva asked, seeking the affirmation as positive reinforcement of their intimate time together.

'I'm feeling… different,' Anna said, searching for the right word, holding Eva's gaze with intensity.

'Different in a good way?' Eva pressed.

'Yes.' Anna smiled, reached for Eva, cupped her face, and pulled her in for a lingering kiss.

13.

Lauren looked at the small square padded box that sat in the corner of her dressing table draw, as she had done many times in the last few weeks. Reaching to pick it up, she hesitated. It had been six-weeks since Anna had visited her neighbour and she had asked Rita to help her get her head straight. Physically she was feeling much stronger having ditched the cane, and her mobility and strength were good, and still improving daily. Her mother had disowned her over her behaviour towards Anna, which brought with it an ironic sense of familiarity - security even. Being alone with her thoughts wasn't a unique experience. Whilst the red-rage anger that seemed to have had control over her had now dissipated, twinges of guilt regularly caused her a fitful night's sleep. The reoccurring dream, the scent of vanilla and the faceless seductress was starting to haunt her, creeping into her daily thoughts. She always awoke before they made love, her body throbbing with vivid desires that the dream had evoked. She had never seen the face of the woman but deep down she knew it was Anna. Frustrated, cold morning-showers were fast becoming the norm.

She picked up the padded box and ran her thumb over the soft suede cover. The Eiffel Tower card stared up at her. She gathered it up, carefully studying the back of the lighter haired woman. The resemblance to the woman in her dream was unquestionable. So what stopped her reaching out to Anna to rekindle what they had? Having talked at length with Rita she still didn't have the answers. Rita had moved on to another job under the pretext of a family crisis, following an incident between them. An incident in which Lauren had been stupid, behaved badly, and she had even had Rita lie for her about meeting her friends. *Had she really lost her mind?*

She stared blankly out the window. A dense fog lingered as the clouds sat motionless on the ground. She could barely see the eucalyptus tree at the far end of the gardens. It had only been a week ago that she had asked Rita if she wanted to see the workings of the vineyard. Antoine had given her an introductory talk, with much less enthusiasm than his normal presentation, and Lauren had assumed he was going down with man flu. She had been feeling exhilarated, for no apparent reason other than she was feeling better, fitter, and more alive, than she had done since as far back as she could remember. They had wandered around the vines talking and laughing. They had then spent the late morning tasting a variety of home produced wines, Lauren taking great delight and pride in explaining the distinctions between the types of grapes and flavours of each wine. Rita wasn't a connoisseur by any standards, but she had easily picked up the different elements with a little prompting from Lauren. Lauren had watched intently as Rita sipped, her soft lips making delicate contact with the rim as she tipped the glass, the light blushing of her skin as the alcohol hit an empty stomach, and the darkening of her hazel eyes. She had become entranced and drunk a little more than she should have. They had held each other's gaze a number of times and she had been sure she had seen the signs, the heat firing through her body had told her so when Rita's hand brushed hers as she handed her the final glass of their most expensive red. Rita had cleared her throat and Lauren hadn't let go of the glass. Instead she had taken a step closer and pressed a soft kiss on those inviting lips. Rita had responded and the glass had hit the floor. The door had been flung open in the same moment and both women pulled back from the contact. Floundering, flustered, Rita had taken a step back from Lauren and started to pick up the shattered pieces from the floor. Antoine had locked eyes with Lauren, lowered his head, turned, and closed the door behind him. Rita had left the Vincenti residence that afternoon.

Lauren pulled the box open and admired the ring. Its subtle blue tints sparkled even though there was no sun for it to reflect off. It was certainly an excellent choice, but she was struggling to believe she would have asked Anna to marry her. Marriage had never been her thing and she'd only agreed to it the first time around to support Rachel's career. That much she did remember. *Anna... Anna... Anna. How did you become so special to me?* She flicked the box closed, puffed out a deep sigh and placed it back in the draw, together with the card. She needed to speak to Carla... now. She picked up her phone and sent the text.

*

'Hey stranger,' Carla greeted her old friend with open arms and a beaming smile as she entered the restaurant. 'To what do I owe this pleasure?' she said, looking Lauren up and down. Lauren seemed to struggle to stand from the table. 'Are you okay? What's happened?' Carla's jovial voice took on an air of concern as she eyed Lauren more carefully. 'Lauren?' she questioned.

'It's a long story, but that's why I wanted to meet rather than chat over the phone. Thanks for coming.'

'Of course, I'll always meet with you. Tell me, what's going on? What happened to you?' Carla intimated towards the apparently gammy leg and the dark bags underneath Lauren's sunken eyes as she sat. 'You look...'

'I know... like shit. But I'm a lot better than I was. I had an accident just before Christmas. Stupidly, I walked out in front of a van and the result...' she rubbed at her leg. 'It still gets a bit stiff if I sit for any length of time.'

'Why am I only hearing about this now?' Carla asked with concern.

'It's complicated. I was in a London hospital for a while. My mother commissioned a nurse and physio and I've been pretty much under house arrest since then,' she said, with the most helpless look she could muster.

'You have a phone.' Carla said pointedly. 'You could have called.' She eyed Lauren carefully knowing full well there was a lot more to the story than she was being given. 'Where's Anna?' she asked. Lauren's head dropped to the floor.

'That's the worst part of it. I can't remember her. Since the accident I have no recollection of who she is, how we met or anything that happened in the time before the accident.'

'But where is she now? Surely, you're still seeing her.'

'Not exactly.' Lauren looked up and out into space. 'I really struggled with her being around and we've sort of drifted apart.' Carla winced and leant back in the chair, staring at Lauren.

She didn't like what she was seeing, and what she was hearing sounded like denial, tinged with self-pity. She had seen it many times in her work as a Psychiatrist, but watching her friend self-destruct had a bigger impact on her than any of her client's cases. This wasn't normal for Lauren, who had always been mentally tough, determined, if sometimes a little single minded, bordering on stubborn. The fragile woman sitting across from her now was a long way removed from that person. 'Drifted apart?' she questioned.

'It was for the best. I didn't want to hurt her.'

'Hurt her how?' Carla asked without judgement.

'I have thought about this a lot. I'm not the same person she fell in love with. I don't know if I still have the same feelings for her now as I did before the accident. I was so angry and I took it out on her.' Carla nodded as Lauren spoke. 'I don't want to break her heart.'

'And you don't think you've done that by withdrawing from her?' Carla asked directly.

'I'm sure I have.' Lauren looked to the sky as she reflected on her behaviour towards Anna over the past weeks. She felt bad, but she had justified it to herself with the story that it was in Anna's best interests for them to go their separate ways. 'I've behaved really badly towards her.' Lauren's glassy eyes reflected her pain, as she looked pleadingly at Carla.

Carla sighed deeply. 'Do you have any memory of her now?'

'Not really. I know what people have told me, so it's a bit confusing. She sent me a hand painted card.' Lauren handed Carla the image of the Eiffel Tower with two lovers sat together. 'It seems familiar somehow. And I keep having the same dream, but I can't see the woman's face. Her hair could be Anna's, and there is a vanilla scent. Oh... and there's this.' Lauren placed the square padded box on the table in front of Carla.

Carla picked up the card and studied it, instantly recognising both Lauren and Anna as the two-people sat on the bench. Not only was the representation clear to her, but the energy between the two women also stood out. There was no mistaking they were lovers. She reached for the box, brushed a thumb across its soft surface and pulled it open. 'Wow. That's a beautiful ring.' She placed the open box back on the table so they both could see the blue diamond as they continued to talk. 'How can I help you?'

'I don't know. I've been a real shit and I don't know how to change things for the better. She must have been really special for me to have gone to these lengths.' She indicated to the ring. 'My mother has disowned me for how I've treated Anna, and rightly so. I came into Ajaccio to avoid her when she came over to work on a project with our neighbours. God, I even got Rita to lie for me to Valerie by saying that we were meeting you when I didn't even try and get hold of you. I couldn't face you guys.'

'Rita?' Carla queried.

'The woman my mother hired to be my nurse. She's gone now. I behaved stupidly and kissed her.' Lauren shook her head as she spoke, admonishing herself.

'Oh. Are you in love with her? Rita that is.'

'I thought I was attracted, but in truth I think it was more that she was the one person I was talking to and I was feeling exhilarated about feeling better. The combination… and I got ahead of myself. I pushed her professional boundaries, even though she kissed me back, and I feel bloody awful about that. It's just not me.'

'No. That isn't you. That's the whole point. You've experienced a traumatic event and it sounds as though you haven't really sought professional help to work through the mental and emotional aspects.'

'I know. I thought I could deal with it myself. I just seem to have tied myself in knots and made some really crap choices.'

'Hey, nothing's insurmountable. We all make stupid decisions from time to time,' she teased, lightly brushing her hand on Lauren's arm. 'Do you want to get back together with Anna?'

Lauren avoided eye contact and gazed at the ring. 'Why would I get her this if she didn't mean the world to me?' Lauren reflected aloud.

'Exactly. And from what we saw you meant the world to each other. You were… are… soul mates. You were planning a family together, remember?'

'A family. No, I don't remember that. No one's mentioned that, not even Anna. Holy shit. How exactly were we planning to do that?' She asked, as something intangible transcended her awareness and thumped her in the chest. She knew she couldn't have children.

'Oh.' Carla lowered her gaze a fraction before facing Lauren. 'The last time we got together you two were made up, talking about Anna having IVF and having your eggs implanted.'

Lauren turned white, her eyes glazed over and her breathing stopped. 'Holy fucking shit! I have so fucked up. Is she… is she…' Lauren couldn't get the words out.

'I don't know if she's pregnant. Like you, we haven't heard from her since the last time we saw you both. I assumed you guys were living in Paris having great sex and a wild life together.' She shrugged as she sighed. 'How wrong one can be.' Carla stared at Lauren. 'How would you feel if she were pregnant?' she asked.

Lauren held her head in her hands, palms covering her eyes, as she tried to process this vital piece of information. *Why hadn't Anna told her? How would Anna being pregnant change things?* Lauren couldn't process the question as wave after wave of emotional turmoil wracked her body. Her mother's behaviour towards her, which at first glance had felt familiar, yet on the other hand there had also been something odd about Valerie's response. At the hospital, her mother had even been jovial with her, and more open than Lauren had previously experienced. In fact, it had been Lauren who had pushed her mother away. It had been Lauren who had been angry and detached. Lauren who had ceased contact with Anna: Lauren who had pushed Anna away: Lauren who had befriended Rita for her own gains. Lauren, Lauren, Lauren. Whichever way Lauren looked at the events since her accident, she had been in the driving seat. Everyone had been treading on eggshells around her - even Antoine. *Fuck, fuck, fuck*. The dawning realisation hit her hard. *What was her fear?* She had been asked the question many times recently and been unable to answer it. Could it really be to do with the pregnancy and becoming a parent? A wave of anxiety shot through her solar plexus as if to confirm her thoughts. She picked up the ring and stared at it. As the blue reflected back at her, her heart sank. 'I need help.' she sobbed.

Carla moved to sit next to her, placed an arm around her shoulder and pulled her into her chest. 'I know people who can help,' she said.

14.

Eva pressed a soft kiss on Anna's head as she sat at the easel, assessing her work. She swivelled on the high stool, instantly locked into the sea-green eyes that held hers, reached behind Eva's neck, and pulled her hard against her mouth. The urgency of the kiss sent fireworks through Eva, goose bumps broke out down her spine, and her crotch throbbed, agonisingly. Teeth clashed as they deepened the kiss together, raw passion fuelling Anna's hunger as she pulled at Eva's t-shirt until her hands clasped fiercely at the small, pert breasts. Stumbling to the floor, she moaned into Eva's mouth when Eva's hand delved into the warm wet sensation between her legs and two fingers penetrated her forcefully. Rhythmically thrusting deep inside her, Anna screamed out long before she came. Shaking uncontrollably her mouth clamped onto Eva's nipple and she bit down hard. Eva jerked at the sharp pain, intensifying her arousal. Anna flipped her onto her back with uncharacteristic strength, her hand moving beneath the band of Eva's joggers, she thrust into her with two fingers, then three. Eva came within seconds and Anna collapsed into her arms. 'I needed that,' she said as she swept her fingers through the blonde spikes, dragging her nails up the back of Eva's shaved neck. She raised herself up slightly and pressed a tender kiss to her lips before resting into her shoulder again.

'You're welcome.' Eva said, pulling her closer, a broad smile on her face. She had loved Anna for as long as she could remember, but it hadn't been until recently she had realised those feelings had taken on more of an erotic nature. For months she had held back, almost drinking herself into oblivion to prevent herself acting on her feelings. Even when Anna had returned from Corsica devastated, Eva had simply been there for her. Collected her from the airport, cooked for her, listened to her, rubbed her back as she vomited in the morning, and held her when she had cried herself to sleep at night. She still couldn't quite believe that they were now lovers, and at the same time part of her felt unsettled by that fact. Anna seemed content though, and for that she felt happy. She was into her work again, which was always a good sign and she hadn't mentioned Lauren since the first time they had kissed. She didn't know if Anna loved her. Frankly she didn't want to know. She wanted to be there for her and the baby and hoped that Anna's feelings for her would grow with time, or so she tried to convince herself. She pulled Anna tighter and kissed the top of her head. 'You okay?'

Anna snuffled into Eva's shoulder. 'I am now... mmm, you smell good. Baby's moving.' She took Eva's hand and placed it gently on the spot. 'There... did you feel that?'

'Umm... would you be offended if I said no?' Eva asked tentatively.

Anna laughed. 'No. That was only a little prod.' She placed her hand on top of Eva's for a few more moments waiting for the next tiny shudder.

'Fancy going out for a drink tonight? I mean... I know you're not drinking, but how about dancing?' Eva asked.

'Maybe. Can we decide later?'

'Sure.' Eva pulled them both to their feet, holding Anna as she stared at the image forming on the canvas. 'That's looking good,' she commented. 'I should leave you to your inspiration.' She smiled at Anna and kissed her on the forehead.

'I'm feeling even more inspired after that,' she nodded towards the floor. Eva blushed. 'Cute.' Anna kissed her softly on the lips. 'Right,' she said, turning towards the canvas. She tilted her head in thought, unaware that Eva had left the loft.

Hours had passed before Anna finished for the day. Eva had taken her a sandwich for lunch, kept her topped up with water and an afternoon tea, and allowed her the space she needed. She had tried to focus on her own work but been unable to settle.

In just a short space of time her relationship with Anna had taken on a new dimension. One she had dreamed about often since the previous autumn. They were lovers, though they hadn't yet shared the same bed. Their lovemaking was always intense, quick, and fierce. Eva yearned to slow it down and wake up with Anna in her arms, but she needed to let Anna lead. She had had too much time for thinking, she mused, disconcertedly. The unsettled feeling, which had been building over the time since they had become intimate, seemed to be taking hold. She worried she had made a big mistake.

Eva sipped at the chilled wine in her hand, flicking through her phone, sniggering at the Facebook banter. She hadn't realised she had been missing anything, but the familiar pull was calling her. The cooked bolognaise sat on the stove. The bottle resting in the cooler sat more than half empty. Her eyes were drawn to the last of the setting sun through the kitchen window, as a band of blood red light descended slowly on the horizon.

'Hi.' The soft tone jolted Eva from her phone.

'Hi. Good day's work?'

Anna's eyes rose, envisioning her creation. 'I'm pleased with progress,' she said with tired eyes.

'What do you think about going out later?'

Anna sighed deeply at the thought, as she plonked herself heavily onto the stool. 'I think I'll give it a miss, but you go. You deserve a break from me,' she said with sincerity. 'I think I'll get back to work after some food, while I'm in the flow.' Eva turned the gas on the stove.

'Are you sure?'

'Of course. Go... have fun. It's been a while since you went out on the town.'

Eva looked over her shoulder, stirring the bubbling mince before turning her attention to the rice. Anna pulled herself a glass from the cupboard filled it with water, downed it thirstily, and placed a peck on Eva's cheek. 'Can I help?'

'It's okay, I've got it.' Eva served up the two plates and placed them on the table.

Eva filled her own glass again, and Anna glanced at the empty bottle as it was placed on the side. She had always known Eva liked her alcohol but the difference in their drinking habits seemed amplified since Anna had stopped completely with advancing pregnancy. The awareness now niggled her. She brushed the feeling aside as a burst of flavour hit her taste buds. 'Mmm... This is great. You're getting really good at this,' she smiled. 'I'm ravenous.' Her fork dived into the plate, her thoughts consumed by fulfilling her hunger.

Eva raised a tentative smile, absorbed in Anna's gratification as she polished off the plate. Eva had barely touched hers, picking at it pensively.

'You okay?' Anna asked.

'Yeah, just not that hungry.'

'Why don't you go out and get a break from the house?' Anna asked. 'We've been cooped up here for weeks.'

'I think I will.' Eva's eyes gave a hint of a sparkle, but her mood shifted dramatically. She rose from the table, took the plates to the sink and paced out of the room, placing a kiss on Anna's cheek as she passed. 'Thank you,' she said. Anna squeezed her arm, refilled her glass, and headed back to the loft.

*

Eva perched on the red plastic stool, her eyes scanning the environment for familiar faces. The blonde who had served her previously was nowhere to be seen, for which she breathed a sigh of relief. The last thing she needed was to have to watch her back all night, politely fighting off admiring hopefuls who didn't take rejection well. She downed the clear liquid savouring the burning sensation in her throat and subsequent warmth in her belly. The last time she had visited *Le So What* had been the weekend Anna had travelled to Corsica. The smell of the place hadn't changed; stale alcohol, a mix of perfumes, a hint of sweat and the residual smell of sex, merged to form the 'nightclub aroma'. An obvious anchor for lust filled erotic behaviour, illicit sexual encounters, and a guaranteed hangover from hell. Week in, week out, the same faces frequented the rundown bar with one thing in mind. Sex. Seeking a feeling. It wasn't really about finding a lover, and definitely not a soul mate. It was purely and simply about fulfilling a need, chasing a high. Eva had been here many times before. Felt the longing, the urges that drove her to take home the girl in the red skirt; the white jeans; the black slacks. It hadn't mattered. It didn't count back then. But, now she and Anna were lovers, so why was she here? She had asked herself that question each time she had ordered the straight vodka on ice. Five-times now and five-times she had no answer.

Her eyes tracked the dark-haired woman across the room as she headed for the toilets. She was tempted to follow her and it took every effort to stay put. Within moments the woman returned to her group. Eva watched. She nodded at the bar woman, holding out her empty glass. The woman approached, swapped the glass for a fresh drink and gave her a wry smile. 'Go easy honey, the night is still young.' Eva nodded. Taking the drink in her hand, she cruised the bar again with her eyes.

'Hey.' A surprisingly tall Arabic looking woman said, as she brushed Eva's shoulder, approaching her from behind. Eva looked up from the seat, surprised at the combination of the woman's ethnicity and height.

'Hey.' Eva stared, trying to recall any previous encounters with the woman and coming up blank. 'Do I know you?' she asked.

'I don't think so,' the woman said, shaking her head, her eyes searching her own memory bank. 'You looked like you needed a friend though.' She squirmed slightly at her own words and smiled warmly. Eva laughed.

'Do I look that bad?'

'Not bad... just... lost.' The deep brown eyes of concern caressed Eva's worried face. 'You've been frowning a lot.'

'You noticed?' Eva cheeked lightly.

'Well it's been quite obvious. You've been a bit 'cat-on-hot-bricks' for the last hour and alcohol seems to be a good friend tonight.' She smiled broadly. 'Do you mind if I join you?' She motioned to the seat next to Eva.

'Sure. Be my guest. You're not a therapist are you?' she asked nervously.

'No definitely not,' she smiled again. Eva visibly relaxed.

'So, what do you do?'

'I'm a pilot.'

'What are you doing in a place like this?'

'Same as you I guess?' She shrugged.

'Ha ha. Maybe. I'm not sure why I'm here.'

'Me neither.' She started to laugh. 'I'm Hanan by the way.'

'Hanan. Where are you from?'

'It's Arabic. My family are originally from Morocco but we've lived in London since before I was born. My father's work is there. He's in banking. I've two brothers who are also in banking. I rebelled for a life of travel and now I'm on the London to Paris shuttle run,' she sniggered. 'I'm on a break: the first of four-days off. I've never been in here before, and probably won't come back again,' she said, scanning the room with

137

disdain. 'But at least I've found someone interesting to talk to now,' she said, eyeing Eva cautiously.

'Wow...' Eva shook her head as her inebriated brain struggled to keep up with the fast flow of information coming at her. Captivated by the tall dark stranger's eyes and the ease with which she shared her life history, she opened her mouth to speak and then closed it again.

'You do talk?' Hanan teased.

'Sorry. Yes, I do... Eva.' She held out her hand. 'Can I get you a drink?'

'No thanks, I don't.' She held up the glass of clear fluid. 'Water I'm afraid...'

'Don't apologise. It's the smart option. Is that a religious thing?'

'No, just personal choice. I haven't found a beverage I like the taste of, and I prefer to be in control,' she said sipping at the glass.

Eva stared into her glass. 'Mmm... I think control is overrated,' she said, before bringing the glass to her lips. Hanan watched with interest. Eva locked eyes with her over the top of her glass, noticing the clarity in a stare that came with being sober.

'Want to talk about it?' she asked. Eva averted her gaze.

'About what?'

'Whatever it is that troubles you? Apparently, it can help to talk to a stranger,' she said, smiling warmly. Eva recoiled, though she didn't go unaffected by the infectious smile.

'Maybe later?' she conceded, as Hanan continued to stare at the glass in Eva's hand. She placed it on the bar, feeling the heat of guilt warm her cheeks.

'Want to dance?' Hanan asked.

'Sure.' Eva slipped off the stool, losing her balance slightly as she set off for the dance floor. Hanan grabbed her arm, supporting her as they worked their way into a space big enough for them both to move without being forced to bump and grind each other.

The music shifted gear and Eva suddenly froze at the slower pace, causing Hanan to smile. 'Want to get out of here? A coffee, or something to eat?' She shouted to be heard, so as not to get too close to a clearly uncomfortable Eva.

'Sure.' Eva virtually ran to the exit and out into the street with Hanan close behind. She breathed in the cool evening air. 'Thanks.'

'For what?'

'Saving me?'

'From what?'

'Myself.' Eva shrugged and pinched the bridge of her nose.

'You want to eat something?'

'I think that would be a good idea,' she nodded.

Hanan linked her arm through Eva's. 'Come on. I know just the place.'

Eva staggered pace for pace with Hanan's long stride. After a couple of turns and crossing the river, Hanan stopped outside a quaint Moroccan restaurant. 'You like Moroccan?'

'I do,' Eva said.

'Hanan.' A middle-aged Moroccan woman greeted them warmly with open arms and gleaming white teeth.

'Hello aunty.' Hanan kissed the woman on both cheeks before succumbing to the familial embrace that seemed to go on for a long time. The small space, authentic in design, seated no more than twenty-people in one sitting. At 10pm, only two tables were occupied. Two men stared longingly at each other across the table. An elderly couple sipped at their tea. The ambience was unhurried, warm, inviting. 'Aunty, this is Eva and she needs something special to eat.' Hanan motioned towards Eva who stepped into an equally warm embrace.

'A friend of Hanan's is a friend of ours,' she said, pulling them to a table at the back of the restaurant. 'We are all family,' she continued, tilting her head as she hurried through to the kitchen.

'Are you going to order?' Eva said after a few moments, her elbows resting on the bare wooden table, her hands supporting her head. The fresh air had heightened the effect of the alcohol and her eyes were unable to hold an image still for more than a couple of seconds. Hanan's aunt bounced through the door from the kitchen answering the question, with a basket of flatbread, a dish of fresh herbs and a range of dips. The aroma cleared Eva's blurred vision and she dived hungrily into the food. 'Mmm, this is awesome.'

Hanan tore off a piece of bread and swept up a healthy portion of the aubergine dip. 'It's a favourite of mine,' she said, chewing and watching Eva.

'What's not to love,' Eva said, munching through the fragrant herbs.

'I'd ask if you want a drink, but I'm guessing...' Eva held up her hand in protestation, shaking her head at the suggestion.

'I've had enough don't you think?'

Hanan smiled and shrugged. 'I guess that depends how much you need to escape from what it is you can't face right now?'

'Perceptive,' Eva said, holding the dark eyes, forcing a smile.

'Well you didn't look like you were getting hammered for fun.'

'And what are you running away from?' Eva asked. Hanan's brows shot up in question. 'You said we were in the bar for the same reason.' Eva clarified.

'Ah, yes. I did say that.' A slow smile crept across her face. Another piece of bread dripping with humus passed her lips. Eva noticed their full shape, and bit down on her top lip as she watched.

'So?' Eva questioned, not willing to let her off the hook too easily.

Hanan stared deeply into Eva's eyes. 'The truth,' she said. The words ricocheted through Eva's mind looking for a place to settle.

'What truth?' she asked, her curiosity piqued.

Hanan's eyes glassed over. 'A recent break up,' she confessed.

Two more dishes were added to the table with another basket of freshly cooked flatbread. The spices tickled Eva's senses. 'Were you in love with her?'

'I thought so,' Hanan said, trying to raise a smile. 'Do you ever know?' she questioned, more to herself.

'I don't know?' Eva said, honestly.

'Had you been together long?'

'Fifteen years.'

'Fuck.' Eva blurted, spluttering on her food. 'Sorry,' she apologised, swiftly, raising the napkin to her mouth. Eva had never been in a relationship for longer than a few months and even then, she doubted anything she had experienced would qualify as a real relationship. 'That's...'

'A lifetime,' Hanan added with a wry smile.

'What happened?' Hanan hesitated, as if searching for the answer in the stream of memories passing before her eyes.

'I don't honestly know. It came as a big shock to me, so I guess I must have been clueless to something,' she shrugged. 'How's the fish?'

'This is all amazing.'

'What about you? What's your truth?'

'Love. Relationships. I think I'm in love with someone who'll never love me back?'

'Ah!'

'Or maybe I just thought I was.'

'Okay, now I'm confused.'

Eva slowly broke off a piece of bread and scooped up the spicy fish allowing time for her thoughts to crystallise. Maybe it was easier to confess to a stranger, she reflected, as she lifted the food to her mouth.

'It's complicated,' Eva started.

Hanan nodded as she bit into her bread, covered in chicken and fresh herbs. 'Isn't it always?' she said, matter-of-factly.

'I guess. It's just that this really is tricky. I've known Anna since we were kids and we've only recently become... intimate. Mainly, because her lover was involved in an accident before Christmas and can't remember who she is, and now doesn't want anything to do with her.'

'Ouch!' Hanan stopped eating. 'That sounds really messy.'

'Oh, and she's pregnant. They had planned to have a family and Anna underwent IVF with Lauren's eggs.' As Eva recounted the last few weeks aloud a realisation dawned.

'Wow, that's all happened really quickly.' Hanan said, voicing Eva's thoughts.

'Yes. Exactly. It's complicated,' she reiterated.

'Complicated... and really, really quickly too,' Hanan stated. 'How do you feel about it all?' she asked.

'I thought I was good with it.'

'But?'

'But...' Eva frowned at her own thoughts, her eyes lowered to her plate, her hands stilled. 'I'm not convinced I'm the one she really wants. I mean I know she cares about me, but we never make love. It's just about sex: fulfilling a physical need, for her. I haven't slept in her bed and we don't wake up together,' she confessed, her eyes watery. 'But, more than that, I've also got doubts now.'

'Have you spoken to her about it?' Hanan asked, giving Eva her full attention.

'No. It's only just dawned on me today that I'm not entirely happy.'

'What about the baby? How do you feel about that?'

'I'm not sure. I thought it would be great and I enjoy being a part of it all, but the reality is, her family isn't something I, or we, decided. I've inherited it.' Eva shrugged.

'Yes. I can see that too. What do you want Eva?' Hanan asked.

'I want a deep and meaningful relationship. I'm sick of clubbing and cheap thrills. I thought Anna was the one, but I'm beginning to wonder if what I really have with her is just an amazing friendship. She's easy to be around and we laugh a lot together. Since having sex I've wanted more, but she's not on the same page. And then, when I think about us raising the child together, I'm still haunted by the fact that this is another woman's baby and what will happen if Lauren remembers Anna in the future and tries to get her and the baby back? Lauren's the one she's really in love with. It's really confusing, and all I can see in the future is more pain and heartbreak.'

'You need to talk to Anna.' Hanan reached across the table and squeezed Eva's arm.

'I know, but I'm not sure how to approach it. I don't want to let her down. I promised to be there for her and I will. And the sex is intense,' she added with a wry smile.

'You never know, she might be feeling the same way?' Hanan said, raising her eyebrows.

'Maybe,' Eva said, as she continued to process her thoughts. Her eyes rose to meet the dark brown assessing look and both women smiled. Even though she knew she loved Anna, she also wanted to see Hanan again. 'Why don't you come over sometime?' The words escaped before she had thought through the consequences.

143

Hanan laughed. 'That would be nice. Don't you think you should check with Anna first?' she asked.

'Sure, but I'm sure she'll be fine. How about tomorrow, while you're here?' She looked at her phone. 'That would be this evening now,' she chuckled, unable to hold back her eagerness. 'I'll check with Anna and confirm by text. What do you think?'

'If it's okay with you both? I've got nothing planned and the bars aren't overly inviting at the moment,' she smirked.

'Deal,' Eva said with renewed energy. 'I owe you after tonight. You've saved my liver, as much as anything else I might've got caught up in. Where are you staying?'

'Here,' she motioned to the ceiling with her eyes. 'How're you getting home?'

'Taxi.'

'We'll order one now then. Coffee?'

'Please.' Eva said, wiping her mouth with the napkin and placing it on the table. 'Thank you for listening.'

'You're welcome.'

*

Eva woke to the smell of coffee wafting through her bedroom door. She hadn't got home until gone 2am. Glancing at her phone it was 9.30. She groaned, moving her head from side to side, testing the damage. Pleased to find the hangover she was sporting rated lower than it would have been had she not met up with Hanan, she smiled to herself. As she recalled the conversation of the previous evening she felt lighter, as if something had shifted inside her mind. She had enjoyed Hanan's company and couldn't wait to tell Anna about her.

Slipping on her joggers and hoody, she skipped down the stairs and into the kitchen. 'Hey.'

'Hey. How was your evening?' Anna asked, pouring the egg mixture into the pan. 'Coffee's in the pot. I'm doing omelette.' She held out an empty mug and nodded at Eva.

Eva grabbed the mug. 'It was good, thanks,' she said, trying to sound matter-of-fact and averting her gaze from the back of Anna's head, as she shuffled the eggs around the pan. 'How did your work go?'

'Great...' Anna said, preoccupied with catching and buttering the toast.

'I met someone interesting and I invited her around here tonight,' Eva blurted out, interrupting Anna's flow. In the cold light of day, having just spouted the words, the situation seemed a little odd. Anna's look told her so too.

'You've invited someone here tonight?' Anna clarified with horror written across her face.

'Erm... well, only if you're up for it.' Eva's excitement didn't go unnoticed. Anna's mouth rested open for a few moments as she tried to process the situation. It wasn't as if she and Eva had discussed their *relationship* or whether they were exclusive. They had drifted into a level of sexual intimacy to fulfil a mutual need, Anna told herself.

'Who is this woman?' she asked.

'She's a pilot. Her name's Hanan, and she saved me from a serious hangover this morning. We had dinner at her aunt's restaurant.' Anna's head tilted backwards with her eyes following. 'She lives and works in London; her parents are Moroccan and she has three brothers. No, two I think. They're both bankers, and so is her dad. She's smart and doesn't drink alcohol.'

'Wow, you know her life story already.' Anna raked at the eggs, threw them onto the toast and rested the plate, more heavily than she intended, in front of Eva.

'Umm... she certainly can talk.' Eva said reflectively, apparently unperturbed by Anna's defensive stance. 'I said I'd check with you first of course. She's on a four-day break in Paris and the bar was really shit,' she mumbled, as if having been chastised by a parent and needing to justify herself.

Anna fought the rising anxiety, trying to put herself in Eva's shoes. They had, after all, stumbled into a physical relationship. Unsure how she was really feeling and unable to fully process her reaction to this new friend of Eva's. 'Sure,' she said. 'That's fine with me. I mean, it's not like we have a huge network of friends,' she continued, trying to sound nonchalant, whilst feeling a little stunned.

They ate in silence. Eva wolfed her food down, and had drained two mugs of coffee before Anna had finished her breakfast. 'You okay?' Eva asked, not really wanting to know if the answer was no. She was feeling high, refreshed, and more alive than she had done in a long time, and she didn't want that bubble burst any time soon.

'Yeah I'm fine.' Anna lied. 'I forgot to mention I'm going to mums' for Easter weekend. Do you want to come?' Eva placed her plate in the sink as she pondered the question.

'No. I've got work I need to catch up on, if that's okay with you? I'll spend time at the flat while you are gone,' she said, turning towards Anna and kissing her lightly on the forehead. 'Anyway, it will be great for you to have some quality time with your mums.' She smiled, but there was something different in her eyes. Anna faked a smile in return.

'That's okay. Right, I'm going to the loft. You going to let your friend know about tonight?' Anna said, as she made for the stairs.

'You sure it's okay?'

'Sure. I look forward to meeting her.'

Anna felt her increasing weight more heavily as she climbed into the loft. She puffed and stood still for a few moments, before seating herself. She removed the work in progress from the easel, placing it carefully against the wall, and replaced it with a blank canvas. She needed a diversion from the

146

pet project today. She felt tired and a little anxious about meeting Hanan, unsure of the real impact the woman had had on Eva. Even though deep in her heart she knew her relationship with Eva wasn't the same as it had been with Lauren, she didn't feel ready to contemplate life without her. They had become lovers but more than that, she felt secure and safe with Eva. She sat shaking her head as she mused. Is that what she wanted out of her life? A relationship based on security? Sure the sex was intense. But for Anna there was something missing between them. Hard as she tried, she didn't feel the same level of intimate connection with Eva as she had with Lauren and Eva probably knew that too. She loved her as a friend. A friend with benefits even. But Eva was not the love of her life. That space had already been taken and Anna knew that if it came to it, she would take Lauren back in a heartbeat.

15.

Anna knocked on the door before turning the key in the lock of her parent's house. She always knocked before opening the door out of politeness, even though her parents insisted she just enter at her will. The door was flung open, whilst she was still attached to the key in the lock, pulling her forcefully over the threshold and into her mum's open arms.

'Good grief mum. You scared the shit out of me, and I nearly floored you. Were you sat behind the door?' Anna blurted out, in shock.

'And a welcome home to you too,' Lisa joked unable to keep the beaming smile off her face. She gave Anna a long hug, kissing the side of her head as she squeezed, unwilling to let go.

'My how strong you are,' Anna squeaked out, huffing a breath as Lisa eventually released her. 'It's good to see you looking so much better,' she said, appraising her mum with a smile. 'You really do look great.'

Anna hadn't seen her mums for nearly four-months, which was a record for them. Historically, she would have travelled back to visit every month but with morning sickness, work, and the Lauren situation, she hadn't felt up to it. During the early days following the accident, Anna had stayed with them. She had spent many nights in deep discussion with Lisa regarding her thoughts of termination, and feeling unable to face the journey of pregnancy alone. Now though, with her mum on the other side of her cancer treatment and Anna nearly halfway through her pregnancy, those early days seemed light years away. She pulled Lisa in for another full-on hug as she absorbed how far they both had come in such a short time. 'Where's mum?' she asked.

'She's buying a kiln.' Lisa said with raised brows. 'She insisted she needed to go into town for a very specific one she's discovered. It's her new hobby. It's all my fault. I got her a potter's wheel for Christmas. It was a bit of a joke present really. I thought it would give her something to do with her hands. You know, help with the arthritis.' Anna raised a brow. 'Turns out she's quite good at it, so now we're inundated with pots and artefacts of various shapes and sizes. Some of them are quite phallic, though I'm not sure that was the intention.' Anna sniggered at the image. 'I'm sure you'll get the guided tour when she's back. Fancy a cup of tea?'

'Love one.'

'Anyway. You look positively radiant. How're you feeling?' Lisa looked tentatively, gauging Anna's physical response to the question.

'I'm feeling much better now the sickness has stopped.'

'Well pregnancy seems to be suiting you. You do look quite beautiful.' Lisa wandered into dreamland as she filled the kettle.

'You look well mum,' Anna said, as if repeating the phrase would cement the fact that her mum had been cured, drawing her mother gently out of her reverie.

'I am, very well actually. So glad that horrid experience is over.' She shuddered. 'The results so far are clear. Just got to go for regular check-ups now,' she said.

'That's great news.'

'Any update on Lauren?' she asked, softly.

'No.' Anna fidgeted.

'As hard as it is Anna, I think you are right to let her go for now,' Lisa said, still watching her daughter's face. 'And?' She sensed there was more to come.

'Eva... You remember Eva?'

'Yes of course. How is she?' Lisa tried not to presume anything and allowed Anna to continue.

'We've become... sort of... close.'

'Oh.'

'She's been really supportive and great company. She makes me happy and right now that's what I need.'

'I sense a but?'

'It's a bit confusing. We haven't talked about *us* and we haven't agreed to be exclusive and I'm not sure about the future, but right now...'

Lisa approached Anna and put her hands on her shoulders. Looking her in the eye she smiled. 'Darling. Your welfare is the most important thing to us.' Anna's mouth moved. 'Wait, I need to finish.' Anna held her mother's gaze. 'I love you dearly... we both do. We also saw how in love you and Lauren were, and it breaks our hearts that this accident has driven such a wedge between you. It seems, a wedge that is insurmountable. Being a single mum wasn't something you wanted to do. If Eva makes you happy and it works for you both, then I am happy for you. I only hope neither of you get hurt in the process,' she continued. 'I'm sure you'll have thought about it already, but what are you going to do if Lauren wakes up one day and tries to reconnect with you... and with her child? Or if Eva falls in love with someone else and leaves you?'

Anna's shoulders slumped. 'I know. I have thought it through from every direction, and you're right. But I don't think I can do this on my own, and Lauren might never come around. I feel so stuck. But, I also care about Eva and we get on really well. We laugh together about silly stuff,' Anna said, still feeling insecure following the supper with Hanan, even though the meal had gone well and she had seemed a genuinely sincere person. Eva was clearly enamoured with her and Anna could understand why.

'Well it's certainly a good thing to laugh.' She nudged Anna's shoulders with fondness. The kettle whistled. 'Anyway, we're delighted you could make it over here for Easter. I need to hear all about...' she nodded towards Anna's growing bump with a broad grin. 'Now, let's get that tea.'

Anna released a long deep breath. 'Great, thanks,' she said taking the mug from her mum. 'I've got that exhibition in Paris coming up,' she said changing the subject.

Lisa beamed as she sipped her tea. 'Yes, you need to tell us more about that too. Come, let's sit and have tea, then I'll show you the latest pieces I'm working on. Brace yourself though, they're rather erotic in nature,' she said, a slight colour rising to her cheeks.

Anna sat in the armchair, which provided more support than the couch, and raised her legs. Her ankles were feeling the weight of her pregnancy and her feet ached. 'It's a small display at the Musée d'Art Moderne over the summer, dedicated to local artists. We each provide up to five-pieces,' she said, even though she had told her mum some of the details previously, over the phone.

'That's so exciting. Have you chosen yours yet?' Lisa's eyes sparkled with pride, but Anna's unenthusiastic response dulled them.

'I guess I'm feeling tired. I'm not sure what to show. I've got a couple of older pieces, but I think some of my latest work is better.'

'Whatever you show will be perfect. You're very talented Anna and I know you don't see that, but you won't be able to hide forever.' Her mother squeezed her shoulder, as she passed to refill her mug. 'I've spoken to Viv and we'd like to come to the opening event,' Lisa said.

Anna's eyes lit up at the idea. 'Would you?'

'Well it can be intimidating if you don't have your own friends at these things. Agents, critics boosting their own egos, and collectors bragging, whilst slating a new artist: acting like they are messengers from God about to create the next big talent. I remember it well.' She stared out the kitchen window, head shaking back and forth, reminiscing.

'It would be great if you could come.'

'Of course, we will darling. We wouldn't miss it for the world.' Anna smiled warmly.

'Will you help me choose? I've bought photos of what I think are my best works.'

'How exciting. I can't wait,' Lisa bubbled with joy. 'Come and have a look at my latest?' she nodded towards the door. Anna leapt to her feet, somewhat inelegantly. Taking her mum by the arm they ambled towards the back room.

'Brace yourself,' Lisa said with a wry smile as she opened the door.

Anna's jaw dropped and her eyes widened at the graphic sexual images, set out in a biographical sequence, representing the transformation of female sexuality through a lifetime. Tears welled at the back of Anna's eyes. She stood still, fixated on a particular set of five-images of a woman in the process of giving birth. The explicit nature of the images might revolt some people, but to her this was real art - a demonstration of feminine strength and beauty. The mother shifting from exquisite pain to ecstasy, culminating with the new life still attached by the cord that brought it into this world. Tears flowed uncontrollably. 'It's...' Words failed her and she threw herself into Lisa's open arms and sobbed.

'Well that wasn't quite the response I expected,' she said with light humour, brushing at Anna's tears.

Anna's smile grew into a spluttering laugh. 'I'm sorry. These are really powerful,' she said.

'Yes they are,' her mother said proudly. 'I love them.'

'You've been busy,' Anna said, flicking through a row of canvases stacked against the wall.

'Vivian has been driving me to distraction, so I've escaped to my hideout regularly. It's been very therapeutic,' she explained nodding in affirmation.

'Has anyone seen them?' Anna asked. 'You'll get them shown?' she asked.

'Maybe I'll let them out of here at some point,' she said with a wry smile.

16.

Anna had worked all morning and then ventured into the garden mid-afternoon to capture the late afternoon sunshine. Temperatures were creeping up into the late-teens and she had spent some time potting seedlings and tidying the garden. She had cut back the hedging, a little more severely than intended, and given the grass its second cut of the season. The snowdrops had been and gone but daffodils and pansies were still in full bloom, and giving a real sense of late spring. The magnolia tree, bulging with dark and light pink blossom, dominated the garden with its overpowering fragrance and beautiful bowl-shape. Sitting on the decking at the back of the house admiring her work, enjoying the warmth of the sun on her face, Anna rested.

'Can I get you a tea?' Eva asked, interrupting her reverie. Anna looked up and smiled warmly. Eva was already dressed for a night out, her blonde spikes perfectly coiffured, wearing tight jeans and a casual shirt, and hopping around like a cat on hot bricks, she seemed oblivious to her own excitement and the message that was sending to Anna.

'Thanks, that would be lovely,' Anna responded, watching as Eva scurried back into the house. She felt strangely calm, content with the day. She had released herself through her work, and the physical exertion in the garden had also had a positive effect. She had had the chance to breathe and felt mentally more prepared to continue the pregnancy alone. 'Thanks,' she said, reaching for the steaming mug. 'Sit,' she said, patting the space next to her.

Eva sat beside her in silence, and sipped from her mug, whilst taking in the garden. 'It is truly beautiful here,' she said after a moment.

'It is. That tree is one of the reasons I bought this place,' Anna confided. 'The barn was just that, a barn. But that tree was magnificent and it has been every year. It brings life to spring and is a sure sign that summer is on its way,' she said.

Eva tilted her head, studying the tree's intricate branch system, taking in the strong scent, watching, as a petal fell delicately to the ground. 'It's majestic,' she said. 'Are we okay?' she asked, out of the blue, still staring at the tree.

The sudden change of topic caused Anna's stomach to flip and her heart to race. Even though she had settled at the idea of being on her own, she hadn't prepared herself for a discussion with Eva, about ending their relationship, just yet. Eva looked at her with a seriousness she hadn't seen before. 'Sure,' she said, with a smile. She reached out and touched the side of Eva's face, tracing the outline of her jaw, brushing a thumb across her lips, all the while knowing that the contact felt subtly different. Maybe she was just preparing herself for the inevitable. Maybe she was misreading the whole Hanan situation, and creating a problem between her and Eva for no good reason. 'Are you okay? With us, I mean.' she asked.

'Sure,' Eva responded, but her eyes were evasive, unwilling to hold Anna's gaze.

Eva kissed the thumb passing her lips, but the touch was fleeting; friendly rather than intimate, Anna mused. 'Are you sure?' Anna asked again, sensing the time was right. 'It's okay, you know. We did kind of fall into this relationship,' she said, trying to ease the obvious tension between them. *Why was communication so difficult?* 'Look Eva, we're both adults and we've had a good time together, but let's not spoil our friendship over the fact that we had a few weeks of sexual intimacy. I mean, don't get me wrong, you're a great lover, but what we have is...'

'Complicated,' Eva finished.

'Yes it is. There are still so many unanswered questions, and it would be a lot to ask of you to become a parent to a child that you hadn't conceived of in your own mind.'

'It's...' Eva started.

'Listen.' Anna interrupted. 'I love you. I always will. You're my best friend and I've been blessed to have you in my life at what has been the shittiest time of my life to date. And maybe we shouldn't have taken it as far as we did, but I for one don't regret that we had sex.' Anna said with fortitude, gathering strength with each articulated thought.

'I don't regret it either,' Eva said, with more of a whimper.

'Are you attracted to Hanan?' Anna asked directly.

Eva looked into Anna's eyes with deep sadness. Anna cupped her face in her hand, watching as her eyes glazed over, and tears started to well. 'I don't know,' she said honestly, warring with the words that hovered at the front of her mind: words that would remain unspoken. *It's you Anna. It's always been you, but I'm not the one you want, and I can't be someone you just turn to for sex.*

'Hey,' Anna said softly, as tears rolled down Eva's cheeks.

'I don't know.' Eva clarified. 'She's different, kind, intelligent and it's not about the sex.' Eva said honestly. One of the things she had liked about Hanan was the way that they had talked so easily without the pretence that goes with bar chat-up scenarios. Hanan had seemed like a genuinely good person, and they had something in common. They had both been in love with someone who didn't love them back. Anna's contact still burned Eva where she touched her skin, still caused a wave of adrenaline to course through her body, still caused her to throb with desire, but she needed to preserve herself. She needed to control the hurt, and the only way she could do that was to pull back from the physical contact between them. She vowed, in her mind, to still be there for Anna, as a friend.

'Then what's up?' Anna asked, seeking Eva's face for answers.

'I'm struggling…' She paused, beginning to sob.

'Hey, it's okay. I'm here for you too you know. Whatever it is, we can work it through together.'

'I'm struggling with us being lovers.' There, she had said it. The release transformed everything. Eva's body softened and her breathing started to settle, as Anna pulled her into her arms. The tears slowed and she pulled away gently to see Anna's face. Her eyes had glassed over too, but she was smiling with loving warmth.

'It's okay. We can just be friends Eva. Perhaps we shouldn't have crossed the line after all,' she remarked, tears starting down her face, sadness in her eyes.

'Maybe,' Eva responded, pulling Anna into a tight embrace. 'Thank you.'

'For what?' Anna pulled back to see Eva's face.

'For making this conversation happen.' She shrugged. "I was too scared,' she added. Anna put her arm around Eva's shoulders and pointed to the sky. 'A red kite,' Eva commented. They both watched the bird sweeping and gliding, as they adjusted to their new relationship status. The distraction worked.

'I do feel relieved,' Anna said as they stood.

'Me too,' Eva responded honestly, even though her heart still ached and probably always would.

'Will you still come with me tomorrow?' Anna asked.

'I'd be honoured,' Eva said with a genuine smile.

*

'Oh my God. That was so incredible,' Eva said, her eyes bulging as she stared with awe at the black and white images in her hand. They had spent a good twenty-minutes watching the screen as the technician had checked the baby from all angles. Both women stared, wide-eyed, engrossed in making head and

157

tail of the wriggling, clearly definable, image on the screen. At one-point Eva had jumped up in the seat, pointing excitedly as she spotted the profile of a beautifully round head, snub nose and visible sucking of thumb. Anna had laughed, relieved at the sight of all limbs growing normally. The technician had checked and rechecked and was as convinced as she could be that Anna was carrying a baby girl. Tears had flowed down Anna's cheeks as she stared in wonder at the tiny human being forming inside her, thoughts of Lauren on her mind. For the first time in a long time she had felt an overwhelming desire to reach out to her.

The set of four-photos were laid out on the kitchen table and they sat staring at them for what seemed like an eternity, neither inclined to stop admiring the perfection. 'Thank you for coming with me,' Anna said cupping Eva's face with one hand and kissing her lightly on the cheek.

'You're amazing,' Eva remarked, as she held Anna's eyes. 'This is amazing,' she pointed at the images. 'I mean...'

'It is.' Anna smiled holding her belly, feeling a ripple of movement in response. 'She's speaking to us,' Anna said.

'That's kind of freaky,' Eva squirmed a little, still beaming from ear to ear. 'I'm going to celebrate,' she said, grabbing a bottle of wine from the fridge and a glass of water for Anna. 'Cheers,' she toasted. 'A little girl... Oh my God! It's really real,' she started to blabber her streaming thoughts.

'Cheers,' Anna responded with a raised glass, sipping the water, drifting in thought.

As soon as she realised she was carrying a baby girl, she couldn't get the image of Lauren out of her mind. For some reason, the gender mattered... a lot. She hadn't thought about it before. Perhaps she had been trying to convince herself that it was a boy, to make it easier for her to move on alone. Now though, all she could see was Lauren's face. Lauren's dark eyes, Lauren's dark curls, and Lauren's tanned skin. Lauren was a part of her. Lauren was inside her. There was no escape from Lauren.

She looked at Eva sat across from her and tried to smile, but it wouldn't come.

'You okay?' Eva had been talking to herself for the last five-minutes and had called Anna's name three-times without being heard.

'Sorry... yes. I'm fine,' she frowned. Smiled. 'I must have drifted off.' Anna stood from the stool and took a sip of the water. 'I need to get back to work,' she said, barely making eye contact, before leaving the room.

'Sure,' Eva responded with her own look of concern. She finished her wine and refilled the glass. Picking up her phone her finger tapped on the keys. She needed to talk to someone, and there was only one person she wanted to listen to her.

Hey, you busy?

Hi Eva. No. Not long landed. Two hour break then back over your way. How's things?

Good. You?

Yeah all good.

An uncomfortable pause seemed to sit in the air as Eva pondered what to say next.

Do you want to meet up?

Eva waited, anxiety buzzing in her gut.

Sure. When?

In town later?

Eva fought with mixed emotions, as excitement blended with pangs of guilt, the latter provided by perpetual thoughts of Anna being alone and pregnant, and a deep sense of commitment to her, even though they both now knew they could never really work together.

Lingering on Hanan's response, time passed slowly. She knew that just talking to Hanan, she could easily be tempted into something more with her, and she wasn't sure she would be able to resist. In fact, she fretted that she might initiate more intimate contact between them, then agonised over whether she was on the rebound from Anna. She wrestled with competing thoughts and feelings, but in the end the thrill of the chase outweighed the guilt, and drove her on. How Hanan might respond to her advances she couldn't be sure, but there was definitely something between them, and now she felt ready to explore that connection further. She hoped it would be the real deal this time. She had to get over Anna, and quickly.

Yeah, I'm staying overnight. Have the early flight back to London

Fancy supper?

Sure. Where do you want to eat?

I'll think of somewhere and text you later ☺

OK

Fly safe

I'll do my best ☺

Eva's heart thumped through her chest and her legs fidgeted. The next few hours would take forever. She made her way to the loft.

'I'm going to stay at my flat tonight,' she said quietly. Anna looked up from the canvas and smiled softly, knowing she had to let Eva return to her previous life, and aware that she had to work out what she really wanted to do about re-connecting with Lauren.

'Sure.' Eva turned away, unable to hold eye contact. 'Hey.' Anna called after her. 'I'm okay being on my own you know. You are free to go and live in your own home.' She stood and stepped across the room and taking both of Eva's hands, forcing eye contact between them. 'I'm fine, seriously. Thank you for being there for me, and for being the best, best-friend I could wish for. Now go, and have fun.' She released Eva who kissed her lightly on the cheek, smiled briefly, turned, and skipped down the stairs.

Anna breathed deeply and smiled to herself. She was on her own now, and felt an unexpected sense of relief pass through her. She would make a plan. Her daughter was the most important thing in her life. Perhaps it was for the best that she would create a future for her daughter, and maybe that would be alone. At least there wouldn't be any parental struggles - no interference because of different beliefs and styles. She nodded to herself resting her hand on the growing bump. 'We'll be fine,' she said. 'Just fine.' She picked up the brush and continued to paint. She would let the dust settle on her thoughts of Lauren and see how she felt in a few weeks' time, rather than doing something rash that might only rekindle old hurts.

17.

The buzz in Eva's stomach kept her legs moving as she paced around her flat. She had whizzed around earlier, cleaning and tidying in the event that the evening didn't end with her sleeping alone. She smiled to herself at the end result. The scent of freshly cut flowers filled the entire space and a hint of lemon zest emanated from her now sparkling bathroom. She closed the windows, cutting out the noise from the busy street below. Even though it was a balmy evening, as the sun set it could still close in chilly by late night, and she wanted the place to feel warm and cosy, in case Hanan returned from dinner with her. She hoped. She brushed her sweating hands down the leg of her jeans, moved the remote control of her television unnecessarily into a different orientation, and fiddled with her DVD collection - moving *Homeland* ahead of *House of Cards*. Nodding to herself at her achievement, she turned her attention to the kitchen. She had all she needed to make coffee, with toast, eggs and yogurt options, for breakfast. Two beers sat at the back of the fridge, having been there for months, still within their sell-by date. There was a distinct absence of wine, which she would normally have collected on her way back to the flat. She had made the choice to avoid temptation, a choice that seemed to result in her emotions turning her inside out. She took a second look at the beers and involuntarily licked her lips. The bleep of her phone made her jump out of the trance and her heart raced.

I'll be free in an hour. You still want to meet up?

Eva's hands shook as she read the message, and she was unable to prevent the broad smile taking over her face or her cheeks heating up. It was 7pm. They could eat a stone's throw from Eva's flat, which sat in the heart of the city, surrounded by the cuisines of many parts of the world.

Sure, fancy Italian?

162

My second favourite food

Great, I'll text you the location and meet you there - 8pm okay?

Can you make it 8.30?

Eva didn't know how she would survive the next hour and a half just waiting for Hanan to arrive.

See you at 8.30 Mancini 20 rue Bachelet.

I know it, 8.30

Eva smiled and pocketed her phone. How the hell was she going to occupy herself? She headed for her bathroom. She'd take a long bath even though she hadn't long showered, and change her clothes again. She picked up her phone and called the restaurant to make a reservation.

*

'Oh my God. She's totally beautiful,' Lisa gushed adoringly.

'She is. Amazing,' Anna said, her whole face smiling as she stared down at the tiny black and white image resting on the kitchen island.

'Do you want me to come and stay with you for a bit?' Lisa asked. Anna had phoned to chat, having sent her mum a text with the image of her granddaughter. 'I'm more than happy to come over,' she insisted.

'It's up to you mum. But there's no need on my behalf. I'm fine. It was the right thing for Eva and me and I'm honestly fine with it.'

'Are you sure?'

'Yes, I am,' Anna said, rubbing the bump softly, feeling more settled than she had expected. Something about the certainty felt more comforting than the conflict of being with Eva, whilst still, deep down, still craving Lauren, even though she had tried to deny that conflict - deny her true feelings. 'You can come and help me decorate at some point soon. Maybe after the exhibition?' She offered.

'Darling, you'll be eight-months pregnant by then for goodness sake. Do you really think you'll want to decorate when you're the size of an elephant, with the flexibility of one too?'

'Nice image mum,' Anna retorted lightly.

'It's true. You think you're feeling big right now. God help you in another two-months' time. How about we get started before the exhibition? I can come over any time. Vivian can't come right now, she's got one of her important medical events coming up,' Lisa said with a hint of fondness and teasing. 'She's coming over for the exhibition of course, so I'm guessing she'll leave the decorating to us anyway,' she laughed. 'You know the only world travelling she does now is in the interests of the medical profession, and her daughter. I'm hoping we can both be with you for the birth,' she added, as her thoughts jumped forward in time.

'That would be nice,' Anna said.

'Are you sure you don't want to come back here to give birth?' she asked, even though they had gone over the birth plan a number of times.

Anna intended to have a home birth, even though it was deeply frowned upon in Paris and even more so for a first child. She had been as adamant about the home birth as she had been about eating liver, and had already arranged for a private nurse to work with her. When she had contacted the clinic, she recalled the conversation Lauren and she had had, with Francesca offering her services. But Francesca was in Corsica and Anna didn't think rekindling those links would do her any favours, and in any event, she didn't have a contact number. She had promised herself a complete break from Corsica for a while and so she had arranged for a nurse from Paris. They had already had their first meeting and Anna had no inclination to change her mind about the plan.

'You know the answer to that one mum. I am not changing my mind,' she said authoritatively.

Lisa sighed down the line. 'Sometimes I wonder where you get your stubbornness from,' she said with a titter. 'You're just like Vivian. Drives me insane,' she added, in jest. 'Anyway, if you change your mind, talk to me, but in the meantime, you can be sure I'll be there from the beginning of August,' she finished.

'But the baby's not due till the 24th.'

'Yes, and it may be early. Maybe I should be there from after the exhibition in July?' Lisa asked.

'Hell no. The beginning of August is early enough thank you,' Anna said, continuing the banter between them. Whilst she enjoyed her mum's company and knew she would be a great birthing partner, she wanted to enjoy the space and time she had alone before the birth. There would be a significant enough invasion after the baby arrived, and she planned to enjoy the peace and quiet of this summer, her last without a dependent. She pondered at that thought.

'Are you still there?'

'Sorry, I drifted. Anyway, I'll keep you informed about the decorating. Maybe in a couple of weeks we can do it. I need to plan the room out first, and before that I want to get the last piece of work finished so I can be ready for the exhibition.'

'Right, well just let me know. I don't have anything in my diary except bridge and tennis, and both of those I can skip and they probably wouldn't even notice I was gone.'

'I'm sure your doubles partner might notice,' Anna said, beginning to chuckle.

'Oh darling, I wish. Derek is all over the court like a teenager. Half the time he's flailing his arms so wildly I just stand to the side and leave him to it. He's blind as a bat, but tall and lanky and still wears his cap on back to front. I think he wins just because he puts the opposition off, being so tall... and wild looking. He does well at seventy-five but I swear Polly Dorett

165

could take my place and he wouldn't even remember who he was supposed to be playing with.' Anna laughed loudly, enjoying the light release.

'Good, well that's sorted then. I'll let you know about the decorating,' Anna said by way of ending the call.

'Take care darling,' Lisa finished.

*

'Hi,' Eva said through a dry mouth, as Hanan approached the restaurant. She had managed the early evening without a drink, and couldn't recall ever going on a date sober, which was a sobering thought in itself. She had arrived ten-minutes early and waited outside, watching with urgency as traffic graced the warm evening with tooting horns and fumes, and tourists scurried past pointing and looking at the maps on their phones. The buzzing sensation in her gut increased. *She* had labelled this as a date, she reminded herself. Hanan was just a friend who she had hooked up with a couple of times when she stopped over in Paris. A friend who had no idea she was on a date. Trying to downplay Hanan in her mind's eye didn't help the situation as the tall woman approached.

Hanan brushed a kiss on Eva's cheeks and she stiffened at the touch. 'Hi,' she said as she pulled away. 'You okay?' she asked as Eva's eyes averted hers, her mouth devoid of sound.

'Sorry... yes, I'm fine. I was daydreaming,' she lied.

'Well, must have been a good dream,' she said, eyeing Eva with a knowing smile. Eva's blush darkened. 'Shall we?' Hanan asked, motioning towards the front door.

'Sure. I booked a table.'

Eva followed Hanan into the restaurant then stepped beside her to confirm the name of their reservation. The waiter smiled and indicated with his hand to the table in the front corner of the room. 'Follow me please ladies,' he said, with just a hint of an Italian accent, though he looked every bit the part with his short dark hair, tanned skin, and piercing blue eyes.

Eva indicated for Hanan to choose where to sit, and was surprised when she elected to face the wall rather than taking the seat that faced into the restaurant. Eva always preferred to have her back to a wall rather than face one, and smiled inwardly at their compatibility. 'How was the flight?' she asked, as they took their seats and the waiter handed them both a menu.

'Can I get you ladies a drink?' he asked.

'I'll have water please,' Eva responded quickly, hiding the grimace that she felt.

Hanan looked at her oddly. 'Water. Are you sick?' she asked, with an element of sincerity and no inclination to hide her surprise.

'Umm. No. I'm not sick. I just thought I'd join you and stay sober for once,' she said with a wry smile.

'Ah. I see. No need to do that on my account. Seriously. It really doesn't bother me that others like to drink,' she said with a shrug of her shoulders.

'In that case I'll have a glass of Sancerre please. In fact, make that a bottle.' Eva visibly relaxed at having ordered herself a proper drink. She smiled broadly and Hanan laughed. 'What?' she asked faking naivety.

'I love your predictability, and thanks for trying with the sober thing, but I could see it was nearly killing you.' Hanan's dark eyes had softened, and Eva could feel the gentle pressure of them touch her in places that were starting to throb.

She cleared her throat and allowed her eyes to gaze at the menu, even though she knew exactly what she would order. 'So how was your flight?' she asked without looking up.

Hanan was studying the menu. 'Fine, same route: same issues. Though at least the French aren't striking at the moment.

167

That's always fun and games,' she said, looking over the top of her menu with a smirk on her face.

'Hey, I'm English remember,' Eva said, louder than she intended, then sniggered, shifting her eyes quickly back to the menu.

The waiter approached with the wine, pouring a taster for Eva. Hanan watched her as she sniffed and swilled the liquid around the glass, before delicately sipping and nodding her approval. 'It's an art.' Hanan commented, placing her hand over the top of her glass as the waiter approached it with the bottle. 'Not for me, thank you,' she said with an endearing smile. The waiter nodded and placed the wine inside the cooler on the side of the table. Eva fiddled with the cutlery and red napkin before lifting the glass and taking a good slug of the wine. She held the chilled fluid in her mouth, taking in the soft tones before swallowing. Hanan watched. 'Are you sure you're okay tonight? How's Anna?' she asked as if knowing the answer.

'Anna's good. We're good. We agreed to split.' Hanan frowned. 'Well, I mean we agreed to revert our relationship back to the status of friendship. I think we both knew it wasn't working.' Eva's eyes glazed over as she spoke.

'I'm sorry to hear that,' Hanan said, reaching for her water.

'No, it's okay. We're both fine about it. In fact, I think it's only now I realise I didn't feel quite what I thought I did. I mean; I love her deeply - I always will, but that has to be as a friend. It was great that I could be there for her when she needed me. But, the idea of bringing up someone else's child, and one that I wasn't involved in the decision about... and then there's the not so small issue of what if Lauren comes back at some point? It was all getting a bit much, and I guess with hindsight we should never have crossed the line and slept together. Not that we did ever sleep together actually, and that was also part of the problem... I'm not making sense. Anyway, I feel a sense of relief, in a lot of ways,' Eva rambled, partly justifying the situation to herself. Hanan listened, a considered look on her face. Eva smiled. 'You look serious,' she said.

'Sorry. I was just processing what you were saying,' she said softly. 'So, you're celebrating tonight?' she questioned.

'That's a good idea,' Eva responded, raising her glass to Hanan. 'To...'

'The future,' Hanan finished for her.

'The future.' Eva took another large slug of her wine and instantly relaxed. Bathing in the familiar sensations, numbing her senses. 'You have amazing eyes,' she said, suddenly.

Hanan averted her gaze and flushed. 'Thank you,' she said, modestly. The waiter interrupted the moment to take their food order, giving enough time to shift the subject.

'So, tell me more about your family,' Eva said, slightly choked.

Hanan stared into space momentarily. Eva watched her face intently, unable to decipher the emotion etched there. Hanan sighed as her mind filtered the images in her mind. 'That's a long story,' she said with a hint of sadness, unable to raise a smile.

'Sorry,' Eva responded, seeing the question had hit a nerve.

'It's okay. It's just...'

'No, honestly. Please don't feel you have to tell me anything.' The waiter interrupted the conversation, presenting two plates of food. Both women turned their attention to the sumptuous meal, with a sense of relief. They ate in relative silence, an awkward tension between them, smiling and nodding on occasion with reference to the food.

Eva placed her knife and fork on the empty plate and sat back into the seat with a contented sigh. 'That was great,' she said polishing off the last of the wine in her glass. 'Do you fancy a nightclub?'

'Where are you staying tonight?' Hanan asked, without answering her question.

'I have a flat here in town, not far from here actually. I'm living back at home now.' Eva's eyes lowered. 'Well as of this afternoon,' she clarified.

'Oh, okay. Club sounds good, but just for an hour or so as I've got an early start. There's a new one, '*Girleze*'. Fancy trying it? It's supposed to be more up market... allegedly,' she said with a slight smirk.

'Sure. Let's go,' Eva said, raising an arm to the waiter and indicating for the bill. 'I'll get this.'

'Okay.' Hanan watched Eva fidgeting whilst they waited for the bill. The intensity had been different between them during the meal, though she was unsure why specifically she had, personally, felt off key. 'You seem edgy?' she asked.

'Sorry,' Eva responded, stopping her leg from jumping up and down and holding Hanan's gaze.

Hanan smiled warmly, toying with the subtle change inside her. 'As long as you're okay?' she questioned. Eva nodded.

Stepping into the street they walked, watching for a taxi, hailing one that passed, and shrugging when it failed to stop. The mild evening made for a pleasant saunter, so they took the short cut through the park, keeping a respectful distance between them, enjoying the semi-quiet. Heading south, they crossed the river leading back into the heart of the city. The noise and bustle assaulting their ears, breaking the trance, and thrusting them back into conversation. 'What's it like being a pilot?' Eva asked, as she scanned the dark night sky. 'I mean, what's it like flying at night?'

'Dark,' Hanan said with a serious look, before breaking into a beaming smile.

'Very funny,' Eva said with a laugh, grateful for the break in tension and injection of humour.

'Well it is.' Hanan shrugged. 'Very dark at times. We navigate through the controls of course, so it doesn't matter that we can't see where we're going, so to speak.'

'That must involve a lot of trust.'

'I've never really thought about that. I guess it does. You just get so used to it. I suppose if I thought about that too much, I might not want to fly!' she said, as she fleetingly pondered the consequences of a failure in their guidance systems. 'We take a lot for granted,' she said, philosophically.

'Here,' Eva said, pointing up ahead at the classy sign above the bar. 'Looks interesting,' Eva said peeking through the windows, as they approached the door. Hanan smiled and reached to open the door.

The first thing that hit Eva was the absence of stale alcohol, replaced instead by a subtle flowery scent. Not too overpowering, and also with a hint of musk that made the place feel neither feminine nor masculine. Plush leather-topped stools adorned the bar and small tables with metal chairs gave the place an authentic, artisan, feel. Most of the women were dressed up rather than down, and there was a general aura of 'exclusivity' about the place.

The barwoman eyed them both as they approached the bar, but not with anything remotely seductive in her eyes. She assessed their suitability for the venue, nodding her approval as her eyes locked onto Hanan's tall frame. 'What can I get you ladies?' she asked. Her smile seemed much warmer than her eyes.

'I'll have a white wine, Sancerre if you have it, please?' Eva asked.

'Of course,' the dark-haired barwoman said, with a tone that suggested she had almost been insulted at the idea that they might not hold a wine of quality. 'And what about yourself?' She held Hanan's gaze with more interest Eva noted, and she was intrigued at the sudden rush of irritation that flooded her senses as she watched Hanan respond with her characteristically friendly smile. The woman winked as Hanan requested a non-alcoholic cocktail, allowing the barwoman to choose one for her.

'What if she makes you something you don't like,' Eva asked out of curiosity.

Hanan smiled, aware of Eva's slight discomfort towards the woman. 'There's no fruit I don't like, so I think the chances of that are pretty slim,' she said with a tilt of her head. 'I like this place,' she said, her eyes scanning the room. The music was loud enough to be heard, and yet people were chatting and laughing without having to shout.

Eva huffed, and her eyes followed Hanan's around the room as they waited for their drinks. She had to admit, it was a lot more up market than the regular haunt. The two drinks appeared on the bar, and the barwoman's smile was directed at Hanan. Eva was sure the woman snarled at her. She huffed again as she followed Hanan towards a vacant table at the other side of the room.

'Hello.' The unfamiliar voice came from Eva's right. She caught sight of the flowing dark curls on the tall tanned woman before her eyes focused on the face that was smiling at her.

'Um, hello.' Eva said, looking around to confirm the woman was speaking to her. Heat rose to her face, as her eyes locked with the Italian-looking woman she had spied at *Le So What* months earlier. *It's her.* The one who had piqued her curiosity, the night she had bailed out of the club and gone to Anna's for supper. The one who had caused Eva to make a promise to herself that she needed to change her life, settle down, and stop the mindless clubbing sexual encounters. The one she had kept an eye out for, and never thought she would see again. Eva's jaw dropped. The woman was smiling, beginning to laugh. Her dark-brown eyes were lighter than Eva had imagined, from across the bar all those months ago, and their intensity pierced straight through her. Her heart pounded in her chest.

'You don't remember me,' she said. 'There's no reason why you would,' she said, with a tilt of her head. 'We never actually got to speak to each other the last time I saw you, though I wanted to,' she continued confidently, and without regard for Hanan who stood for a moment, before leaving Eva's side and taking a seat at the table.

'I...' Eva started, but stuttered as the dark eyes on her - piercing inside her - threw her off balance. 'I do remember you,' she managed, before taking a gulp of her wine to wet her mouth. Remembering Hanan, Eva turned and indicated towards her. 'I'm sorry, I don't know your name,' she said. 'This is Hanan. Hanan this is...'

'Rosa,' the woman finished for her, holding out her hand and shaking Hanan's firmly, before moving in and placing a kiss on both cheeks. Eva looked around Rosa's shoulders, seeking out the butch friend, but couldn't see her anywhere.

'And you are?' Rosa asked with a broad grin. Eva fidgeted, clearly flustered by the obvious blunder of not introducing herself. Even though they had never spoken, they had caught each other's eye in a way that had created a common bond between them - connected them.

'Oh, yes... sorry, I'm Eva.'

'Well hello Eva,' Rosa said, her eyes admiring Eva from head to toe.

'Why don't you join us?' Hanan asked.

Rosa smiled, shaking her head, before looking back towards Eva, her eyes boring into her, causing heat to rise to her face. 'No. Thank you for asking. I'm here with friends and you two seem to be... together.'

'We're not together,' Hanan clarified calmly, catching a smug look from the dark eyes as they assessed Eva with renewed interest.

173

'Well, in any event I need to get back to my guests. It was lovely to finally meet you,' she said holding Eva's hand, and pressing a kiss on her cheek that lasted for longer than it customarily should have. The touch set fire to Eva's skin, and the flames ripping through her caused the sensitive parts of body to erupt.

'Yes. You too,' Eva mumbled, as Rosa nodded towards Hanan again, turned, and moved elegantly across the room. Eva watched her until she had disappeared behind a group of women who were laughing at something that had passed between them. She wondered if the butch woman was one of the guests in Rosa's party. She had been staring a while before she turned back to the table to face a smiling Hanan.

'Seems you're a popular lady,' she teased. Eva released the breath she had been holding and took the seat opposite Hanan. The aftershock rumbled inside for some time.

Hanan watched, as Eva stared vacantly for a long moment. 'I saw her once at *Le So What,* but she seemed to be with someone so we never got to speak.'

'She's a very good-looking woman,' Hanan remarked. Eva nodded unconsciously as she sipped her wine, lost in thought.

'Sorry?' she asked as she reconnected with Hanan, thinking she had missed something. Rosa's image was stuck firmly at the front of her mind and now sat between them.

'She is clearly attracted to you,' Hanan said, watching Eva's eyebrows rise at her comment. 'She is. She must have undressed you three-times,' Hanan said with a laugh, finding Eva's stunned look, and apparent naivety, endearing.

Eva locked onto Hanan's gaze, momentarily confused. Her pulse raced and her lower region throbbed, and as she dived into the dark brown irises that were not too dissimilar in colour to the Italian-looking woman's eyes she knew there was a big difference. 'Maybe,' was all she said, but she wasn't sure what the question was that she had answered. Something about the dark-haired, sophisticated woman had been very alluring back then, from a distance, and to have met her up close just added to the draw that seemed to pull Eva in.

18.

Lauren stared at the abstract print on the wall of the room above her therapist's chair, noticing it wasn't quite horizontal and it wasn't quite in the middle of the wall either. The lack of symmetry caused her to feel mildly uncomfortable, irritated even, but the print still drew her in. There was something hypnotic about it, and she wondered if that was deliberate on the part of the woman who sat opposite her, posing questions to her that she didn't always feel she wanted to answer. But, having committed to Carla that she would work with Georgina Dente, she had been religious in attending the weekly sessions. If she were honest with herself there had been some benefits to the work they were doing together. The virtually constant anger she had felt since the accident had subsided and she was beginning to feel ready to address the issue of Anna, and the possibility that she was pregnant. Even her relationship with her mother had improved, and they were now on speaking terms, though a distance remained between them. Perhaps it always would.

'So how did you feel about your sister's sudden death?' Georgina asked, seemingly out of the blue. Lauren sat up in the chair stiffly, it's softness no longer providing the comfort she had succumbed to as they had revisited the previous week's session. Lauren's heart raced and she could feel a bead of sweat forming under her hairline. She squirmed before resting back in the seat, as Georgina's eyes assessed her every movement.

'I don't know,' she answered, too quickly - evasive - her eyes wandering then locking onto the print on the wall.

'I'd like us to explore this event Lauren, if that's okay with you?' she asked directly. The sincerity in her voice resonated with Lauren. She too was aware that there was probably something about that time that was still unresolved. She took a deep breath and returned her eyes to Georgina.

'Okay,' she said softly. 'I really don't know how I felt. I was angry, confused, and upset, I guess.' She continued searching for relevant memories, maintaining her gaze on the image above Georgina's head. Georgina made no sound and simply nodded, the tenderness and compassion that carried through her eyes felt reassuring. Lauren dropped her eyes to her lap and continued, 'I remember coming home from school and both my parents stood next to each other in the study. It was the room in the house where business was carried out. Mother stood slightly behind papa and their faces were stern. I think she had been crying because her eyes were red and swollen, but she didn't speak. Father told me that there had been an accident and Papi and Corry had been killed. I remember running into his arms and sobbing uncontrollably. He held me for a short time and then released me curtly. There was stiffness in his body that surprised me. I started to scream, and mother left the room. He allowed me to shout, but then quietly said that we needed to be strong and move on as a family together. After that he became more distant. He had always been the one I went to for a hug as a child and he had always taken time to show me things. He was patient, kind and loving, and that all changed. Mother was always distant, even before the accident.' Lauren's brows furrowed. 'I felt so alone.' She looked up, pain in her eyes. 'That's what I felt. Alone. Very, very alone... isolated, with no one to talk to. And a great deal of pain, burning through my chest, I remember. I couldn't get rid of it no matter what I did.' She paused, Georgina nodded. 'I remember my father crying at the funeral, but after that neither Papi nor Corry were ever mentioned again. I wanted to ask questions. I wanted answers, but that discussion was off limits. I moved to London to study Law and found peace in that, I guess.' She looked up.

'And how do you feel about that time now?' Georgina asked. Lauren reflected, but the tears that flowed answered the question. She reached for a tissue from the box on the small table next to her chair, and blew her nose.

'Sorry,' she said sniffling, and wiping at her eyes.

'You have nothing to be sorry for Lauren. Please allow your feelings to flow. You're safe here, and doing really well.' Georgina smiled with kindness, as she allowed Lauren the space she needed. Lauren sobbed, as she never had sobbed before, as the pain of twenty-five years ago surfaced, gripped her hard, and turned her world upside down again. Tears gave way to rage, as she grappled with the unfairness of what had passed. Not only the loss of her sister for all those years, but also the loss of her parents who had deserted her in the most excruciating way possible - being physically present, yet emotionally absent. Then there was the impact on her life, and specifically the emotional withdrawal she experienced in her relationships. She could see that now. Maybe that's why being with Rachel suited her for so long. Questions replaced the rage, then guilt replaced the questions.

Leaving the session, she had felt lighter, though utterly drained. They had talked for another half an hour about Lauren's feelings of loss and the penny had dropped in terms of the link with her reaction to Anna. It had even made sense with respect to her lack of real commitment in her relationship with Rachel. Her fear of loss had prevented her from allowing emotional intimacy in any of her relationships, and that stemmed from her relationship with her parents, their rejection of her, and particularly her mother's detachment. And yet here she was doing exactly the same thing as Valerie had done over the years: withdrawing from those she felt closest to, being independent to the point of isolation, and emotionally detached. She had clearly let her guard down with Anna, hence the blue-diamond ring. It even made sense that the idea of becoming a parent had tapped this defensive part of herself - threatening her sense of security. The security that she had founded in avoiding the emotional empathy that, in effect, she craved. As she walked back to her car she felt taller. With the sun on her back, and a light breeze coming off the sea, she breathed deeply and vowed she would let go of the past. She didn't quite know how she might achieve that, but she knew she needed to re-engage with Anna, and hoped that it wasn't too late for them to try again. And, she needed to speak to her mother.

*

Lauren had arrived home early in the afternoon, and spent a couple of hours sitting under the eucalyptus tree talking to her father. The sun was warm and the sky a deep blue. The red wine she had taken with her had enabled the words to flow more easily, and after an hour or so she felt she had made peace with him. There were still many questions unanswered, and she still didn't understand why he and her mother had behaved the way they had for the sake of the Vincenti name, but she had resolved to let the past be, so that she could get on with the future. What was more important was that she was able to forgive him for making choices that had hurt her deeply. She could do that now, knowing that he had simply been human, with human fallibilities, rather than the perfect father her child-like self had wanted, and needed.

A feeling of deja-vu had passed over her as she had cast her eyes across their vast estate. She wondered whether it had been worth it for her parents? She had felt their pain at the loss of their youngest daughter, and wondered about Anna being pregnant - carrying their child, her child. If she didn't reconnect with Anna she would be losing everything that meant anything to her. It was bad enough that she had missed the last six-months, she didn't want to miss another day.

'I don't know whether I'll be as good as you papa,' she had said, staring at the vines in the valley below, whose green leaves were already beginning to close over the chalky ground in which they sat. 'I don't know if running the business is the right thing for me, but I promise I will try. I need to see if I can make things work with Anna too,' she had said, as she finished the last of her wine.

*

'How was therapy?' Valerie asked, as Lauren entered the living room for pre-dinner drinks. The t-word still grated on Lauren a bit, but she couldn't deny the fact that the sessions with Georgina were making a positive difference.

'Therapy's really good actually,' Lauren responded.

'That's good.'

'Can we talk, please?' Valerie's eyebrows rose to her silver hairline, though she also seemed to visibly relax at the request.

'I'd like that,' she said, with a heartfelt smile. She walked towards Lauren with her arms open and Lauren fell into the embrace, holding her mother with the same desire to reconcile their past. 'I love you Lauren,' Valerie said, softly, into her ear.

'I love you too,' Lauren said, hugging her tightly. Valerie matched her movements, as they swayed together momentarily, before Lauren released the hold. 'I need a drink,' she said with a wry smile.

'I've already started darling,' Valerie said with a wink. 'Henri won't be joining us tonight. He's out with a friend. That's called a *bromance* these days I think,' she said with a light chuckle, as she strode out to the bar and topped up her champagne. Lauren stared at Valerie, for the first time seeing her lighter side. She rubbed her eyes, sighed, and chuckled with her.

'I'll have a glass of that please,' she said. 'I feel like celebrating.'

Valerie looked up, but the smile had gone. 'I'm so glad you're more like yourself,' she said seriously. 'I've been so worried about you… and poor Anna,' she continued as she poured.

'I know. Shall we talk? I'd like your advice please.' Valerie's eyes sparkled, as she handed Lauren the glass.

'How about over supper?' she asked.

'Perfect.'

19.

Eva turned into the cold space on the other side of her bed. Hanan had left it in the early hours. She had been aware of the movement, as the covers had been softly pulled back and she had slipped out, and tiptoed across the wooden floor. Her clothes had been left in the bathroom so as not to disturb Eva, a habit they had become accustomed to over the last month.

Becoming intimate with Hanan had been a premeditated act on her part. Not for malicious or manipulative reasons, simply because she felt attracted to the tall Arabic woman and they seemed to chat easily together. She had tried to execute her plan after their date at *Girleze*, but Hanan had resisted, and for all the right reasons. Then, one evening, as they had walked back from watching a movie together, Eva's eyes had locked onto an intense stare, and she had instinctively moved closer and kissed her. Hanan had reciprocated. Eva had been sober, and to kiss Hanan had felt like the most natural thing in the world in that moment. The kiss had been brief, tender, and warm. They hadn't made any promises. In fact, their relationship wasn't something they talked a great deal about, which was slightly out of character for the easy going, chatty pilot, and especially given the basis upon which they had found each other. They were relaxed together though, in a way that even she and Anna weren't.

She stared at the shards of light reflecting onto the dark-blue accent wall in her bedroom. The sun had weaved through the spaces between the curtain and window, forming an almost uniform set of lines, as the rings that held the material in place failed to provide any form of darkness in the room. She smiled, breathing in the scent that had suffused the now empty pillow. She smelled of sex, *nice* sex. Hanan was always a tender lover, unlike her previous experiences, which had often been frantic, even aggressive, by comparison. But there was something else pricking at her - something lacking. She had hoped the stability of a long-term relationship would settle her. It didn't. The absence of intensity, of fire, left her feeling unfulfilled, though she had no doubt that Hanan cared for her, and vice-versa. They had only been seeing each other a few weeks, and even then, only when Hanan was on a stopover in Paris. But she didn't want to think too hard about that - about what was lacking. She would enjoy what they had while it lasted and if it didn't last, then so be it - she told herself every time Hanan left for work. Anna had given her blessing, which had helped her relinquish her guilt at leaving her alone in the barn. She didn't want to let her down either. Her phone pinged, pulling her out of her daydream, and she reached for the table at the side of her bed.

Eva?

The message had no contact name. Her brows rose as she tried to recall if she knew the number. She didn't.

Who is this?

She responded immediately, noticing that it was already gone 11am. She rarely slept in late, even on a weekend.

It's Rosa, from Girleze

The name instantly caused her heart to race, and heat rose to her face, as her finger tapped at the keys.

How did you get my number?

Your website and social media ☺

Eva smiled wryly to herself. Of course, she wouldn't be that hard to track down, if someone was intent on finding her. She breathed deeply, realising she felt more than a little anxious.

Ah! How are you?

Good. Are you coming out tonight?

I hadn't planned to

I'd like to see you. Will you come to Girleze so we can be properly introduced? ☺

183

Eva paused, to allow the offer to penetrate. Her body responded in a way that she hadn't expected, and she felt embarrassed at the instant betrayal. Hanan wouldn't be back in Paris for a week, her schedule having expanded, and they hadn't put any rules in place about one going clubbing without the other, she justified. In the last month, they had generally avoided bars and clubs and, instead, tended towards sampling the vast choice of restaurants in the city. Eva's love/hate relationship with the clubbing scene played out in her mind. She sometimes missed the buzz, the thrill. But she had also come to enjoy the feeling of having someone in her life whom it seemed could be more than just a short-term fling. She could go out and let her hair down without compromising what they had together, couldn't she? A surge of adrenaline answered the question, reminding her she needed to do the right thing by Hanan. She was in two minds as to whether she trusted herself.

Maybe

I'll be there from 9. Hope to see you later

The response came back immediately and she decided to save the contact, just in case, before slumping back on the bed. The familiar feel of anticipation pumping through her veins caused her mind to wander. Her phone, resting on her chest, bleeped again.

Hey x

It was Hanan and another surge of emotion, of a different kind, exploded through her gut. She stared at the phone thankful Hanan couldn't see her.

Hey x

In Athens now x

Eva felt the bile rise in her throat. What was she thinking?

Sounds hot! Be safe x

Eva's response seemed inadequate. She felt the need to talk with Hanan, to reaffirm their connection, as if doing so would ensure she made the right decision and stayed away from *Girleze*, and particularly from Rosa. Since their chance meeting in the up-market bar, Eva had managed to push the tall, dark temptress to the back of her mind, even though she had been more beautiful up close and Eva had swooned in her presence. There was something about the elegant woman that intrigued her. She wanted to find out more about her. Maybe she could become a good friend, she tried to convince herself, as she jumped out of bed and padded towards the bathroom, rubbing her fingers roughly through her short hair. Standing in front of the bathroom mirror she verbally committed to her reflection to be faithful to Hanan, but her eyes told a different story as they held her intense gaze with a dark green hue. Her mind seemed to find many reasons to justify any digression from the plan, especially the one that said they hadn't labelled their relationship as anything other than casual. The butterflies in her stomach warred with her concept of honour. She tried to tell herself that her feelings towards Rosa might have changed since the last time they saw each other, but she was far from convinced and already accepting how the evening might turn out.

*

Eva caught sight of herself in the glass frontage before she opened the door to *Girleze*. She smiled, pleased with the fact that she looked hot in tight faded jeans and a white string-vest. Even at 9pm the temperature was still in the mid-twenties, having hit a high of twenty-eight degrees that afternoon. She didn't want to start the evening sweating so she had walked slowly from her house to the bar, enjoying the vibrant feel that summer invariably bought with its lighter nights.

'What can I get you?' The dark-haired bar tender asked with a wry smile, having recognised Eva.

185

Eva noted her piercing light brown eyes for the first time. The look was intense, flirtatious even. She hadn't noticed that before. She smiled politely, turned, and glanced around the bar. No sign of Rosa. 'Sancerre, please. A large one,' she confirmed, as the woman turned her back, reaching for the chill-cabinet. She continued to scan the room, smiling, and nodding briefly to acknowledge a familiar group of four occupying the table by the window, but without holding their attention for too long. 'Thank you.' She handed over a twenty-euro note, ignored the barwoman's gaze, and waited for her change. Moving around to the other side of the bar to a small, round, high table, she checked her phone. Nothing.

'Hi.' The singsong voice came before Eva caught sight of Rosa, and made her jump. Her heart raced, her mouth parched. Her eyes locked with Rosa's over the top of her glass as she came into view. 'Do you always hide behind pillars? she asked, but Eva was too entranced by the dark eyes and broad white smile, that seemed to be undressing her, to respond.

'Hi,' Eva croaked, the colour deepening in her cheeks. 'I didn't see you,' she said.

'I was watching you. You look good,' Rosa said, eyeing Eva with raised brows, sipping at the wine in her hand. 'I didn't know whether you'd come,' she added, with a questioning tilt of her head.

'I thought about not,' Eva responded, matching the sipping of wine, any ounce of guilt about meeting up having fled at that first smile. There was something about Rosa that had intrigued her from the first time she caught sight of her. Yes, she was stunningly attractive, athletic, and oozed confidence. But more than that, there was something else about the dark stranger who seemed to have a knack of sending fire through her blood.

'And you decided to come?' Rosa said, searching Eva with a sparkle in her eyes.

She cleared her throat. 'Seems so,' she offered, trying to remain cool and feeling anything but, as a bead of sweat started its journey down the side of her hairline. *Damn heat*. An image of Hanan smiling flashed through her mind, bringing her out of the trance, allowing her to pull out of the seductive grip Rosa seemed to have on her. 'How are you?' she asked, breaking the spell.

'I'm... good thank you,' Rosa said, less than convincingly, something passing across her eyes, fleetingly. 'I haven't seen you around,' she said, focusing her attention back on Eva. 'You weren't too difficult to track down though, even with just a first name,' she continued, smiling again. 'Your look is... distinctive,' she said, her eyes scanning Eva's face, neck, and body.

'Facebook?' Eva asked, nodding rhetorically. Rosa tilted her head, neither confirming nor refuting Eva's assumption, just admiring. 'Do you want to sit?' she asked, following a brief silence.

'Sure.' Rosa headed deeper into the bar and Eva followed close on her heels, her attention firmly fixed on Rosa's swaying hips and cute, tight, backside.

'So, what do you do?' Eva asked, as they settled into a vacant booth. The seats were still warm and two half empty beer bottles sat on the table. Eva pushed them to one side and placed her glass on the table.

'I'm a surgeon,' Rosa answered, her eyes deepening, her tone suddenly more serious. She lowered her glance a fraction, and seemed to avoid contact with Eva momentarily. Eva straightened in the chair, feeling the shift in connection between them.

'That must be...' Eva started slowly.

'Challenging,' Rosa finished.

'Interesting I was going to say,' Eva corrected her.

'Interesting...' Rosa repeated, with a hint of sarcasm before shaking herself out of whatever seemed to be irking her.

'Sorry. It's been a rough day. We lost someone today,' she continued, her eyes focused on something in a space beyond Eva.

'I'm sorry.' Eva lowered her eyes to her wine, and fiddled with the stem of the glass.

'No, I'm sorry,' Rosa countered in a more upbeat tone. 'I try not to bring my work out with me, but today we lost a young child and that's always hard to handle.' She shrugged as she spoke, before sipping at her wine.

The slight fracture in the otherwise rock-solid confidence Rosa had exhibited earlier caused Eva to feel something she had felt only once before - with Anna. Her breath stalled. The buzzing in her gut at the subtle vulnerability she had witnessed softened, as it dawned on her that she had the same overwhelming desire to wrap Rosa up, protect, and defend her, as she had with Anna. Her eyes held compassion for the kind surgeon, who had clearly been affected by the events of her day. This time the silence between them was of a different quality.

'I gather you're a graphic designer,' Rosa stated, as she finished her wine. Eva nodded, curious that Rosa had clearly done her homework. 'I like your website,' she said with a smile. 'You've done some great work.'

'Thanks,' Eva responded, feeling a little on the back foot, given her lack of knowledge of the woman who had clearly sought her out.

'Cute,' Rosa remarked with tenderness, as her comment reflected in the rise in colour in Eva's cheeks. The butterflies took flight in Eva's stomach again, and her tongue felt lost in her mouth. 'Do you want to get out of here?' Rosa asked, but there was no sign of the earlier overt seduction, which had been replaced by genuine sincerity. 'I'd like to get to know you better, and the noise is only going to increase in here as the night goes on. And, I could do with some fresh air,' she added.

'Sure.' Eva smiled. Leaving her wine, she stood, to find herself just inches from Rosa's face. She backed off instantly, feeling the heat between them, drawing them closer. Rosa turned on her heels and worked her way through the gathering clientele, holding the door open for Eva as they stepped out into the street. Eva looked up at the darkening sky and breathed in deeply. Rosa watched, her eyes tingling Eva's skin. Without saying a word, they walked in silence. 'Where are we going?' Eva said after a while, more out of curiosity, feeling content just ambling next to Rosa as they wandered through the small park she had led them into.

'I have a place just over there?' Rosa pointed to the ornate buildings bordering the Seine. She stopped walking and held Eva's eyes. 'Sorry, I should have asked. Would you like to come back to mine?' she said, mildly embarrassed.

'Sure.' Eva responded, without thought or concern for the consequences, or for Hanan. Driven by a strong sense of *something,* she followed her into the gated building.

Eva admired the architectural design, as Rosa opened the door. They entered the pristine hallway. Eva followed Rosa through to the back of the house where she opened the large French doors, leading to a flower-laden courtyard. Two decorative metal chairs and a matching small round table sat on the stone patio. Stepped beds full of colour, and a series of small solar lights rested against the high walls, with the scents of summer wafting around the moderate space. It wasn't large by any standards, but it was totally private and enchanting, with a light trickle of water drawing Eva's ears to the small water feature in the far corner.

'Very Feng Shui', she said with a smile, her eyes catching Rosa's, which seemed to have become even darker.

'Drink?' Rosa asked, her mouth clearly parched and her demeanour softer.

'Thanks,' Eva responded, her hands sweating, her heart racing. The electrical charge running through her had intensified with the heat of Rosa's eyes, and remained even after the surgeon disappeared back into the house. She breathed deeply and allowed her eyes to feast on the garden, inhaling the scents, hoping it would settle the rising tension. This feeling wasn't just the sense of the chase or the thrill. There was something else, something more than a little disturbing, yet also very compelling.

The light sound of bare feet on tiles eased Eva out of her trance. Rosa handed her a glass of chilled wine and stared towards the stars. 'I love it here.'

'It's beautiful.' Eva looked to the sky, following Rosa's arm as she pointed to, and named, the constellations above them. She could feel Rosa's calm presence at her side, sensed the residual sadness occupying the surgeon's heart. The ambience felt sombre, intimate and unhurried. Lust had taken a back seat, whilst tenderness and respect filled the space.

'I've never brought anyone here before.' Rosa said earnestly. Eva remained silent, aware of the magnitude of the statement. 'But then I've never blurted out about losing a patient to a stranger either,' she said with a wry smile, turning to face Eva, holding her gaze. Eva swallowed hard, but her throat rebelled. She was suddenly aware that she didn't want to drink the wine in her hand.

'Want to talk about what happened today?' Eva asked, genuinely concerned, observing the grief in Rosa's eyes.

'There's not much to say really. A mother and daughter were ploughed down by a deranged ex, and father, of the child. She was only seven-years old. They were on their way back from school and he mounted the pavement to get to them. She didn't stand a chance. The mother's still critical.' Tears welled in her eyes as she spoke with compassion, her head shaking in disbelief at the atrocity.

'I'm really sorry,' Eva said softly, her heart aching.

'I'm glad you came out this evening. I'm not sure why this incident has had the effect it has on me,' she said, briefly staring towards the starlit sky. 'I'm glad you're here.' Her eyes settled on Eva's.

'I want to kiss you,' Eva said softly, without thinking.

Rosa leaned in, all the while holding Eva's eyes with her own. The intensity stunned Eva, and she was shaking by the time Rosa's lips met hers. The touch was intense and sensitive, her lips soft, and the connection between them deep. She pulled away slowly, her eyes still focused intently on Eva's. She offered her hand and Eva took it, placing the wine on the metal table before following Rosa's lead. Wherever she was taking her, Eva would go willingly. Whatever she offered her, Eva would take. If only for this one night, Eva was all in, and perhaps for the first time in her life.

20.

Anna stood back, rubbed her lower back, and nodded to herself as she admired her work. 'What do you think?' she asked, turning to face a smiling Lisa.

'It looks lovely darling, as do you,' she said, moving to take the brush from Anna's hand, thumbing a splash of paint from her cheek. She had watched Anna putting the finishing touches to the room, full of admiration and pride. The pastel colours gave a calming feel. The crib with its hand-made mobile, using various combinations of black and white stripes, circles, and squares; providing appropriate contrast and stimulation, could have been something out of a children's magazine. 'It's perfect,' Lisa said, as she sealed the lid on the light sky-blue paint. It had taken them the best part of a week, but Lisa had loved every minute of it. Vivian had even sent across a range of ceramic pots she had made and Lisa had decorated, as a baby shower gift, even though Anna wasn't planning to have a baby shower.

'I love it,' Anna said, beaming, still puffing from the exertion required to simply get from bending over to standing upright. 'I'm shattered, but I think it's utterly beautiful.' She scanned the room with an approving nod. 'Right, I need to get changed.'

'Are you sure you don't want me to come with you?' Lisa asked, Anna wiping the sweat from her brow with the cuff of a sleeve.

'No, it's okay. I think I'd rather do this alone.' She watched her mum's response hoping she didn't feel disappointed.

Lisa smiled. 'I understand. I'll cook something up for supper,' she offered.

'Great.' Anna pulled her mum in for a quick hug. 'Right. I'm disgusting and need a shower,' she admonished, sniffing at her armpit.

'Me too, but I'll clear this lot up first so you can get there on time.'

'You sure?' Anna asked. Lisa nodded. 'Thanks mum.'

'Go, get changed,' Lisa waved her away.

Anna swayed out of the room, with the weight of pregnancy now fully impeding her normal movement. She felt heavy and tired, but excited about her first antenatal class. She had already read all there was to read on the topic, but the idea of being with other first-time mum's felt somewhat reassuring. She plodded into her room, dropped her clothes and stepped into a cool shower, washing away the added discomfort of the summer heat. She allowed the water to flow over her, watching intently as her belly changed into a bizarre shape with her daughter's wriggling and stretching. She wondered briefly about Lauren, and how the little one would resemble her - she knew she would. She smiled, comforted at the thought. For now, Lauren would remain in her life in the form of her daughter. She had come to accept that that might be all she would ever have of the woman she had fallen in love with. She would wait until after the birth before planning how to re-engage with Lauren. At this time, she needed to give her full attention to her unborn child. Wrapping a towel around herself she wandered to the bed, sat, raised her legs and then sunk into the soft mattress, enjoying the light breeze through the open window.

*

Anna entered the pristine, white painted building with trepidation, and sweating from having rushed to get dressed and out of the house in good time. She had fallen asleep, and had it not been for her mum she would have missed the meeting altogether. She waddled, following the directions to the meeting room, and another - also waddling - young woman who seemed to be alone. They both reached the seminar room door at the same time and tired smiles passed between them, just as a young man jogged up to help.

'Thanks,' Anna said, as the young man held the door open for them both to enter.

'Thanks love,' the young woman said, smiling. She clearly knew the man. Perhaps they were together Anna wondered, instantly feeling the jolt of absence in her own life. She had worried that she might be the only single mum in the room, and most definitely the only lesbian. As her eyes searched the tense faces, her fears were confirmed. She suddenly felt heavier, as she crossed the room to a table hosting water, juice, tea, coffee and biscuits.

'Hello, I'm Jennifer.' The only slender woman in the room bounded towards her, hand outstretched; kissed Anna's cheeks lightly, and smiled warmly. 'You must be...' she consulted her clipboard. 'Anna,' she confirmed, satisfied with appraisal.

'Yes, hello.' Anna returned the smile but lacked the enthusiasm of her host.

'Welcome to the class. Please do help yourself to a drink and then grab a seat,' she said pointing to the semi-circle of chairs in the middle of the otherwise sparsely decorated room, before turning her attention to another couple who had just arrived.

'Thank you,' Anna said quietly, to Jennifer's back.

The room was clearly used for a variety of purposes, and its simple decoration would fit a board meeting as well as it did their antenatal class. Anna wondered what the stickers might be about, as she scanned the white board and easel at the head of the room. She hoped she wouldn't need to contribute to a discussion, and panicked at the thought. She took a glass of water from the table, found a seat, eased herself into it, and noticed the last couple being accosted by their lively host. She smiled as they both stood stiffly, listening intently to the instructions they were being given. As they turned to move into the room, Anna breathed a sigh. The two women caught her eye and a knowing glance passed between them. They sat in the only two seats available, to Anna's right, and smiled briefly in her direction. Anna had wanted to say hello, but their host flailed her arms as she commanded centre stage, so she just slumped back into the uncomfortable seat and listened.

The customary introductions had revealed that the two women were sisters, named Jacqui and Natasha. Anna wasn't convinced, but the other three couples had clearly bought into their story and marvelled at how wonderful it was that the younger sister was so supportive. They had looked as though they wanted to hold hands the whole session and clearly seemed on edge, in spite of the best efforts of their host to make them feel welcome.

The session had started with them working in groups of four, writing down their fears around childbirth, to share with the wider group. Anna had worked with one of the young couples, Alicia and Mario, who had already mapped out their birthing plan, not seeming to miss any scenario. They were having a boy, and he would be called Marco after Mario's father. Anna sat in stunned silence, horrified at the list of fears the couple reeled off. She couldn't think of anything specifically that worried her about giving birth, and had kept her birthing plan very simple. She hadn't really thought that much about names either. A wave of anxiety passed over her, and she began to wonder whether she would be better off not attending the group. As they revealed the contents of their list, she realised that the pair she had worked with were more extreme than the others in the group, and vowed to work with someone else next time.

At the break, she received great sympathy for being a single parent. She had omitted the fact that she was a lesbian, not because she was embarrassed in any way. It was just easier, and she didn't feel like fielding the inevitable questions that the topic would raise, though she did feel drawn to sharing that information with Jacqui and Natasha.

The post-break session involved more activities around the necessary equipment and useful items that would be needed after the birth, although she suspected every couple in the group would possess every item available whether it was actually needed or not. They had talked about baby names and she was surprised to see which couples had already chosen names for their unborn baby. Jacqui and Natasha were having a boy and adamant that he would be called Christophe. She had explored names in her mind during the session, but hadn't been able to decide. She couldn't say why, but had settled with the idea of waiting until she saw the baby. Next week they would be moving onto breathing techniques and birthing options they were informed, as the session was wrapped up by a, still enthusiastic, Jennifer. She breathed a sigh of relief as she exited the building, taken aback by the heat of the afternoon sun, feeling unsure, but strangely obligated to attend the following week. She wondered briefly, and not for the first time, what Lauren might make of it, shook off the thought and headed home. She needed to finish the last piece of work for the exhibition.

*

Lauren walked tentatively towards the unfamiliar front door. It had taken a while to track down where Anna's parents lived, but fortunately getting hold of information was something she had always been good at as a lawyer. She was shaking, and her heart raced out of control. She breathed deeply, and raised herself up to her full five-feet, eight-inches, aware of the slight stretch down her recovering leg. She hadn't been back to London since she had been discharged from the hospital, but the mental scars from the accident had still stirred in her body as she approached her old office building. She had needed to finalise business once and for all with McDermott, Knight and Davies, her ex-employers. The meeting had been civil and both parties could now go their separate ways. They had agreed to release her from any contractual obligations, on the basis that she dropped all allegations of harassment and bullying. In her former life as a Lawyer she would have wanted to sue their arses, but the accident had changed all that. She had more pressing issues than to waste her time with the likes of John McDermott and his inflated sense of self-importance. She felt tense, anxious, but committed to her decision. She needed to speak to Anna's parents before she headed back to Corsica. She knocked on the door with as much confidence as she could muster.

Vivian jumped at the heavy thud invading her concentration, and cursed as the pot she was shaping squirmed and collapsed onto the wheel.

'Damn it.' She wasn't expecting anyone and for a moment considered not answering the door, until the thump came again. Whoever it was, wasn't going away easily. 'I'm coming,' she yelled as she picked up a cloth, wiping her hands, heading towards the door. She squinted into the lowering sun, raising her hand to enable her to focus. 'Lauren,' she exclaimed.

'Hello,' Lauren said, with slight reservation. She smiled at the state of the older woman, with clay splashes on her face and a tatty cloth in her hand. The anxiety she had felt approaching the door receded the instant Vivian smiled back at her.

'Come in, come in.' She ushered Lauren through the door with excitement. 'Can I get you a drink?' she asked, as she followed her through to the living room. 'I was just about to take a break,' she lied with a beaming smile. 'Please join me. Would you like a glass of wine?' Vivian busied herself, pouring them a drink before Lauren had even answered. 'It really is lovely to see you,' she said, looking into Lauren's eyes. 'Lisa and I have missed you dreadfully, and I know Anna has too,' she added, failing to hide the genuine sorrow she had felt.

Lauren's eyes lowered slightly. 'I know. I'm sorry. I...'

Vivian cut her off, waving her hand for her to stop speaking. 'Please don't apologise. You were involved in a terrible accident. The rest is...' she paused looking for the right words. 'Well, the rest is just as it is. People respond differently to trauma. What's important is that you're here now. Have you spoken to Anna?' she asked.

'Umm.' Lauren stumbled at the direct question, even though she knew it was the obvious question to be asked. 'No... not yet. That's why I'm here. I want your advice. Is Lisa around?' she asked, looking towards the door, expecting Anna's birth mother to appear at any moment.

'No, she's with Anna, in Paris at the moment. They're decorating the baby room...' Vivian looked up, aware that the words were out of her mouth before she'd thought about the consequences. 'Did you know?' she asked, holding Lauren's gaze.

'Not until recently,' Lauren said with a sigh. 'And even then, I hadn't had it confirmed until you just...' Lauren looked away as tears pressed the back of her eyes.

'Then, I'm sorry for spilling the beans.' Vivian shrugged, placed the wine on the coffee table and reached for Lauren, pulling her into a hug.

'It's okay. I wanted to know. I'm so sorry, I've completely fucked up,' she said, welcoming the embrace, fighting the tears.

Vivian released her only to look sternly into her eyes. 'I said, no saying sorry, remember,' she teased lightly, brushing a tear that had fallen onto Lauren's cheek.

'Thank you.'

'For what?' Vivian said with a look of confusion.

'For being so... understanding.'

'I'm a Doctor remember... no you probably don't,' she said with a slight chuckle. 'Now, come on. Let's get that drink, and talk.'

'I need to get Anna back,' Lauren blurted.

'I assumed that was why you were here,' Vivian responded with a gentle smile. 'Now drink. The wine's too good to let it go warm.'

21.

Anna's eyes scanned the alcove space in awe. Her work sat alongside the most revered young talent in Paris, and every piece she had selected was worthy of a space here; at least that had been the view of one of the main critics attending. In the end, she had selected her original of the *Two Lovers* piece, from which she had created the Eiffel Tower card she had sent to Lauren. Alongside that sat her work, titled: *One Love.* She hadn't shown the piece to anyone until now. It had been intended as a Christmas present for Lauren, but that hadn't materialised and the canvas had sat wrapped in her loft ever since. It was a profile picture of Lauren sitting in the crook of a tree looking out over the valley close to her barn. She had taken the photograph during one of their sessions for the family portrait and the image had touched Anna deeply. Lauren looked relaxed, content, and there was a quality of softness in her energy that seemed to connect her with her surroundings. It held the essence of peace, openness, and it stood out. Her third choice had been a collage, incorporating the vineyard, the eucalyptus tree, local faces, and some of Claudia's pets, which she had titled: *Life's Loves.* The collection told the story of the different dimensions of love. Finally, she had created a piece she had titled: *A Mother's Love.* The image of a baby in its mother's womb sucking its thumb had been taken from the last photos she had received at the scan. She had turned it from a black and white piece into colour. She smiled, happy with the finished result.

Rowena bundled towards her with flailing arms, looking more pregnant than Anna's eight-plus months. Anna allowed herself to be bear-hugged as their two bellies clashed, Rowena's giving where Anna's didn't; Rowena's puffy cheeks making dainty contact with Anna in a flamboyant air kiss. 'Look at you?' she said, holding Anna away from her and eyeing her up and down. 'You look radiant. And your work is stunning,' she said as her eyes darted towards the wall. 'I've had an offer for the entire collection already,' she said, squeezing Anna's arm.

'And you know they're not for sale,' Anna said, smiling ruefully.

'200,000 Euros is a lot of money to turn down,' Rowena said, wagging a finger at Anna. 'Especially with a baby on the way,' she added, nodding at the protruding bump.

Anna's brows rose. 'Wow... who's buying?' she asked, having no intention of selling no matter what the price.

'An American collector. Think about it, eh?' she frowned at Anna who forced a smile. 'Now, where's that vagrant daughter of mine,' she asked, searching the room.

Anna shrugged. 'I'm not sure. I haven't seen her yet.' Anna's eyes scanned the wider room through the open archway but couldn't see Eva's characteristic blonde spikes anywhere. It had been a couple of months since they had agreed to resume their relationship as friends. Eva was living back at her flat and they were back to their old ways: Eva out clubbing, and Anna slouching at home in the evenings, preparing for the baby's arrival. Eva had come round in the early days for the occasional meal but she hadn't even heard from her in the last few weeks. 'Have you seen mums?'

'Not yet. I'm so excited to see them. It's been years.' Rowena cooed, hopping from toe-to-toe with excitement. At five-feet two-inches, she was unlikely to see too far into the fast-filling room of people. 'How are you? I've missed you coming into the office?'

'I'm good. I've been busy.' Anna smiled evasively. She had been avoiding Rowena since her relationship with Eva had taken on the *friends with benefits* status and subsequent reversion to *platonic friends*. She didn't know what, if anything Eva had said to her mum about their arrangement and didn't want to draw attention to something that, as it turned out, was short lived and ill conceived. 'I promise to come by more regularly, after the birth,' she said, looking down at her belly.

'Good, good. Ooo I've just spotted Lana Aventa. I need to catch up with her. I'll be back.' She patted Anna firmly on the arm and wriggled her way towards the renowned artist. Anna went to speak, but Rowena had already disappeared into the crowd.

Anna breathed deeply and glanced around the room, looking for her mums. She sipped at the glass of water in her hands, having refused a glass of Champagne. Her eyes locked onto the back of an elegant head, it's shape familiar. Dark curls with auburn hints rested on strong shoulders. A white, high collar shirt sat above the dark grey suit jacket. Anna's mouth parched and her heart raced. She couldn't breathe, couldn't swallow. The brown curls jolted backwards as the woman laughed. Anna swore she could hear the slightly gravely tone over the other voices in the room. Her focus narrowed and her legs started to shake. She gulped at the water in her hand and tried to breathe slowly and deeply.

'Are you okay?' A waiter asked in passing. Anna shifted out of trance.

'Yes, I'm fine. Thank you.'

'There's a chair, if you need to sit down,' he said, his eyes locking onto her bump as he pointed to a cosy-corner in the room.

'Oh… yes. Thank you.' Anna's breathing calmed slightly and she glanced back around the room. The woman had gone, and she instantly wondered if she had been seeing things. She sighed at her mind's trick, tried to relax, shocked at the strength of her visceral response to the illusion.

'Hi Anna.' The soft voice came from behind her, causing her to turn sharply, the bump occupying more space between the two of them than expected.

'Lauren,' she blurted, stumbling backwards as her legs started to fold. Lauren reached out and took her arm firmly. Anna's mouth remained open.

Lauren smiled warmly, though tension dominated her features. 'Sorry, I didn't mean to shock you. Are you okay?' Anna nodded slowly, unable to bring the words to her mouth. 'Do you want to sit down?'

'Yes,' she squeaked almost inaudibly, still nodding her head. She moved slowly towards the cosy-corner the waiter had pointed out, Lauren holding her arm protectively. Lauren took the glass from her hand just before she sat heavily into the seat, then sat next to her, her eyes eagerly appraising Anna. 'I'm...' Anna tried to speak but couldn't.

'I'm sorry Anna.' Lauren said, interrupting her. 'I'm so sorry. I don't know where to start, and now I nearly scared you half to death.' She winced, her eyes looking down towards her clamped fists. She looked paler than Anna remembered, and thinner. There were lines on her face that hadn't been there before.

Anna locked onto the deep brown eyes she had fallen in love with almost a year ago. A sharp pain cut through her chest. Images of her and Lauren before the accident clashed with the movie that had been running since Christmas. She fought not to dry-wretch, her face grey. Lauren moved to comfort her but stopped, shy of making physical contact. 'I...' Anna tried to speak but the words still wouldn't come.

'Anna, I'm so sorry about how I've treated you. I need to explain but I know now is not the place or time. Please, give me that chance, please?' she begged. Her hands were shaking, and the earlier confidence she had worn effortlessly had disappeared in a flash, as she pleaded for an opportunity to explain.

Anna's eyes lowered to the floor, the pain of eye contact too great for her to handle, her hands covering her belly, protecting her baby, her head shaking in disbelief.

'Please Anna?' Lauren's voice was almost at a whisper. Anna looked up at the sheen of water coating her dark eyes. The pain carved into her face ripped through Anna's heart. She knew then that she would always love Lauren. She couldn't stop herself. She didn't want to.

'How did you know I was here?' she asked, regaining some composure.

'Your mum, Vivian,' she clarified, tentatively holding Anna's eyes, searching for her reaction. Anna's eyes rose up into the spot-lit room, her head nodding.

'Why didn't you contact me?' Anna asked, determination building as a surge of anger coursed through her body, the red mist settling before her eyes.

'I know. I know.' Lauren spoke quietly, her eyes on the floor, head shaking, flicking her hands through her brown curls, searching for answers. 'I have behaved badly. I know that, and I'm truly sorry. You didn't deserve that.'

'No, I didn't,' Anna interrupted sharply, though feeling torn at the sight of Lauren crumbling before her.

'No, you didn't.' Lauren looked up. 'You didn't deserve any of this.' Her glance lingered on Anna's pregnant belly, before rising to meet her eyes. 'I am so sorry. I didn't know you were...' She paused. Something resonated as she held Anna's steel-blue eyes, noticing their dark rims widen. 'Pregnant. I didn't know. Why didn't you tell me?' she asked tentatively.

Anna shrugged and winced at the same time, as she recalled her decision not to leave the photograph of the positive result of the home pregnancy test. Now wasn't the time or place to bring up the past, but she didn't know if she could stop herself from spilling the months of agonising; the confusion, the betrayal. She turned her eyes away, as she recalled asking

Lauren's mum and Claudia not to say anything about the pregnancy. Anna challenged the feeling of guilt rising in her; justified it through Lauren's unresponsiveness, her anger, and eventual withdrawal. 'You were too stressed and you didn't want anything to do with me.'

'I know. I was angry and confused. I rejected you. I rejected everyone. I was scared,' she confessed.

'What's changed?' Anna asked. 'What makes you think you can just come waltzing back in here and everything be back to normal? Christ, I don't even know what normal is anymore,' she said.

'I don't. I know I can't. But I had to start somewhere. I know I've got a lot of work to do, and I also know you might not want to see me ever again. It's a risk I had to take.' Her eyes glazed.

'So, is your memory back?' Anna asked, her eyes scanning Lauren's face for clues.

'No.' Anna's heart sunk. 'I keep thinking things seem familiar and I have a recurring dream, but that's about it.' She shrugged, unsatisfied with her reality. Anna's eyes dropped, as a wave of deep sadness consumed her.

'Oh. So where does that leave us?'

'I don't know. All I know is that I've behaved inappropriately and treated you badly, and I want to make amends for that in whatever way possible. I want to try and find the memories of us and the only way I'm going to be able to do that, is if we spend time together.'

'And what does that mean?'

'I don't know the details Anna. I just know I'm ready to try… when you are. I realise this has come as a shock to you, and you've probably already carved out a life for you and the baby.' Lauren's eyes pleaded, tears rolling down her cheeks. 'I can only hope you'll accept me as a part of that life too, at some point.'

Tears pushed through Anna's eyes and flooded her face. She collapsed back into the seat, releasing the tension she hadn't realised she had been holding. Her hands covered her face and she rubbed vigorously at her forehead. 'I need time.' The words came out as a whisper.

Lauren's posture straightened. 'Anything you need. Anything,' she said, holding back the smile that was trying to break through at the slither of hope she had been given.

'There you are.' Vivian's familiar voice jolted Anna from her thoughts. She wiped the tears from her face and stood to greet her mums, who approached at pace. Lauren stood swiftly and held out a hand for Anna to help her up. 'We've been looking all over. Oh. I see you've caught up?' She squeezed Lauren's shoulder as she came to a halt by her side. Lisa eased herself between Vivian and a stranger to get to her daughter, pulling her in for a motherly embrace. Vivian patted Lauren's back before hugging Anna. 'I'm glad you two found each other,' she said, looking from one to the other, acknowledging the distress in their faces, before moving the conversation on. 'I've just seen your work darling. It's utterly brilliant. Have you seen it yet?' she asked Lauren, hoping to shift the mood between the two women.

'Umm. No. I haven't,' she said apologetically, with downcast eyes to Anna.

'There's plenty of time and a lot of amazing artists to see,' Anna said, dismissive of her own work, feeling mildly irritated at her instinctive desire to defend Lauren... and to be held by her.

'None as good as you though darling,' Lisa stated with authority. Anna squirmed under the adoration. Lauren caught Anna's eye and smiled warmly at her. She returned the smile, weakly.

'I'd love to see it,' Lauren said, her eyes holding Anna's. Anna wound her way across the room to the alcove, heat rising

206

in her cheeks as her eyes focused on the image of Lauren hanging on the wall. She could see Lauren appraising the piece through the corner of her eye, her mouth agape.

'This is incredible, Anna,' Lauren said softly, as she absorbed the display, her heart fluttering with the intensity of the emotion coursing through her veins. A strong sense of pride, mixed with something far deeper, painful even, touched her.

'See, I'm not the only one who thinks it's great,' Lisa said, smiling with smug satisfaction. 'It's the work of a genius.'

'Mum,' Anna admonished, trying not to blush, and rolling her eyes.

'It is,' Lauren insisted, her eyes locking onto Anna's, closing the space between them, clearing the past, homing in on the future.

'Thank you all,' Anna said, recovering herself from the overt praise. 'I'm tired. I think I'll go back to the hotel now,' she said, suddenly feeling claustrophobic, closing the evening prematurely.

Lisa nodded, pulling Anna towards her and kissing her on the cheek. 'It's been a long day,' she said. As much as she wanted Lauren back in her daughter's life, she was well aware of the adjustment that might be needed. Anna feigned a smile.

'Where are you staying?' Lauren asked coyly.

'The Trocadero La Tour. It's not far,' Anna responded.

'We'll come with you,' Lisa added.

'It's okay you don't need to. Stay here and we'll catch up for breakfast,' she directed to her mums. Vivian had insisted that they all stay overnight and make a celebration of the event, without the need to travel to and from Anna's barn. It had been her treat to Anna, and probably her last opportunity for a luxury night's sleep before the baby came. Anna had resisted at first, on the basis that her sleep was already affected and it would have been a waste, but Vivian had won that battle.

'Can I escort you back?' Lauren offered, bashfully.

Anna sighed deeply, feeling suddenly weary, even though it was still relatively early in the evening. 'Okay,' she conceded. Lauren raised a twitch of a smile. Lisa and Vivian nodded in unison.

'Right, we'll say goodnight then,' Vivian said, kissed Anna on the cheek. Lisa leaned in and kissed both women, squeezing their hands, willing them together.

'Thanks mum.' Anna said, aware of the butterflies that had awakened at the idea of being alone with Lauren. Leaving her parents, she made her way through the room and exited the gallery into the clammy summer evening. Temperatures had hit thirty-two degrees earlier in the day, and even though the current twenty-five degrees was light relief, it was still sticky and humid, especially compared with the air controlled gallery environment. She broke into a hot sweat within seconds and groaned.

'You okay?' Lauren asked.

'Yeah. Just hot! High temperatures and pregnancy don't go too well together,' she said, with a wry smile.

'I can imagine,' Lauren responded with a slight grimace, acutely aware that she needed to follow rather than lead any conversation between them, not wanting to push the delicate balance a step too far.

'Can you?' Anna asked harshly, a flash of anger fuelling her words.

'No. You're right. I'm sorry, I can't possibly imagine what you've been through.' Lauren looked desperate. Anna's heart ached. As much as a part of her wanted payback for what Lauren had put her through, and even then, only a small part, the biggest part of her felt nothing other than compassion, tinged with sadness.

'I'm sorry. I didn't mean to bark at you.'

'It's okay. I understand. I deserve it.'

'No. You don't actually. I can't imagine what you've been through either. Or what you're still going through.' Anna stared. The evening sky had a silver-blue hue; the sun, sitting low, was still glowing white, and a warm haze hovered in the air, seemingly absorbing the oxygen. It felt oppressive. The situation felt oppressive. She needed some space. 'I'll make my own way,' she stated, turned, and walked away.

'Anna.' Lauren called to her retreating back. Anna didn't stop walking, the distance between them increasing with every pace. 'Anna,' she called again, this time with greater intensity. Tears flooded Anna's face as she tried to block out her name, turned the corner out of sight, and doubled over, gasping for breath. Her heart thumping through her chest, she glanced over her shoulder hoping she was alone. Yet, in part, hoping Lauren had chased after her. She hadn't. Standing, she breathed deeply to compose herself. The tears had dried, but the pressure in her head remained, along with the burning behind her eyes. What had she just done?

*

Anna woke to the sound of birds singing loudly, and twinges pulling low in her cervix. It was just past 4am, the feeling a familiar one. She groaned as the spasm took hold of her, breathed to release it. Opening her eyes slowly, she debated turning over and going back to sleep, but her bladder screamed and she obeyed. By the time she returned to her bed, she was wide-awake. *Damn* she cursed to herself. Perhaps it was her body's way of making sure she would be ready for the baby, but all she wanted was a restful night's sleep. She hadn't had one of those in as far back as she remembered and the bags under her eyes had become a permanent feature.

Lauren had texted her several times a day since her impromptu appearance at the exhibition. Anna had played every permutation of every option she could think of, with respect to re-engaging with her, and was still without a resolution. So many times over the previous eight and a half months she would have welcomed Lauren back with open arms. And then, all the other times, she had settled on the idea of life as a single mum. She had adjusted to the idea of being on her own, and was now thrown by her body's response to the possibility of a life with Lauren. The family that they had originally conceived together was a real possibility.

She winced as the Braxton Hicks kicked in again. Lauren was clearly making an effort to engage with her, but she still felt torn. Exhausted from the mental energy of processing the pros and cons of her situation with Lauren, she collapsed back onto her bed. Staring mindlessly at the ceiling to stop her mind spinning, she drifted into a light sleep.

*

'I'm worried I've blown it,' Lauren said sighing, slumped in the seat, and faced her old friend with a questioning gaze.

'What makes you say that?'

'Just a feeling… and the fact that she's over there and I'm here and we don't get to talk properly.' Lauren frowned, frustration appearing between the lines.

'But you are communicating?' Carla asked, hoping the answer was yes.

'We've been texting a lot. I know it's only been a few days since the exhibition, but that meeting didn't go too well, and… well… I need to talk to her, properly,' Lauren confirmed.

'Properly in what sense?'

'About the baby. About us as a couple, and as a family. I get the impression she'd rather go it alone, which I sort of get.'

'It's been hard for her, needing to deal with the fact that you might never have reconnected, and having to parent alone.

She needs time to adjust.' Carla reminded Lauren of the facts she was already well aware.

'I know and I get that, I really do. It's just...'

'Just?'

'I want to be there when the baby's born. I want to be a part of its life. More than that, I want to make a life for us all, and I'm scared she doesn't want that now.'

'Have you asked her, directly I mean?'

'Not exactly.' Lauren confessed, feeling edgy at the idea of broaching the subject with Anna, for fear of rejection.

'Ask. Surely it would be better to know either way and deal with the consequences, than play a waiting game.'

'Maybe.' Lauren sighed again. The depth of her pain just got deeper.

'Anyway, how's your mother?'

'She's good.'

'What does she say about...'

'To talk to Anna.' Lauren raised her eyebrows at her admission.

'What can I say?' Carla smirked, teasing her old friend lightly. 'Right let's order food, I'm starved.'

'Sure.' Lauren's appetite had deserted her, but she stared at the menu and pointed at something when the waiter arrived.

*

'Hi mum.'

'Hello darling. How are you? Have you gone into labour?' Lisa's strained voice, bordered on panic as she took the unexpected call. She was due to fly to Paris at the end of the week and suddenly worried that she wouldn't make it in time for the baby's arrival.

'No, I'm fine,' Anna said, though far from convincing.

211

'What's wrong darling?'

'I'm confused.'

'Ah.' Lisa knew exactly what Anna was referring to… or rather, to whom.

'I'm so torn. I'd just got my head around being a single mum and then this…' she waited for a response from Lisa, but the line stayed quiet. She continued. 'I want her back so much, so that we can be a family together,' she admitted.

'So, what's stopping you?' Lisa questioned, knowing the answer.

'I don't want to get hurt, I guess,' Anna replied, in thought.

'And what about the baby knowing its heritage, and the life you and Lauren had planned together?'

'I know, you're right. That's exactly what I wanted… but that was then and this is now. I intended to re-engage with her after the birth. I didn't expect to be thrown into this… this turmoil again, and just before…' Anna groaned down the line as a sharp pain ripped through her.

'Anna,' Lisa almost shouted down the line. 'Are you alright?'

'Yes. It's just Braxton Hicks.' She breathed deeply to regain her composure. 'I'm so glad you're coming over,' she said, the tiredness noticeable in her voice.

'Me too darling. I'll be there soon.' Lisa faltered. 'And… I'm really sorry if Lauren turning up at the exhibition threw you. I… we… didn't think. We thought you'd be happy. I'm so sorry darling,' Lisa apologised.

'It's okay. On one level, I'm glad you did. I just need to get used to the idea… and maybe stop worrying about her leaving me again. I'm just not sure how to do that yet.'

'Talk to her darling.' Lisa offered.

'Yes, I will.' Anna wandered, in thought again. Lisa waited on the line. 'Right, I'd best let you go,' Anna said, finally.

'Yes,' Lisa responded. 'I've got a flight to catch at the end of the week and I haven't even packed yet.' She chuckled.

22.

'Where are you staying?' Anna asked.

'Hotel Plaza Athenee.' Lauren responded. Anna smiled wryly. 'You know it?' she asked, quizzically.

'We stayed there together.'

'Oh. Sorry,' Lauren winced. Anna stopped walking and turned Lauren to face her.

'If we're going to move this forward,' she waved her hand between the two of them, 'then you've got to stop saying sorry for everything you can't remember.'

Lauren gave a timid smile. 'Okay, sor...' She stopped herself and shrugged apologetically. Anna smiled, amused by Lauren's cuteness. Linking arms she resumed the walk. She directed Anna down to the river, the Eiffel Tower sitting proudly in the near distance, the bench just a few paces away. Anna slowed the pace. 'You okay?' Lauren asked, looking to her swollen belly.

'Sure,' she faked a smile.

'Come and sit with me, please?' Lauren held out her hand and Anna took it. The bench was dry; unlike the previous time they had occupied this spot. The oppressive heat left the air feeling stuffy and heavy. For Anna, it was like negotiating life in a steam bath, as the additional weight caused her to perspire at the slightest of movements. 'It's beautiful,' Lauren said, looking down the river, the water rippling with the movement of traffic, the scent of flowers in full bloom wafting down the pathway lining the river. The occasional toot of a ferry horn, chattering tourists as they meandered past, birds singing, and trucks throwing up black smoke on the road behind them. Lauren reached down and took Anna's hand. Anna nuzzled into the strong supportive shoulder, yielding to the weariness that seemed a permanent feature in her life. 'I've looked at your picture so many times,' Lauren reflected aloud. 'You're an amazing artist.' Anna squeezed her hand in response, feeling too tired for words. 'Will you have dinner with me tonight?'

Anna rose in her seat, her eyes tracking Lauren's face intently. She had come into town for work, with the intention of returning home mid-afternoon. It had been an opportune time for them to meet up without any added pressure or expectation. Something in Lauren's gaze penetrated Anna to the core. She wanted to not need her, but she couldn't. She wanted Lauren more than she had ever wanted anything or anyone in her life. 'Yes,' she said. Lauren smiled and leaned closer, subtly confirming her place in Anna's life. 'I haven't got anything to change into,' Anna said, as an afterthought.

'You look amazing just as you are,' Lauren said, cringing.

'Yes, that sounded horribly corny, but thanks,' Anna giggled.

'It did... and you do... look amazing I mean,' Lauren said, in seriousness.

'What time's your meeting?' Anna asked eventually, breaking the comfortable silence between them, as they watched Parisian life in action.

Lauren looked at her phone. 'Oh shit. It's in fifteen-minutes,' she said, jumping out of the seat. She held out her hand to Anna, who took it and heaved herself up to standing. Lauren looked at her with eyes that were asking for permission to leave.

'It's okay. I'll make my way back to the office. What time...?'

'I'll meet you at 6.30 back here, at this seat, if that's okay?' she said, dashing towards the road to hail a passing taxi.

'Sure.' Anna sniggered at the sudden panic and rush of activity, reminded of Lauren's passionate nature. Cute. She meandered back towards the office, enjoying the sun on her back and the warm feeling gathering in other parts of her body. It was a feeling she had never experienced with Eva. This was something completely different. *This* consumed her in a positive way, and reaffirmed her connection with Lauren on a non-physical level. It was the difference that made the difference and the reason why, no matter what, she could not let Lauren go again.

The afternoon flew by and Rowena took great pleasure in regaling her of all the positive feedback from the exhibition, still managing to slip in the good reasons why she should sell her exhibits - a counter-offer of 250,000 Euros, being a key reason. Anna was flattered but still unwilling to sell. She couldn't put a price on the portrait of Lauren and the baby, and the other pieces seemed inextricably linked: they belonged together.

Eva had popped in, full of apology about her absence from Anna's life. She was bustling with energy and looked different, but they were back to their old selves, the three of them eating donuts and drinking coffee. Rowena had nagged her daughter about her work tardiness, which seemed a constant bone of contention between them. Apparently, Eva had been wrapped up in 'other stuff', to which Rowena had thrashed her podgy arms around in despair and cussed at the youth of today. Anna had mouthed the word 'Hanan' to Eva and she had shaken her head, with a sparkle in her eye. Clearly Rowena was unaware of the latest love in her daughter's life, but that was the way Eva liked to keep it between them.

Eva had shown genuine concern for Anna as they talked about Lauren's return. Eva needing to feel reassured that her best friend was making the right choice, still protective of both her and the baby. Anna had promised that they were taking things slowly and hadn't made any rash promises. Eva had backed down, but the way she looked at Anna had said that she too would be keeping an eye on them. Anna had felt somewhat comforted by the knightly gesture, knowing full well that Eva was actually too consumed by her own affairs of the heart to be of any assistance in the near future.

Anna meandered the route she had taken earlier. The curly brown hair, slightly tussled from the soft breeze, caught her breath as she approached the bench. 'Hi,' she almost croaked.

'Hi,' Lauren responded, instantly standing and swinging round to face her. She leaned in and placed a soft kiss on Anna's cheek. The touch set fire to her skin, and she flushed. 'Sor...' Lauren started then stopped, as the steel-blue eyes threatened her menacingly.

'How was your meeting?' Anna took the outstretched hand in hers and they stood staring, a slightly nervous embarrassment between them.

'Really good. We've secured another distributor that will help us get into the UK and the rest of Europe on a larger scale.' Lauren said with the enthusiasm of an excited child.

'That sounds brilliant.'

'How was your afternoon?'

'Fine. Rowena keeps hassling me to sell the collection that I exhibited the other week. Apparently, there's a new buyer who's offered 250,000 Euros for the complete works.'

'You going to sell?'

'Nope.'

'Oh.'

'Why? Do you think I should?' Anna asked, suddenly struck by a bolt of insecurity.

'That's not for me to say. It's up to you. It's a lot of money though.' She shrugged nonchalantly as she mused.

'It is, and it would really help with the baby...' Anna wandered off into deep thought. Lauren watched Anna's dream-face and pined. Anna was a very attractive woman, and pregnancy only added to her allure. Lauren could easily see how they would have become lovers. She smiled softly as Anna slowly drifted back out of her reverie. 'Sorry... I went off...' she chuckled.

Lauren's soft smile caused the heat to rise into Anna's cheeks again. She was beginning to perspire. 'That's fine. Shall we go to supper?' Lauren said, softly.

Anna released the breath she had been holding, her skin still buzzing with Lauren's proximity. 'Sure.'

Much to Anna's surprise, Lauren chatted with enthusiasm about the impact of her meeting on the future of their family's vineyard. Previously she had been torn between her work as a lawyer and her obligations as a function of inheriting the family business from her father. Unbeknown to Anna, she had resigned from the London law firm and walked out the day of the accident. It was intended to be a surprise, but in the end even Lauren hadn't remembered and ended up surprising herself. 'You seem really excited about the vineyard,' Anna said, more as a question than a statement.

'I am, now. I've spent a lot of time with Antoine, and a lot of time thinking. I clearly made some choices before the accident, and even though I can't remember what or why, I've worked out that I need to honour my previous self and then just work out the details over time. I think I was fighting the truth before, trying to pretend nothing had happened. I felt a void and filled it with anger and frustration, and pushed away the people I needed to help me.' She shrugged, stopped walking, and turned Anna towards her. 'I was scared Anna. I hope you can forgive me.' Anna pulled her into a tight hug, melting at the contact, whilst also navigating her bump. They giggled, and Lauren gazed longingly at Anna's swollen belly. 'I'd like to find out more about the pregnancy, if that's okay with you,' she asked tentatively.

Anna placed a chaste kiss on her cheek and pulled out of the hold. It had been a topic they had avoided on the phone, both aware of the significance of such a discussion, and both realising it would be better undertaken face-to-face. 'I'd like that too,' she said, resuming the walk.

Lauren stopped them outside the entrance to Epicure and steered Anna into the doorway. She smiled, the same smile as earlier when Lauren had said where she was staying. 'Don't tell me, we've been here before too?' she asked with a wry smile.

'Yes, we have, and it was spectacular.' She reached up and squeezed Lauren's arm. '*We* are looking forward to this time around too,' she said, tenderly rubbing her free hand across her belly. Lauren smiled softly, her eyes stinging.

The same waiter welcomed them as had previously, recognising the two women instantly, his familial smile uncharacteristic for the more formal style of the restaurant. He seated them at the same table and Anna flushed as she recalled erotic memories of that surprise stopover in Paris. 'It was your birthday.' she recalled. 'Only you didn't tell me in advance. I found out at the end of the night,' she teased. Lauren looked sheepish and squirmed in her seat.

The waiter returned with a bottle of mineral water and took their order. The restaurant was empty, but for one other table where an elderly couple sat and pondered the menu in their hands. 'How are you feeling?' Lauren asked, her eyes tracking down to the round shaped belly. 'I mean, how has the pregnancy been?' the pressure behind her eyes increasing with the reality of all that she had missed.

'I think I got off lightly. I was sick in the early days... well weeks actually,' she corrected. 'But now it's really good. I just feel tired a lot, and my feet swell... a lot.' She winced.

'I'll massage them for you,' Lauren said spontaneously.

'I'm having a baby girl,' Anna blurted, not registering the offer Lauren had just made, taken aback with the urgency behind her own words. Staring into Lauren's eyes for a response, seeing the tears trace down her face, she gulped, barely able to swallow past the painful lump blocking her throat. Lauren held her head in her hands, pressed her fingers hard into

219

her eyes to push back the tears, averting Anna's gaze. Anna reached across and took Lauren's arm, the tenderness of the touch adding to her inner pain as she continued to sob.

'I'm so sorry I wasn't there for you... for us,' she sniffed, using the pristine white cotton napkin as a towel for her eyes and tissue for her nose. Anna tried to smile, Lauren's sadness causing a searing pain in her heart. She wanted to hold her close, tell her everything would be fine, and she wanted most of all to believe that it would be.

'Hey, you're here now.' She traced her fingers down the side of Lauren's face. Lauren captured the palm of her hand in her lips, took in her scent, and tenderly kissed the soft skin.

'I'm lost for words. I can't believe you've been through all of this on your own.' Anna lowered her gaze.

'When's the baby... when's she due?'

'Twenty-fourth of August.'

'That's just a couple of weeks away?' Lauren looked aghast. 'What are you doing here? Shouldn't you stay close to home just in case it all kicks off?' she asked with sudden concern. Anna smiled warmly, enjoying the fact that Lauren really cared.

'I'm fine. We're fine. Chances are she'll be late anyway... and there's no way I'm sitting waiting for weeks on end.'

'Have you always been so determined?' Lauren asked with a coy smile, regaining her composure slightly.

'Yes.'

'I like it,' Lauren smiled broadly. 'Have you thought of a name yet?' she asked.

'No.'

Lauren's face shifted quizzically. Anna too had wondered why she hadn't spent many hours pouring over names, as the others in her antenatal group had. She thought she had decided to wait until the baby was born to see what might suit her, but with Lauren sat directly opposite her she realised she had always wanted them to make that choice together.

'I wanted to see what she looked like,' she said, maintaining the illusion she had been living under for the previous months.

'Ah.' Lauren accepted the response and took a sip of the water that had been poured for them. 'How did we first meet?' she asked, curiously.

Anna smiled with the memory of her spilling her drink at Sardo's and Lauren gallantly coming to her rescue with a napkin, before insisting that they dine together. She had been captivated by Lauren's unassuming confidence and the ease with which she entertained. 'Eighteenth of September, at Sardo's. I tipped my drink over myself at the sight of you,' Anna recounted in humour. 'Then you insisted I dine with you. You were very persuasive.' Lauren blushed, feeling a long way short of the confident woman Anna was describing.

'That was my favourite place to eat in London. And this is one of my favourites in Paris,' she said in a more upbeat manner. 'And you sampled both with me. That's good to know.' Lauren smiled sipping at her water.

The waiter approached with two plates of food. Lauren ordered a glass of chilled white wine, offering Anna out of politeness, though expecting her to refuse. 'Tell me more about the pregnancy.' Does she wriggle much? Have you seen any scans?' Lauren buzzed, firing questions at Anna who answered each one in great detail, hesitating before admitting that Eva had supported her and been there with her. Lauren recoiled noticeably, seemed to process the information, and then leaned forward again. 'I'm glad Eva was there for you,' she said, with sincerity.

Anna talked at length about the pregnancy, going over the details of their IVF experience, trying to give as much information as she could, in the hope that there might be some

221

recollection, and even though none came, Lauren's genuine concern and interest drew them together. Anna was hooked.

'I'd like to be a part of the baby's life.' Lauren announced, as she twiddled the stem of her glass at the end of the evening, the Cognac forming a film on the side right up to the rim. They had talked for hours and Anna looked tired. Exhausted. She stopped the glass and held Anna's eyes. The dark blue rim was thick around her steel-blue irises sending an involuntary shudder through Lauren. Her heart skipped, her stomach flipped, and she could feel the shaking that hadn't yet reached her hands.

A tender smile formed on Anna's lips. Lauren couldn't stop staring as the soft pink flesh pulled her in. She bit down on her own lip in an effort to gain some level of self-control. Delicate crow's feet framed Anna's eyes, and strong fingers tussled her hair, as she pondered the question. Lauren suddenly moved towards her in an unconscious act of bravery and brushed her lips softly across Anna's. Every nerve in Anna's body fired simultaneously, and she pulled back instantly, scolded from the burning heat, reminded of the first kiss they had shared. Anna's lids fluttered open and the near black irises penetrated Lauren. When Anna opened her mouth to speak Lauren had already occupied the space between them and taken Anna's mouth gently with her own. Lauren's heart thumped, the ripple causing her to shake, her body screaming for release. There was no going back now. She had tasted Anna and there was something familiar about it. The essence of vanilla was consistent with her dream for sure, but more than that, she knew she had been *here* before. She wasn't sure if the groan had escaped her mouth or not, but a young couple at a table close to theirs grinned as they caught sight of the display of affection. Lauren pulled back and motioned to speak. Anna pressed two fingers tenderly to her lips.

'Don't apologise.' She said softly, looking flushed, flustered, and enlivened all at once. 'Can we go please?' Lauren looked concerned. 'I'd like to take this somewhere a little more private.' Anna smiled softly, and Lauren stood instantly, taking her credit card to the bar and waiting for the bill. Anna followed her, standing by her side. The waiter looked flustered at the break in restaurant protocol and hurried away to get the maître d'.

'Do you want to come back to the hotel?' Lauren asked.
'Yes, I'd like that.'

They walked at a pace that was almost too fast for Anna, in edgy silence, the sense of urgency palpable. Polite, but brief, greetings exchanged with the concierge, they all but dived into the lift, maintaining a jittery distance between them. Anna's breathing was short and fast, as her eyes traced Lauren's body.

Lauren's shaking hand struggled to fit the card in the slot on the heavy door to her room. She pulled Anna into the room, allowing the door to slam behind her. Trying to slow things down, she closed the space between them and placed a shaking hand on Anna's swollen belly, staring in wonder as a ripple filtered through to her palm.

'Oh my God, did she move?' Lauren's mouth fell open and her eyes widened. Anna put a hand around Lauren's neck and pulled her mouth to hers, pressing an urgent kiss on Laurens lips that sent shock waves down her spine. She deepened the kiss and Lauren reciprocated.

Anna released her hold and fingered Lauren's hair, gathering her breath. Her smile revealed the undeniably intimate connection that had endured between them. As much as Anna wanted to ravish Lauren's body - to plunge deep inside her, take her to the edge and feel her come hard - and she wanted to feel Lauren's fingers penetrating her into a state of oblivion, she needed something else more. Lauren held her eyes in unspoken acknowledgement of their mutual need. She cupped Anna's face with exquisite tenderness, leaving her breathless. 'Will you sleep next to me tonight?' Lauren asked, searching Anna's eyes intently.

Anna took the gentle hand resting on her cheek, kissed the palm, lingering at the feel of her strong fingers. 'Yes.'

'Would you like a drink? A bath? A foot massage?' Lauren asked, assessing the room for ways to ease Anna's physical comfort, acutely aware of the dark rings forming deep shadows under her eyes.

Anna linked her fingers through Lauren's, toying with the feel of her supple skin against her own slightly callused hands. She knew how to make love to her and she knew how to give herself over to her; neither were the cause of the electric sensations that rippled over her in soft waves. She felt on the edge of a precipice of a different kind, the beginning of a new chapter, and one that would last a lifetime. She couldn't conceive of anything less: to do so would destroy her in a way that she might never recover. She studied Lauren's dark brown eyes, long seductive lashes, naturally tanned skin with high cheekbones, and her face framed with curly short locks. She wondered if she felt even more in love with her than the first time around. Strange. Yet undeniably true. Even the pain of the last few months hadn't dented the love she felt. She felt complete in Lauren's presence, and with that came a feeling of security, unattainable through possessions and material wealth. 'Yes. A bath would be great, and my feet are killing me,' she said squeezing Lauren's hand.

Lauren led her into the room. 'Please,' she said, indicating to the soft leather couch. 'I'll get you a glass of water and run the bath.'

Anna lowered herself into the seat, which gave way more than she had anticipated, comforted by the walled feeling of the material pressing against her sides. Leaning her head back, she allowed her eyes to close, soothed by the aromas in the room. Lauren's light musky fragrance merged with the light scent of freshly washed sheets. The scent of a delicate posy, the essence of lavender wafting from the bathroom, and the sound of running water caused Anna to drift off. She felt drained, and not from the pregnancy.

Lauren watched with a loving smile, leaning against the bathroom door. Twitching, concealed, steel-blue eyes triggered a soft flicker of delicate light-brown eyelashes. Relaxed skin smoothed out the lines that had appeared as Anna had frowned and smiled throughout the evening, and her mouth now rested partially open, her soft red lips standing in contrast to her pale skin. The rise and fall of her shapely chest providing reassurance that enabled Lauren to enjoy the sight. As her eyes feasted on the engorged belly, extended unnaturally by Anna's posture in the seat, a tingling sensation crept down her spine and into her solar plexus. Beads of sweat formed lightly on her brow and she wiped them immediately. Her heart raced. She continued to stare. The idea that a part of her, a mini version of her, was being nurtured inside this beautiful woman scared and excited her at the same time. There was no doubt in her mind that Anna was attractive. More than that, they had something intangible between them. She imagined it had been like that from the start, and smiled. A rush of sorrow passed through her, as her mind flashed to thoughts of what she had missed over the past months. All the time that they should have been celebrating every stage of the pregnancy together, and she had been behaving like an ass, in denial, withdrawing. Doing what she had historically done to preserve her sense of self: doing life on her own, cutting off her support network and blaming the world for her problems. She had thought she was over such behaviours, since the death of her sister and her move to London, being successful in her work, and standing up to her mother. But the accident seemed to have regressed her behaviour - the therapist had said - and it had cost her. She only hoped it hadn't taken from her the one thing in her life that really meant something: Anna… and now the baby: their baby. She walked into the bathroom and stopped the tap, relishing the lavender scent and steamy warmth against her face. She walked to the bar and selected the Cognac, poured it into a tumbler, and sat on the seat opposite Anna. Watching, she leaned back into the chair.

Anna swallowed and tried to turn her head side-to-side, stiffness preventing a smooth movement. She groaned, her heavy lids rising slowly. Lifting her head off the couch her focus fixed on Lauren's smiling face. 'Sorry, have I been out long?' She stretched her arms and shook her left arm to regain circulation.

'Not long. I stopped the bath. Shall I start it again or would you rather just go to bed?

Anna stifled a yawn. 'Bed I think.'

Lauren stood with a spring in her step and placed her empty glass on the coffee table that separated them. She moved round the table and held out a hand, helping to ease Anna out of the deep cushions. 'I can sleep on the couch.' Lauren said.

'No. Can we sleep together please? I've missed you.' Weary eyes claimed Lauren's heart again.

'I was hoping you'd say that,' she said softly.

*

Anna woke with a start, momentarily unsure of her surroundings, hoping her recollections of the previous day hadn't been just another trick of her mind. Light filtered through the slit between the two blackout curtains. She turned into the middle of the bed and came face-to-face with Lauren's dark brown gaze. A smile formed on Lauren's face and Anna mirrored her.

'Morning,' Anna said, the sound of her voice sending flashes of electricity through Lauren, setting off the region below her bump. Her stomach flipped, in a good way. Without thought, she leaned in and pressed a kiss on Lauren's lips. Lauren responded, pulling their bodies close together, gently running her hand over Anna's bump. Releasing the kiss, 'Morning little one,' she said, her eyes resting on her hand as she caressed.

'Morning mummy,' Anna whispered and smiled tenderly.

Tears welled behind Lauren's eyes. 'I think I'd like that,' she said.

Anna wiped an errant tear with her thumb, traced the line of her face and jaw, moved in, and kissed her tenderly. 'I'd like that too.'

'I don't deserve you.'

'I never stopped loving you Lauren.'

23.

Turning the key in the lock, Anna stepped into the empty space, dropped her keys on the ledge of the tall stand, and placed her coat on the hook. The air was warm inside yet she shivered, isolation biting through her like the north wind on a winter's day. Her hands rubbed at her temples, as she took in the silence that had previously been her sanctuary. They had only parted three-hours ago, but that might as well have been a lifetime ago given the solitude she now felt. The previous evening had been the start of the rest of their lives together, and it had taken all of Anna's resolve to submit to her heart rather than her head. Now, the barn, her wonderful barn, seemed empty in a way that she had never noticed before. She couldn't wait for her mum to arrive. She reached down as her belly fluttered, reassured by the safety she was providing for her daughter... for their daughter.

Every ounce of her had wanted to go back to Corsica with Lauren and as she stood in her foyer now, her eyes scanning the hollow space, she questioned why she hadn't asked her back to the barn. Lauren had offered and she had declined, too quickly, reminding Lauren that her mum was arriving to help with the birth. Lauren's eyes had taken on a new heaviness, and she had withdrawn. Anna had left the hotel swiftly after breakfast, with the promise of a future together, but without a plan. Lauren had adopted a respectful distance between them, and Anna hadn't taken the lead to close that space - a lead that was hers, and hers alone, to take. She realised that now, as the sinking feeling weighed down on her. Rubbing at her eyes, she glanced at her phone; brushed the screen with her thumb. Coming to her senses, she tapped furiously, and waited.

I can cancel my return
The reply came instantly.

When can you get here?
I have a meeting at 3, so by 7
I'll cook
You sure?
Yes x
What's your address?

Anna gave a wry smile at the need to provide her address. She released a slow breath, gave a satisfied squeeze of her phone, skipped into the kitchen and put on the kettle. Her racing heart slowed as she took stock of the changing landscape from the window; the warmth of summer, optimistic, full of life, infused her senses, abating the hollow emptiness of moments ago. Lauren was coming. She allowed the camomile tea bag to sit in the boiling water, watching as its essence seeped through the paper filter, muddying the water. Stirring the hot liquid, speeding up the infiltration process and releasing the heat, she picked up the mug and sipped mindlessly. The warm feeling enveloped her. Lauren had agreed to come to the barn. It was 2.55. She picked up her phone, pressed the autodial number, and waited for her mum to answer.

*

Poking at the still frozen meat on the kitchen workspace with sharp, indiscriminate movements of the knife, admonishing herself for not taking the chicken out of the freezer earlier, Anna reasoned, there was always the option of a take away. Her stomach flipped and her legs lost all strength at the sound of the doorbell. By the time she turned the latch she could barely breathe. Despite the time they had spent together the previous day, and the fact that they had slept side-by-side, she still felt like a teenager about to embark on a first date, wanting it to succeed, yet also fully aware of the gravity of the pain of failure. Heat rushed to her face, and she looked as though she was in a mid-menopausal flush.

'Hi.' Lauren's soft, slightly husky tone, tall, elegant physique, stunning dark eyes and engaging smile, heightened her dishevelled state, parched her mouth, and caused her lips to move without emitting a sound.

'Umm… hi,' she croaked, clearing her throat. Lauren closed the space in an instant and pressed her lips to Anna's. Anna melted, her arms enclosing Lauren's neck, her fingers teasing at her hairline, their bodies touching down their length, as Lauren wound around the protruding belly.

'Thanks for inviting me.' Lauren said, pulling back, and sweeping Anna's hair from her face. 'You okay?' she asked, raising her hand to the flushed, hot face, testing for a fever.

Anna sniggered, 'I'm fine, just really hot.' *You make me hot.* 'Can I get you a drink?' she asked, pulling free and moving with a purposeful-waddle towards the kitchen. Lauren's presence was reassuring, and any concerns Anna had mulled over earlier had disappeared the instant she locked onto those dark eyes.

'Sure, water will be great.' She threw her coat over the stand and dumped her holdall, followed Anna, and sat at the seat she had always occupied at the kitchen island. 'You have an amazing place.' Her eyes traced the room with the awe that comes with the first sighting of a masterpiece.

'Sorry, I keep forgetting you can't remember having been here before. I'll show you around later,' she said over her shoulder, reaching for a bottle of water from the fridge, and pouring them both a glass. Lauren's hand lingered on hers as she took the offered drink.

'Thank you.'

"I'm sorry about earlier… I sort of ran out on you,' she said hovering.

Lauren carefully placed the glass on the table, locked onto Anna's eyes, and rose into her personal space. Heat fused the short distance between them. 'It's okay,' she said, breathing the words into Anna's ear, setting off sparks that scooted down to her toes. Lauren's lips brushed her ear and down her neck. Anna's head fell back in submission, her eyes closed. Lauren claimed the open mouth with a divine balance of urgency and tenderness, penetrating beyond the physical connection of flesh on flesh.

Anna pulled back slowly. 'No, I need to explain,' she said. Lauren looked with sudden concern as her stomach flipped at the thought of bad news. 'You must think I'm crazy. One minute talking about being our baby's mother, the next high tailing it out of the room telling you mum is coming to be my birth partner.'

Lauren tilted her head. 'It was kind of uncomfortable,' she grimaced. Taking Anna's hand in her own, watching as she pressed her thumbs across the knuckles, summoning the courage to speak. 'Do you want me to leave? Disappear?' she asked softly.

'No. Christ no. On the contrary, I meant what I said about being the other mother of our baby. I just got scared that you might leave me, go back to Corsica and rethink the whole thing. That I might not hear from you again. That we would be back where we started after the accident, so I ran, trying to take control of the situation as if the fear would just go away. Then when I turned up here, the emptiness hit me instantly and I knew I had to see you again. I want to be with you Lauren. Live with you, and love you. I don't want there to be a distance between us ever again, physical or otherwise.' She traced a tear down Lauren's cheek, pressed a thumb across her lips. 'I am in love with you.'

'I love you too.' Lauren said, as naturally as if she had spoken the words six months earlier. Anna leaned in and kissed her tenderly.

'Dinner is still frozen,' she said with a shrug, her eyes focusing on the meat that still sat on the kitchen surface.

Lauren smiled, pulling Anna into her chest. 'How about we go out?'

'There's a local bistro which is really good. It's small, but the food's great.'

'Perfect.'

*

Anna stretched out slowly, aware of Lauren lying into her side, an arm draped over her belly. The bird's early chorus filtered through to her ears, the first sight of dawn barely visible through the curtains. It was very early. Out of the corner of her eye, Lauren slept deeply. Peace seemed to smooth her tanned skin as her eyelashes twitched involuntarily, and her breathing remained slow and soft. Anna bathed in the absence of uncertainty: the warm bubble that had enveloped her the previous evening, as they had chatted openly about their fears and desires for the future together, still remained. She felt something much deeper than happiness. She felt complete.

When they had returned from the Bistro bar Anna had pulled out the folder she had put together, containing all the images, reports and her own diary of events throughout the pregnancy. Lauren had held the photograph of the test stick showing *Pregnant 1-2* for some time before cupping Anna's face with her hands, apologising, and kissing her tenderly. They had promised that would be the last apology they would make in relation to the past.

Anna smiled inwardly, listening to the birds. Her belly wriggled and she tapped the spot. It moved again. She tapped again.

'What are you doing?' a bleary-eyed Lauren asked.

'Sorry, did I wake you? We were just communicating. Watch.' Lauren leaned on her elbow and stared with wide eyes as Anna's bump rippled at her touch.

'She's awesome.' Lauren rested back onto the pillow and pulled Anna into her shoulder. 'It's early,' she mumbled, drifting back into a light sleep. Anna poked her in the ribs, repeatedly, and she began to squirm and chuckle. 'Hey,' she protested. 'I need my beauty sleep.'

Anna eased out of the hold, and threw her legs out of the bed.

'Where are you going?'

'The loo,' she replied, a seductive grin on her face, teasing.

Lauren slipped out of the bed and entered the bathroom just as Anna stood from the seat. Anna stepped into her space, not letting her pass. Her hand reaching into Lauren's crotch, she groaned at the wet heat coating her fingers. 'You smell great,' Anna said breathing heavily, her lips barely touching Lauren's.

Urgency building, she ripped at Lauren's sleep-shirt. Lauren lifted it up to assist her and Anna's mouth descended urgently onto the right nipple, her free hand working the left. Lauren groaned and jerked sharply at the intensity coursing through every cell in her body.

'Fuck Anna,' she murmured, her hands clasping around Anna's head, her mouth pressing the top of her head. 'Ahhh.' Lauren shuddered as the surges of throbbing pleasure and sharp pain vied for pole position in her mind and body. The exquisite sensation created an instant need to touch Anna. She moved her against the wall, reached a hand down past the bump and found the warm wetness she sought. Anna was open, ripe, and Lauren entered her easily with three-fingers. Anna groaned as Lauren thrust deep and slow, teasing her G-spot, her thumb caressing her clit. She fell back from Lauren's breast, her eyes wild with desire. Lauren held her tightly; increasing her pace and depth, each thrust driving Anna closer to the edge. Lauren slowed suddenly, holding Anna just short of release. 'Look at me Anna.' Anna's eyes locked on as the final thrusts sent shock waves of pleasure through her body. Lauren stayed inside her as the shuddering continued, moving slightly, tenderly, to prolong the release until she was spent. She fell into Lauren's hold, tears streaming, wetting Lauren's neck and shoulder.

'You okay?' Lauren asked softly, kissing the tears tenderly.

Anna snivelled. 'I'm fine.' She placed a sensitive kiss on Lauren's lips. 'I'm just happy.' The slow tender kiss escalated, as Anna traced a hand down Lauren's toned body, toying with her muscular stomach before teasing the shaved area below.

Catching her breath Lauren pulled out of the kiss. 'You don't have to… we can go back to bed,' Lauren mumbled, but she was already consumed again. Anna pulled her back and claimed her mouth urgently as her hand moved between Lauren's legs, claiming the swollen sex with nimble fingers and thumb. She entered her with such force that Lauren rose up allowing Anna to reclaim the nipple she had started on earlier. Lauren screamed out with the intensity of the sensations firing through her body as she was driven over the edge. The urgency sent Lauren spiralling into another orgasm. Anna kissed her hungrily, adjusting her pressure in tune with Lauren, as she tensed and shook again, and then again.

'Enough,' Lauren begged, every part of her body shuddering uncontrollably. She pulled back, but her eyes locked on deeply. 'I love you,' she said. Her irises looked almost completely black.

'I love you too,' Anna said, with a beaming smile. *Welcome home*, she thought but didn't say.

24.

'So, how come the change of heart,' Rowena asked with a frown that seemed to have etched itself permanently since Anna stepped through the door. 'You were adamant about not selling, to the point that I really believed the prospect was closed.' She shook her head, unable to fathom the turnaround in her protégé's mind-set.

'I just feel it's the right thing to do. I suppose it's about letting go of the past, the past-pain that is, and moving on. Lauren and I are getting on really well and going to make a go of it, so I don't need an image to remind me of her. I have a print for keepsake,' Anna said, as she processed her thoughts.

'Okay, I'll see if the buyer is still interested, but it may be too late now,' Rowena said with irritation, calculating the potential loss of a sale. 'Anyway, how are you?' she said, as her eyes held the growing bump with an affectionate smile.

'I'm good. We're good. Not long to go now,' Anna said, with a slight grimace. 'And she's very active,' Anna finished, as she flinched at a kick just below the ribs.

'Eva was a wriggler. Didn't stop, the whole nine months. Hasn't stopped since, frankly.'

'How is she?'

'She's in love apparently,' Rowena said derisively, brows raised. Anna blushed.

'Really. Who's the lucky lady?' Anna asked, faking ignorance.

'I haven't met her but she's a Doctor I think. Or is it a pilot?' Rowena searched her memory. 'She seems to have been through a few in the last couple of months. I think the last one was a pilot and this one's a Doctor, or maybe the other way around. I don't know what's wrong with the girl. But anyway, she seems to be very loved up at the moment. I think her name's

Rose something or other,' she said, bringing her attention back into the room.

Anna frowned. 'Oh.' She had expected Eva to be hooked up with Hanan and was more than a little concerned that Eva had been apparently playing the field again.

'She should be in later,' Rowena said as she eased herself into her director's chair, filling every ounce of space snuggly, puffing heavily and sweat forming on her forehead. 'Right, let me drop a line to this buyer while you grab a coffee, or water. I've got more work we need to discuss, if you're up for it?' Her eyes locked onto Anna's bump. 'For after the baby's birth of course,' she added.

Rowena's tapping and huffing was interrupted when the door thrust open and a lively Eva carrying a box of donuts came bouncing into the room. 'Hi all,' she sang, a beaming smile covering her face.

'Well hello stranger,' Anna said, pulling her in for a one-armed body hug, squeezing and rocking back and forth gently.

'Wow,' Eva said, pulling back swiftly. 'You're huge.' Anna slapped her on the arm with more force than she had intended and Eva juggled the donuts momentarily before lowering them to the coffee table. 'I didn't mean it like that,' she sniggered.

Anna laughed and slapped her again. 'That's what happens when you stay off line for weeks on end and I get even more pregnant,' she teased.

'How far off are you?' Eva asked as she eyed the bump curiously.

'One week from the due date, could be up to three weeks though.'

'Jesus Christ, what are you doing here?' Eva asked with her mouth open, beginning to panic.

'Eva,' Rowena chastised, as she looked up from the screen.

'Don't look so freaked out,' Anna said calmly, picking up a chocolate donut and sticking it in the gap between Eva's teeth. 'Here, chew on that before speaking again,' she said, with a wink. Eva walked to the coffee machine chewing and mumbling.

Rowena hoisted her body round the desk, a bright sparkle in her eyes. 'Yum.' She dived into the box with both hands, ecstasy written across her face as the sugar danced on her tongue and infiltrated her veins. 'Two sugars in mine please,' she said, making her way back to her chair. Eva frowned, head shaking, as she watched her mum negotiate the short space back to her desk.

'Lunch?' Eva mimed, pointing between her and Anna whilst Rowena found her seat, landing with a deep exhalation before biting on another donut. Anna smiled and nodded in affirmation.

'What are you two plotting?' Rowena asked, not missing a trick.

'Nothing,' both women replied simultaneously. Rowena looked from one to the other suspiciously before giving her attention to her incoming mail.

*

'I'm really worried about mum,' Eva said as they wandered down to the restaurant for lunch.

'How so?' Anna asked. She was really waddling, and moving slowly.

'She's gotten so big. She eats all the time and she's ratty as fuck most of the time. I think she looks like shit.' Eva spouted, relieved to get her thoughts off her chest.

'She has piled on the weight since Christmas and is a bit moody today,' Anna said reflectively. 'What do you think's up with her?'

'Today? Every day's the same. She's irritated about everything,' Eva corrected, her face taut with the strain. 'I don't know. But I'm worried. She's prime candidate for a frigging heart attack.' Eva thrust her hands in her jeans pockets. 'I've asked her to go see a Doc but she flatly refuses.'

Anna nodded and fiddled with the button on her jacket, which wasn't quite closing around her middle. 'It's tough. We can't force her to go. Do you want me to have a word with her, see if she'll listen?'

Eva looked at Anna with pleading eyes. 'Would you?'

'Sure. I'll find a way. She certainly seemed on edge today, at least before she tucked into the donuts.' Anna linked arms with Eva and pulled her in as they walked. 'So, how've you been?'

Eva jogged herself out of her reverie and sighed. 'Good,' she smiled as recent images flashed through her mind.

'How's Hanan?' Anna asked tentatively, prodding for information.

'She's good. We're great friends but that was as far as it was going. I thought there might've been something more between us, but in truth I think I was deluding myself. She wasn't the one.' Eva smiled gingerly, reaching to open the door for Anna to go through to the restaurant. The waiter pointed them to a seat by the window and within a short time had placed a carafe of house Rosé and bottle of water on the table, and taken their order of the house specials of the day.

'So, who is the one?' Anna asked, as Eva poured herself a glass of wine.

Eva took an uncharacteristically delicate sip from the glass and held Anna's eyes. 'She's a surgeon, and her name's Rosa,' she said, a smile taking over her face.

'Wow.' Anna remarked. 'You're really smitten.'

Eva shrugged dismissively, but her eyes gave away the depth of her feeling. They glazed as she streamed images of Rosa, heat rising to colour her face.

'Hellooo,' Anna waved at her, refocusing her attention. 'So, tell me more. How did you meet? What's she like? When am I going to meet her?'

'We met at a new bar in town, *Girleze*. I'd seen her before, months ago at *Le So What*. That night I came over to yours for dinner and vowed to sort my life out.' She rolled her eyes. 'She was at the bar that night and we sort of connected, but she was with a group of people and we never got to speak.'

'Connected?' Anna queried.

'The same night I was being hit on by that bar tender. You know, the blonde one, big tits, slut,' she animated with her hands for emphasis.

'I get it. I think I know who you mean.' Anna sipped at her water. 'Connected?' she said again, not letting Eva off the hook.

'Anyway, she kept eyeing me, nodding and smiling when she knew I was looking at her. Her short arse friend glared at me, scared the shit out of me, and pulled her in the other direction, and not long after that I left the bar and came to yours.'

'That was it?' Anna questioned.

'I went into the bar a few times after that, but never saw her again until recently, when I get a text from her out of the blue. She tracked me down.' Eva took another sip of her wine. Anna looked expectantly. Eva twiddled her glass on the table, lost in thought. Anna cleared her throat, jogging her out of trance.

'Tracked you down?'

'I was in two minds whether to meet up with her, but Hanan was away and I didn't think...' She stopped. 'That's a lie. I did think and chose to meet her knowing I might do something.

240

In fact, thinking about it, I'm not sure I had much choice. It's like I needed to go, like we needed to be together. I know it sounds a bit cliché, but it's like we're soul mates.'

Anna laughed. 'It's not… or maybe it is… but who cares? If that's how you feel…' Anna flushed at her thoughts of Lauren.

'She's about an inch taller than me, athletic, confident, dark wavy hair, and dark chocolate eyes… really dark eyes. Smoulderingly dark eyes… In fact,…'

'Okay, I get the picture,' Anna interrupted with a snigger.

'She's very… confident, but also kind and chivalrous. It's sort of… endearing and sexy at the same time. She's hot, and smart.'

'A good combination.' Anna nodded.

'And she's funny. We laugh about a lot. Silly things. A bit like you and I did…' She stopped herself and looked for a reaction from Anna. None came.

'We did laugh a lot and I loved that about being with you,' she said matter-of-factly, smiling at the times she and Eva had laughed till they cried over the daftest of things. In some cases, they had even been unable to remember why they started laughing.

'And get this. She's originally from Corsica. It would be funny if you knew her.'

Anna choked on the water she had just sipped, frowned, and held Eva's gaze. 'She's from Corsica and her name's Rosa?'

'That's what I just said,' Eva said, looking confused.

'What's her surname?' Anna asked intently.

'Bartoli. Why?'

Anna released a breath, not knowing whether to laugh or be concerned. 'Holy shit. That would be Lauren's step-father's niece,' she said.

'You serious? How do you know that? Do you know her?'

'There can't be too many women of that description who are surgeons and from Corsica. If it is we met briefly. She was at Lauren's mother's wedding last year. Quite...' Anna searched for the most appropriate word so as not to cause upset, but failed.

'Quite what?' Eva said, bordering on impatient.

'She was very flirtatious. She tried to hit on Lauren at the wedding, in front of everyone. But, I'm sure she's really not like that...' Anna backtracked at Eva's reddening face.

'Shit. You're kidding me, right?' She looked suddenly deflated. 'You sure Lauren wasn't open to it?' she blurted defensively. Anna's brows rose at the assertion. 'I'm sorry.' Eva sat back in her chair and raised her hands in apology. Anna mirrored her.

'No... I'm sorry. I didn't mean to burst your bubble and I'm sure she's really nice. I don't know her and it would be great to meet her again, under different circumstances,' Anna said, trying to recover the dismal feeling that had built a wall between them.

Eva's eyes drifted around the room. 'So, how are you? How's the baby?' she said, but Anna got the impression she was asking just to fill the space.

'I'm back with Lauren. I mean, we've agreed to give our relationship a go.' Anna said hesitantly.

'Shit. I didn't realise,' Eva said, swigging her wine. 'Does she remember what happened before the accident then?'

'No. Not really.'

'How long has... Is she living with you? What about the baby?'

'Not long. We've chatted... a lot, and she's been staying at mine the last couple of weeks. She's at a meeting in town today. She wouldn't let me come on my own in case the baby arrives while I'm here,' Anna said with raised eyebrows. Her friend, Francesca, is a midwife. She's staying at ours and she'll take care of us, so hopefully we can have the baby at home. Mums arrived last week too, so it's a full house. Another reason to get out today,' she joked.

'Wow.' Eva stared at Anna as she spoke, noting the change in reference from singular to the plural. 'You do look... happy,' she said, noting the difference in Anna since their time together. 'I really hope it works out for you?' She reached across and squeezed Anna's hand affectionately, a little lost in her own thoughts and concerns. Whilst she and Rosa hadn't been seeing each other for long, Eva had been sure they both felt the same way. Anna's comments had thrown a spanner in the works, caused her to doubt, and burst Eva's bubble in the process.

Anna's eyes lowered momentarily. 'I do too. I think we're good together and I think she thinks so too, even though she can't remember our past. We can work around that and hopefully move forward together.'

'Sure,' Eva pondered into her wine, not really hearing anything other than the voice bouncing around her head. 'I'm sure it'll work out fine,' she mumbled. Having felt the pain Anna had been through the previous six months she still felt protective of her.

'And I'm really sorry about my comments about Rosa. I hope that works out for you both, and I mean it about you both coming round for dinner. Lauren will love that too, I'm sure.' Anna searched Eva's eyes for an acceptance of her apology, squeezed her hand tightly.

Eva raised her glass in a toast. 'To love.'

Anna clinked glasses with a smile. 'Is that how you feel about Rosa?'

'Yes, I think I do.'

'Then I'm doubly sorry for what I said. Ignore me. I'm hormonal.' Eva nodded and tried to raise a smile as she took a slug of her wine. Anna winced.

'You okay?' Eva looked at her with concern. She had gone a strange shade of grey.

'I'm not sure. I don't think that food sat very well, I feel a bit sick. I'm going to the loo.'

'Want me to come with you?' Eva asked, still partly lost in her concerns about Rosa.

'No, it's okay. I won't be long.' Anna moved slowly towards the small bathroom. As soon as she entered the dark room she lurched towards the sink and wretched. Immediately her stomach cramped. The damp between her legs meant only one thing. She needed to get to the hospital. She washed her face with the cool water and breathed deeply. Within moments another contraction had her doubled up and unable to move. She breathed through the pain, stood, and headed back to Eva. 'We need to go the hospital,' she said, more calmly than she felt.

'Holy shit.' Eva jumped to her feet, scanned Anna, and waved for the waiter. 'Can you get a taxi... or an ambulance... quickly please?' The urgency of her request, as she focused on Anna's bump, sent him running. Anna groaned again with another contraction. 'Jesus, Anna. The baby's coming.'

'Seems so.' She was already on her phone. 'I think I'm in labour,' she said into the speaker. 'Yes. I'm going to the hospital now.' She paused. 'Yes, Eva's here with me. We'll be fine. Okay.' Another pause. 'Okay. I love you too.' She pocketed the phone and looked up at a wide-eyed Eva, hopping up and down. 'Lauren will meet us there,' she confirmed.

Eva nodded. 'Where's the bloody transport,' she said, more loudly than intended, and walked towards the restaurant bar to investigate. 'Taxi is on its way,' she said with irritation as she returned to the table. Anna was stood, unable to sit through the discomfort of another contraction. 'You sure you'll be okay? Jesus fucking Christ.' Eva's panicked state and vocalisation causing concerned stares from other diners.

Anna placed her hand on Eva's arm to calm her. 'I'll be okay. I'm sure there's plenty of time,' she said smiling, though the lines around her eyes indicated more pain than she was letting on.

The taxi arrived. Anna moved slowly and eased into the back seat. Eva followed her, tapping rapidly into her phone before pocketing it and looking across the space to check on Anna, who was groaning with another shot of pain gripping her. There was no need for words between them and within ten minutes the driver pulled up outside the hospital entrance.

Within moments Anna was whisked into the hospital. Eva followed the wheelchair, tapping into her phone again, whilst answering questions the attendant reeled off as he pushed Anna towards the maternity section of the hospital.

They entered a large, airy room with a bed, armchair, monitoring equipment, and sunlight streaming through a large window, Eva breathed a deep sigh, relieved at the safety of being under hospital care. A nurse followed them into the room, paperwork in hand. The attendant parked the wheelchair by the side of the bed, wished Anna luck, and quietly left the room. The midwife smiled at them both reassuringly. Eva smiled weakly in response. Anna tried to stand out of the chair as another spasm swept through her. Holding the bed with her hands she rocked herself until the pain subsided.

'Right, let's get you onto this bed. We need to take a look at this little lovely,' the midwife said softly, but firmly. 'I'm Elaina by the way. I'll be with you both now, so if you have any questions don't hesitate to ask,' she said, looking from one to the other.

'Um. Anna's partner will be here shortly,' Eva said, wanting to correct the woman's assumption.

'Okay,' Elaina said, with the same kind smile, as she helped Anna onto the bed. The door burst open and a tense looking Lauren rushed to the side of the bed. Anna's eyes smiled even though her mouth looked tense.

'Hi,' Anna said. 'So much for a home birth eh?' she joked. Lauren visibly relaxed, releasing the breath she had been holding. The midwife watched the interaction as she continued her assessment of Anna.

'You okay baby?' Lauren asked.

'Ahhhh…' Anna groaned, more loudly. 'Just great,' she said with sarcasm as she gripped the side of the bed. 'This is our midwife, Elaina. Elaina, Lauren.'

'Hi.' Lauren smiled and moved out of the way as Elaina moved with urgency to connect the monitors.

'Pleased to meet you Lauren,' she said as she worked. 'Well I'm happy to tell you you're already seven-centimetres dilated, so this little one isn't going to be hanging around too long.' She smiled at the shocked looks on the two-women's faces.

Anna pointed towards the quiet figure sat in the armchair. 'And this is my friend Eva.'

Lauren stepped towards Eva as she stood, and captured her in her arms, squeezing tightly. 'Thank you for being there,' she said, with sincerity.

Eva smiled broadly. She could see exactly what Anna saw in the woman who stood before her. There was something familiar about Lauren, something she saw in Rosa. 'You're welcome,' she said as she patted her on the back. 'I'll leave you two to it,' she said looking from Anna who was building for another assault, back to Lauren whose face contorted with anxiety. 'I'll wait in the café,' she said, turning and heading for the door.

'Ahhh,' was all she heard as the door closed behind her.

25.

The guttural-groan brought tears to Lauren's eyes as she watched the tiny baby slip effortlessly from the comfort of its previous nine-months of existence. A miracle. Anna looked exhausted and so beautiful, Lauren thought, as her eyes moved from mother to child, in awe.

'Oh my God, she's beautiful,' Lauren exclaimed as the midwife flipped the baby over and began rubbing her down.

She stared at the pair of surgical scissors being held out to her for what seemed like an eternity, before the message registered. 'Would you like to cut the cord?' Elaina asked. Lauren gulped as a tear trickled down her face. She took the scissors, barely able to control the buzzing sensation infiltrating her body, and positioned them as instructed, squeezing through the tough material that had provided sustenance to their daughter in the womb. Elaina took the pink, flailing baby and placed her onto Anna's bare chest. Anna stared, awestruck, watching as the little one searched, reached out, wriggled and suckled against her breast. Lauren watched them both in stunned silence.

Anna groaned, breaking the spell, as cramps wracked her body for the second time around. 'Shall we pass her to her other mum?' Elaina asked, moving to remove the little one, wrap her, and hand her to Lauren. She looked dumbstruck, but held her daughter with gentle ease, entranced by her first moments in the world; one eye on Anna as she continued to deliver the placenta.

*

Anna watched the crib, unable to remove her eyes from the sight. Lauren sat in the chair next to her bed, holding her hand, her eyes moving from Anna to the tiny baby still lying fast asleep. Three-hours had passed already and they hadn't been able to stop staring, smiling and staring again. The speed of the birth had resulted in Anna going into shock so she was on a drip as a precaution, and feeling very tired. But baby was fine. The Doctors had decided that they should stay in overnight and would be released sometime in the morning. Anna had text Eva to let her know. Anna's mums had been sent a picture, and agreed to stay at the barn, with Francesca at the ready, rather than trek into Paris. A knock at the door broke their trance.

'Hey mums,' Eva said excitedly, beaming a broad smile as she stepped through the door, followed by a tanned woman in scrubs.

'Rosa.' Anna exclaimed. Lauren looked confused until it dawned on her. The pictures of her mother's wedding, the face was vaguely familiar.

'Congratulations you two,' Rosa said respectfully. 'I hope you don't mind me popping by? I work here and had a moment. Eva text me to let me know you were here.'

Eva beamed as her eyes locked onto the tiny baby sleeping softly in the crib. 'Fuck,' she blurted then apologised. 'She's fucking gorgeous.' She hadn't even realised she had cursed a second time, as she moved closer to observe the stillness - the small bundle of perfection. Anna laughed, shaking her head. Rosa shrugged, raising her eyebrows.

'This is Emilie,' Anna said proudly, her eyes holding Lauren's with deep affection. 'Emilie Vincenti.' She spied the tears forming in Lauren's eyes. They hadn't discussed surnames.

'That's a gorgeous name,' Eva said as she inspected the tiny being who was beginning to snuffle, her eyes twitching to open.

'It suits her.' Anna confirmed, staring at her daughter.

'Hi Rosa,' Lauren said, belatedly. Rosa smiled and nodded towards her, before a bleeping sound took Rosa's attention.

'Well congratulations again you two. She's beautiful. Let's catch up sometime?' She reached out and squeezed Eva's arm, smiling as she gained her attention. 'I'll see you later,' she said with a broad smile.

'Sure,' Eva responded, but her attention was on Emilie. 'Can I hold her?' she asked, looking from Anna to Lauren and back again.

'Yes,' they both said at the same time.

*

'Oh my, she's so beautiful,' Lisa said, unable to stop the beaming smile as she opened the door to the barn, her hand covering her mouth. Her eyes sparkled as she took in the tiny little one snuggled in the car seat. 'You on the other hand look exhausted. Radiant, but exhausted,' she said placing a motherly arm around her daughter; taking the seat from her and cooing at the sleeping baby.

Vivian patted Lauren on the shoulder, winked and nodded. Lauren smiled knowingly and followed them all into the barn. 'I've got the champagne ready,' she said. They had been on tender hooks, impatiently waiting for their return from the hospital and had already downed one bottle between the three of them. Vivian sounded as though she had consumed the lion's share.

Francesca peeked into the seat as Lisa carried Emilie into the living room. 'She's stunning. Congratulations,' she said, smiling at the awestruck family surrounding her. Emilie's tanned skin tone, full head of dark curls and eye shape resembled Lauren without any shadow of doubt. All eyes were on her, but her eyes remained firmly shut.

'Drink anyone?' Vivian asked. 'Let's celebrate. Valerie's on her way, she should be here in a few hours, but she said to start without her.' Vivian tilted her head with a wry smile on her face, as if the idea of celebrating would be such a hardship.

'Great, thanks.' Lauren smiled as Vivian staggered slightly towards the kitchen.

'Let me help,' Lisa said with a goofy grin and raised eyebrows. The colour in her cheeks gave away her contribution to devouring the previous bottle. Only Francesca seemed totally sober, for which Anna was grateful.

'You guys take a break. I'll keep an eye on her for a while,' Francesca said. 'What time's her next feed due?'

'Probably in the next half-hour or so,' Anna responded as she noted the time on her phone. 'I'll skip a drink right now and have a little after the feed.'

Lauren pulled her into her arms and placed a tender kiss on her lips. 'I'd do the feed for you but I'm a bit short of... sustenance,' she said, beaming a grin, shrugging her shoulders. 'Guess I'll be okay for a couple of glasses then.'

Anna slapped her teasingly on the arm. Emilie stirred.

'I've got something for you,' Lauren said, holding Anna's eyes softly. Anna's brows rose in question. Emilie started to snuffle before emitting a noise, decibels louder than expected for her tiny body. Lauren smiled at her daughter then held Anna's eyes again. 'After the feed.' She kissed her again, tenderly, and turned towards the kitchen as Emilie opened her lungs fully. 'That's my girl,' she said, laughing.

*

Anna placed Emilie into the crib then fell heavily onto her own bed, intending to rest for a short while before joining the party in the kitchen. She stared at the rise and fall of the tiny body. Lauren interrupted the moment and sat on the bed next to her. 'Are you ready for your present?' she asked. Anna yawned then smiled. As tired as she felt, she didn't want to dent

Lauren's enthusiasm for whatever it was that she had bought her.

'Sure,' she said, Lauren already pulling her to her feet and into her arms.

Enthusiastically Lauren led her up into the attic. Anna's confusion apparent on her face, Lauren laughed. She opened the door, pulled Anna into the room and turned on the light. Anna's jaw dropped at the sight. 'I thought you'd want to decide where to put them,' she said, staring at the images avoiding Anna's gaze, unable to face any disappointment or disapproval that might come. Anna's silence eventually drew her gaze and they locked eyes. 'Please don't be mad at me,' she said urgently. Anna stepped towards her. She wasn't smiling.

'You?'

'Yes. I needed to be sure you'd have enough money if...' Anna silenced her justification with an impassioned kiss that bruised Lauren's lips. Lauren pulled her in tightly and kissed her back, with equal depth and passion.

26

'Are you sure she'll be okay?' Lauren asked with more than a little anxiety as she paced their bedroom at Anna's parent's house.

'Hey,' Anna said softly, catching her by the arms and looking into her dark brown eyes. 'She'll be just fine. She'll most likely sleep the whole time we're out and if there's any problem they've got both our numbers and we're only a short taxi ride away.' Anna squeezed softly and rubbed Lauren's arm tenderly, picking at the sleeve of her jacket as if there were a piece of fluff lingering there. 'We should get going then.'

'You're absolutely sure?'

'Come here.' Anna pulled her into her arms and claimed her mouth with passion. Lauren groaned. 'You look stunning,' she said as she released her. Lauren breathed deeply and headed for the door and down the stairs.

'You two ready then?' Vivian asked, sipping at a glass of wine as she prepared a salad in the kitchen.

'Yes,' Anna responded before Lauren could open her mouth.

'She'll be fine you know. Now go and enjoy your evening. We've got this. We know how it works you know,' she said, laughing at the tension fixed in Lauren's face.

Lisa looked up from the work surface, her hands still wrapped around the bread she was shaping, flour resting on her cheek and tickling the edge of her nose. She wiped her arm across her face and smiled. 'Go!'

Anna smiled, waved off her flour-covered mum who was moving in for a hug, grabbed Lauren's hand and dived for the front door. 'You've got our numbers,' she said as she closed the door behind them.

'Go,' Vivian said, raising her voice in humour.

Anna wrapped her arm through Lauren's as they stepped out onto the street. It had been three months since the birth of their daughter and the first opportunity for an evening out, and whilst she wasn't planning for it to be a lengthy affair, she was going to enjoy being alone with Lauren. The air was cool and the darker early evenings reminded Anna that it was only just over a year ago since they had met. She reflected on everything that had taken place in that time and sighed; snuggled into Lauren's side.

'You okay?' Lauren asked.

'Perfect.' She stared up into the sparkling eyes that reflected the street-lit night, and smiled. Lauren kissed her lightly before heading down the steps into the tube station.

'Ciao Lauren,' the tanned Italian waiter said as they entered Sardo's. He beamed a smile at them both. 'Haven't seen you for a long time,' he remarked.

'Too long Naz,' Lauren responded, moving forward to embrace the familiar man. 'Too long.'

'We have a nice bottle of chilled Livon Friulano' he said with a cheeky grin.

'You know me well,' Lauren said, reaching for Anna's hand. 'This is Anna,' she said.

'I remember the beautiful lady from the last time she was here. A small incident with a drink as I recall,' he said, extending his hand in greeting, bowing gracefully. 'This way to your table ladies,' he said, indicating towards the cave at the back of the restaurant. He poured them a glass of wine from the ice bucket by their table, placed the menus on the table, and returned to the bar.

Lauren had taken the seat she always took at the table and Anna sat opposite her. Anna glanced at the empty adjacent table, where she had spilled her wine, entranced by the warmth and familiar aromas that invaded her senses; her body reacting as it did the first time they had met here. When she turned back to Lauren, a small padded box sat on the table between them. Anna looked at Lauren with a questioning glare.

'What's this?' she asked. Lauren's eyes seemed to be evading hers and she was sweating. 'Are you okay?' she asked with concern.

'Open it. It's for you.'

Anna picked up the box and stared at her shaking hands. She flicked the sprung-hinge, and her eyes widened. Her mouth remained open for what seemed like an eternity, but no sound came. The large light-blue diamond sparkled brightly, dancing within the candle-lit space. Anna nearly dropped the box, then, placed it carefully on the table. When she looked up Lauren's eyes were wet and she too had tears flowing down her cheeks. Her hand reached across to Lauren's, but Lauren had already leaned into the table to claim her mouth, softly, deliberately.

'I love you Anna. I always will.'

About Emma Nichols

Emma Nichols lives in Buckinghamshire with her partner and two children. She served for 12 years in the British Army, studied Psychology, and published several non-fiction books under another name, before dipping her toes into the world of lesbian fiction.

If you enjoy Emma's work then please leave a review on book sites and register on her website for regular updates about up-coming novels.

www.emmanicholsauthor.com
www.facebook.com/EmmaNicholsAuthor
www.twitter.com/ENichols_Author

Thank you.

COMING SOON...

The Hangover, Book 3 in the Vincenti Series,
will be out in late 2017.

Please register at **www.emmanicholsauthor.com** for news
about the release of The Hangover.

Made in the USA
Middletown, DE
17 August 2018